DEAD END

A TRUTH SEEKERS NOVEL - BOOK THREE

SUSAN SLEEMAN

Published by Edge of Your Seat Books, Inc.

Contact the publisher at contact@edgeofyourseatbooks.com

Copyright © 2019 by Susan Sleeman

Cover design by Kelly A. Martin of KAM Design

This book is a work of fiction. Characters, names, places, and incidents in this novel are either products of the imagination or are used fictitiously. Any resemblance to real people, either living or dead, to events, businesses, or locales is entirely coincidental.

1

"He's not my father? What do you mean?" Sierra gaped at her mother seated at the bedside of the man she'd called father for thirty-two years, but now? Who was her *real* father?

"I...I..." Tears filled her mother's eyes, and she clutched her hands in her lap, while she tried to compose herself.

"It's my fault, sweetie," her father said from his hospital bed. As a retired Multnomah County Deputy, he was still in good shape and very active, but his face and lips were pale today, his energy non-existent as he waited for a kidney transplant. "I didn't want you to know. I thought it might change our relationship."

"And I agreed because your dad married me when I was pregnant and alone." Sierra's mother took his hand. "He's been an excellent father to you, and we've both been blessed since the day he came into our lives."

"How...I...this..." Thoughts whirled through Sierra's head. Spinning. Rushing. Taking her down. She collapsed on a hard chair and blinked. Over and over again.

This made no sense.

She lifted her gaze to the pair who felt like strangers.

This man and woman who had raised her. Cared for her. Loved her.

Lied to her.

"This is why you didn't want me to be tested for a kidney donation," she muttered, letting the thought linger in the tense air.

Another lie. They claimed they didn't want her to give up a kidney at her age. She believed them, but what they really wanted was to stop her from discovering her blood type. She desperately wanted to help her dad so she'd gone ahead and gotten tested only to learn she couldn't possibly be this man's biological daughter.

"I hope you can understand and can forgive us," her father said, his tone pleading when she had never heard him plead for anything for her entire life.

"Understand? How?" She shook her head—kept swinging it as if that would make the thought more palatable. Could she ever understand? Ever forgive? Certainly not until she heard their reason for withholding the information from her.

She looked at her mother, the woman Sierra very much resembled. Her hair was still dishwater blond but streaked with gray. Her honey-brown eyes matched Sierra's, too. As did her full lips and broad nose. Looking at her mother was like looking in the mirror at an older version of herself. But she didn't have a hint of her father's features when all five of her brothers were spitting images of him.

Now she knew why. She had a different father. Her brothers weren't her full blood brothers. An ache cut through her body so fierce it took her breath. She clutched her arms around her stomach. Felt like she might be sick.

She swallowed hard and sat up straight. She pinned her gaze on her mother. "Tell me about my biological father."

"His name is..." Her mother's gaze flew around the room

as if looking for a way out. She took a long breath and settled her focus on Sierra. "He's Edward Barnes, but he goes by Eddie. He still lives in Seaview Cove where I grew up."

Seaview Cove. Of course. Things were starting to fall into place for Sierra. "Is that why you never wanted to go back there?"

Her mother nodded. "I really don't like the beach. That wasn't a lie. I got pregnant there." She paused and frowned, but then stiffened her shoulders. "Eddie and I were only eighteen. He didn't want to be a father, and honestly, he wasn't mature enough to be one. Not that I was ready to be a parent either, but after the way I was raised, I was committed to being the best mother ever."

Sierra tried to process the news and compare this information to the stories her mother had told her. "So what you said about growing up in poverty was true?"

Her mother nodded. "I didn't want that life for you, but it was looking like that was going to happen. My parents threw me out of the house when they found out about you."

Her anguish cut Sierra to the quick, melting a thin slice of the anger in her heart. "What did you do?"

"I lived with a friend until I finished a high school secretarial course and graduated. Then I moved to Portland." She gave a sad shake of her head. "I only had the money I saved that last six months of school from my job at the Dairy Queen. But I found a cheap motel and got a secretarial job at the county right away."

"And that's where you met...Dad." Sierra wasn't sure what to call this man lying in the bed, and her hesitation resulted in a pained expression making him look older than fifty-five. With him being extremely frail, the last thing she wanted to do was hurt him, but she couldn't seem to help herself.

God, please help me here.

"You know the rest of our story," her mother said. "Except I was pregnant when I met him."

Sierra had always thought her parents' love story was incredible. They were so in love that they married after knowing each other for only two months. But now Sierra knew her mother's pregnancy rushed them into marriage. "So...your wedding anniversary. It couldn't be when you told me it was, or my birthdate is wrong."

"Your birthdate is accurate." Her mother sat silently for a moment, then shook her head. "Our wedding occurred later than we told you. We didn't want you to know you were conceived out of wedlock. It was a different time then. You would have suffered if you would have known. And you might have been ostracized if anyone else found out."

Sierra looked at her mother and couldn't reconcile this woman who was confessing a lifetime of lies or half-truths with the God-fearing woman who raised her. "Is there anything else I need to know?"

"No." Her mother shook her head hard. "Nothing."

"Have you kept up with Eddie?" Sierra asked, not at all sure what to call him either. "And you're sure he still lives in Seaview Cove?"

She nodded. "I haven't sought him out, but he's in the class reunion information I've received. He took over his dad's property management business. Cove Rentals. It's very successful."

"Married with kids?"

"As far as I know he never married and has no children." She looked down at her hands. "I heard he was still kind of a player. Never really could settle down with any woman."

Sierra tried to picture what this man, this Eddie Barnes, looked like and nothing came to mind. Of course not. She'd never met him. Never even seen a picture of him. She had to

4

go see him, that much she knew. "You're positive he still lives in Seaview Cove?"

Her mother nodded. "In the same beach cottage where he grew up. He inherited the place when his parents passed away."

"Do you know the address?" Sierra worked hard to keep the bitterness from her tone for her father's sake. She couldn't let this make him sicker.

Another bob of her mother's head, and she rattled off the address on Ocean Drive. "And his business is on Main Street."

Sierra got to her feet. "I'm going to see him."

"Right now?" Her mother's mouth fell open, and she stared at Sierra.

"Right now." She looked at her dad lying in the bed, the machines with wires running to his body, beeping a steady rhythm and attesting to his poor health. She wished she could instantly forgive him, as he was already suffering, but she had to come to grips with this news.

She crossed the room and patted his hand. "I need to process this. A drive to the beach and back will help me do that."

"I understand." He gave her a weak smile.

She tried to return it, but knew by his continued pain-filled expression that she failed. "Mom was right. You've been a great dad. The best a girl could hope for, and I appreciate you agreeing to be my father." She patted his hand again, but couldn't find it in herself to hug or kiss him like she usually did after a visit.

She stepped back, and the anguish in his eyes brought tears to hers, but she couldn't stay. No matter how much she wished he wasn't suffering. "I'll spend the night and be back tomorrow. I'll see you then."

"Can you call or text me?" her mother asked. "Just to tell me you got there okay?"

Sierra nodded and fled the room. In the hallway, tears replaced her anger, and she barely climbed inside her red Civic in the shadowy parking garage before she totally lost it. A raw sob erupted from her throat and tears poured from her eyes, running down her face. She swatted at them and took long breaths over and over, willing the tears to stop. She grabbed tissues from her purse and tried to keep up, but the torrent continued.

How had this happened to her? Her!

One of Sierra's partners at the Veritas Center had recently learned she was adopted, and Sierra hadn't been able to fully empathize with the anguish Emory suffered. But now...now Emory could serve as a role model of forgiveness. She'd gotten over her shock, forgiven her mother for not telling her, and Emory had a second family to love.

That thought should stop Sierra's tears, but her biological father didn't sound much like someone who would open his arms to a long lost daughter. Maybe she acted in haste, and she shouldn't go see him. She had no idea how he would react to her. Would it be the second heartbreaking experience in one day?

She continued taking deep breaths, swiped away her tears, and firmed her shoulders. She wasn't a crybaby. She was a strong, independent woman who didn't need anyone in her life to be happy. So what if Eddie laughed in her face or told her to leave? She had to see him. No matter what she found when she got there, he was her biological father, and she at least needed to know her medical history.

But how in the world would she get through that first meeting? What would she even say to him?

Think of this like a difficult investigation. Of the way you collect forensics. Think only of the facts, not how the crime makes you feel.

"Okay. I can do this." She swallowed away the last of her tears and made the short drive to the Veritas Center to pack an overnight bag.

She parked in the lot and looked up at the pair of towers. They were connected on the ground with a lobby and on the upper floor with a glass-enclosed skybridge. She and six partners ran the private forensic lab. Their toxicology and controlled substances expert, Maya Glass, inherited the building from her grandfather when he passed away. The partners pooled their money, built out the labs in the east tower, and the partners moved into the existing condos in the west tower. As the trace evidence expert, Sierra had a lab on the fourth floor. Her home away from home.

But it didn't feel like home now or her sanctuary.

Odds were good once she made her way inside the building she would run into one of her partners, and she really didn't want to see anyone with this discovery weighing heavy on her mind and heart.

No. She couldn't see them. Not yet. She could buy whatever items she needed in Seaview Cove.

She started up her car and whipped out of the lot.

Chicken. Yeah, she was acting like a chicken all right, but so what?

She pointed her car south on I-5, thankful for the busy Saturday traffic as navigating the many vehicles took all of her attention until she was south of the Portland metro area. And then again in Salem and Eugene, and she soon found herself cutting west toward the coast. By the time she pulled up to Eddie's cottage the setting sun cast a rosy orange glow over the beach.

She killed the engine and sat back. Here she was. At her biological father's house, and she hadn't come to any conclusion on how to act or what to think, other than she needed to keep an open mind.

She shifted her focus to the small cottage painted a powder blue with pristine white shutters. A wide deck, also white, held brightly colored Adirondack chairs and faced the roaring ocean. All in all, it was cheerful and beachy looking. The kind of place she might rent on a vacation if she ever took one, which she hadn't since becoming a partner at Veritas. Her job was her life.

But her life had been a lie. At least part of it.

"Stop thinking that way or you will never be able to forgive. Do something positive." She checked her appearance in the mirror and was thankful she'd stopped at a gas station a few miles out of town to clean away the mascara under her eyes and comb her hair. She wished she wasn't wearing her Saturday casual clothing, but she would have had to shop to change, and she wanted to talk to Eddie before it got too late. Besides, he wouldn't care about her yoga pants and top. He might not even care about her.

She stepped out. A gust of salty ocean air buffeted her body with stinging grains of sand, and she struggled to remain upright. Though it was mid-September, the temperatures had already dropped and soon the stormy season would set in. She gathered her shoulder-length hair to stop it from whipping against her face and hunched into the wind. At the drive, she looked for a car or a garage. She found neither. Maybe he wasn't home. Maybe she should go.

No. She wouldn't run again. She strode up to the door and pounded. She waited, time ticking by, her heart racing, but no answer.

She pounded again. "C'mon, Eddie, answer."

She refused to leave and tapped her sneaker on the

wood slats. No one answered. She would take a quick look through the windows, but the blinds were closed.

She waited a few more minutes. The ocean waves roared onto the shore and seagulls called out, but otherwise, silence filled the air. He clearly wasn't home. She gave up and returned to her car. She pulled up the map on her phone, looking for directions to Main Street.

She reached the quaint street lined on both sides with colorful shops, but the sun had dropped out of sight leaving the area shadowed, almost ominous. Streetlights popped on one by one down the street, illuminating the area filled with tourists milling about in search of T-shirts, souvenirs, and salt water taffy. She didn't have to go far before spotting Eddie's building painted red, white, and blue with a large Cove Rentals sign over the door.

She angled her car into a space in front of the building and climbed out, the sweet smell of waffle cones wafting through the air. To reach the glass door, she had to step between a smiling family of four eating ice cream cones, their joyful laughs bouncing on the breeze. Their delight was an even bigger contrast to her shocking news.

The lights inside his office were out, and the door locked. Not here either?

Why had she rushed to Seaview Cove? She should've called. Or should she have? Eddie might not have agreed to see her if she'd talked to him first. She planted her hands on the window and peered inside.

"You looking for Eddie?" the male voice behind her startled her.

She spun to see a lanky bald man she put in his sixties staring at her. He wore khaki pants and a navy blue Mr. Rogers sweater, and stood under the glow of a nearby streetlight.

She smiled at him. "Do you know where he might be?"

"That's the six-million-dollar question." He stepped closer. "You a friend?"

"His daughter." She felt really odd saying that.

The man tipped his head and stared at her. She felt uncomfortable under his watchful eye, but she didn't budge or offer an explanation.

"Yeah, I can see the resemblance." He held out his hand. "Mayor Warren Parks. Also Eddie's landlord here."

She shook his hand. "Sierra Byrd."

He arched an eyebrow, likely at her different last name. "I take it you're not close to Eddie."

"No," she said, not wanting him to know she learned of his existence less than six hours ago. "How did you guess?"

"A, he never mentioned you. And B, he's been missing for four weeks now, and you don't seem to know about that."

"Missing?" She blinked. "How can he be missing?"

The mayor frowned, his thin lips dipping above a sparse goatee. "He just up and disappeared. One of his clients called Sheriff Winfield when they couldn't get ahold of your dad. They cordoned this place off. His house, too. Spent days collecting information and doing that forensic thing you see on TV."

As a trace evidence expert, she knew all about that "forensic thing," as he called it. She collected and handled forensics on a regular basis. But she had no idea how to handle the second shock of the day. "Do you know if the sheriff found anything?"

"Guess you haven't read the papers."

She shook her head, but wouldn't explain her limited knowledge of her biological father. "What do they say?"

"Eddie embezzled from his clients and skated with an estimated quarter of a million dollars in tenant rents and security deposits."

Sierra's mouth fell open, and she couldn't close it. Shock

number three, and like in the game of baseball, she was *so* out. Her father wasn't her real father and her biological father was a criminal. A criminal!

Everything caught up to her. She struggled to breathe. Her legs suddenly felt weak. She grabbed onto the wall and started hyperventilating.

"Hey, hey." The mayor reached into his pocket, and pulled out a full key ring. "You look like you need to sit down."

He quickly unlocked the door, took her arm, and led her inside the small office. She dropped onto the nearest chair and put her head between her knees before she passed out. She concentrated on taking deep breaths, but she couldn't seem to gain control of her breathing.

"Sit tight," the mayor said. "I'll go grab a bottle of water for you."

He bolted out the door. She didn't want him to watch her make a fool of herself and was thankful he left. She stared at her feet illuminated by a beam of light shining through the glass door and counted over and over the eyelets in her sneakers to take her mind off her breathing. She felt her body eventually relax, and her breathing return to normal, but the mayor hadn't returned.

She sat up and noticed for the first time that the office smelled stale with a hint of mildew, like it had been closed up for some time. She looked at the desk in front of her. Even in the dark she could see it was covered in fingerprint powder as were many other surfaces.

Curiosity got the best of her, and she went to a door heading to the back room to examine the wood doorframe where residual black powder lingered. She assumed the sheriff department's CSI team processed this place when the sheriff had responded to the call reporting Eddie missing.

The town likely contracted policing with the sheriff as did many tiny towns on the coast.

She wanted more information on Eddie's disappearance, and the sheriff taking charge of the investigation should work in her favor. Up until six months ago, Veritas's investigator Blake Jenkins had been the county sheriff here, and he might be able to get a copy of the sheriff's file on Eddie's disappearance.

She moved over to a picture on the wall behind the desk taken at a baseball field where the mayor stood proudly with another man at his side, both wearing blue-and-white Seaview Cove uniforms. The other man's smile seemed familiar to her, and it took her a few seconds to figure out why. She'd seen the smile in the mirror her entire life. This was Eddie Barnes, and she had his smile.

She ran a finger over his mouth and quickly searched his other facial features. He had a round face like hers, but deep-set blue eyes and a hooked nose not at all like hers. He wore a ball cap that hid his hair, and she couldn't compare the color to hers.

Tears pricked her eyes again, and she wanted to sit down on the floor and have a good cry. But if Eddie was indeed missing, she needed to call in the considerable resources of the Veritas team to help her locate him. She preferred to think he hadn't absconded with his clients' money, but—criminal or not—she needed to see him.

"FBI, don't move," a deep male voice rumbled through the small space making her jump. "Hands on the back of your head."

"Wait, I..."

"Now!"

She thought to turn, but she was sure this agent had a gun and any sudden move could earn her a bullet in the back. She complied, lifting her arms in the air and slowly placing them on the back of her head.

She heard his solid footsteps cautiously cross the room. She held her breath as she waited. He pressed her against the wall, grabbed one of her arms, and tightly cuffed her wrist. She took a long breath and inhaled his scent of warm cinnamon mixed with citrus and masculine leather.

The law enforcement officers she often interacted with on the job didn't smell this good, and she was instantly curious about him, but not curious enough to forget her anger at being cuffed.

"You're going to regret doing this," she said, but as he jerked her other arm back, she wondered if she was the one who would regret coming on a whim to Seaview Cove.

2

Reed huffed out a breath. Just like a suspect to threaten him. The very last thing he needed in this investigation that was going nowhere. As an FBI Agent, *he* should be doing the threatening.

He flipped on the overhead lights and quickly searched the woman, finding only keys and a cell phone in her pockets. He took hold of her shoulder and spun her around.

Big golden-brown eyes met his. Eyes loaded with fury. Her breath was coming in quick, angry gasps, her chest rising and falling.

He ignored her anger and ran his gaze over her. Slender, tall. Five foot ten, he guessed. She wore tan pants tight at the ankles with multiple zippered pockets, and a knit top that wrapped around at her trim waist and fit like a glove, emphasizing her toned abs. He brought his gaze back to her face, and he had to remind himself to breathe.

"Like what you see?" Her snide tone made him mad. Not because of the tone, but because she was right. He'd basically been ogling her.

"Agent Reed Rice." He held out his credentials. "And you are?"

"Sierra Byrd. My ID's in my car."

"Oh, no," a male said from the doorway. "I didn't mean for this to happen."

Reed reached for his weapon and spun, but relaxed when he saw the mayor standing in there.

"You know this woman, Mayor Parks?" Reed asked, making sure to keep an eye on both of them.

"Just met her. She's Eddie's daughter. I told her he was missing, and she started hyperventilating. So I let her in to sit down and went to get water." He held out a bottle.

Reed locked gazes with Parks. "Eddie doesn't have a daughter."

"But she said..." Parks suddenly looked ill himself.

"She most likely wanted to get in here to retrieve something for him."

"Why don't you both try asking me why I'm here?" Her snide tone was back.

This time it really peeved Reed off. He widened his stance and locked gazes with her. "Like I believe you'd tell me the truth."

She sighed, the breath seeming to go on and on. "Give Sheriff Winfield a call. He'll vouch for me."

Reed never took what a suspect said as the truth, but something about her confident tone and the way she held his gaze said she wasn't lying. "How do you know the sheriff?"

"I'm the trace evidence expert at the Veritas Center in Portland. His former boss, Blake Jenkins, works as our investigator now."

Veritas Center? He knew all about that place. His office had used their services in the past. He knew the word Veritas meant truth in Latin, and they prided themselves on finding the truth using their varied and highly-praised skills. Could she really be part of that team?

"She's right about Blake," Parks said sounding relieved. "He *did* move to Portland to go to work for them about six months ago."

"He's also engaged to our DNA expert, Emory Steele," Ms. Byrd, if that was really her name, added.

"Yeah...right...yeah." Parks blew out a relieved breath. "I knew he got engaged to one of them, and that's why he left his job as our sheriff."

"So you're one of the squints at Veritas," Reed said absently as he thought about how to proceed.

"One of the scientists, yes." She glared at him as if he'd insulted her.

Maybe he had.

"I just learned today that Eddie Barnes is my biological father," she said. "I came here to meet him. As Mayor Parks said, I nearly passed out. I'm not usually one to faint, but one too many shocks for the day did me in."

Reed glanced past the mayor and out the open door. "Which car is yours, Ms. Byrd?"

"The red Honda."

"And your ID is in there?"

"Wallet's in my backpack on the floor in the front seat."

"I'll need your keys," he said remembering they were in her pants pocket, and there was no way he would go fishing in her pocket for her keys. "Turn around."

She did, slowly and with an exaggerated sigh. He ignored her continued irritation and also ignored how well the pants fit her shapely body to unlock one of her wrists. "Get your keys out and slowly hand them to me."

She reached into her pocket, not making any effort to break free, and slapped the keys onto his palm.

He clamped the cuff back into place and tossed the keys to Parks. "Go get her backpack."

"Sure." He scuttled out of the room.

16

"You can turn around now," Reed said.

"Like I want to look at you."

"I'll need to see your face to compare it to your ID." He didn't really need to see her as he'd memorized her face, big eyes with long lashes, and soft-looking hair, but he wanted to keep an eye on her expressions.

She slowly turned. He expected her to call him out on his obvious ploy to get her to face him, but she didn't say a word and stared at him. As an agent he should be irritated at her behavior, but she was feisty. He liked that. Liked it a lot.

Parks rushed back into the room carrying a black leather backpack. He set it on the desk, and Reed got out her wallet then fished out her driver's license. He looked at the photo first, surprised to see she'd taken a decent picture at the DMV when they were often hideous. Next he checked her name and details. At thirty-two, she was three years younger than him. And she was indeed five-ten and weighed one-thirty.

He turned to Parks. "Thanks, I can take it from here. I'll lock up after we leave."

Parks clasped his hands together, his gaze on Ms. Byrd. "Are you going to arrest her?"

"We'll see what the sheriff has to say." Reed looked at her. "Might as well sit while we wait."

He pointed at the chairs by the desk. She strode past him, and he noticed for the first time that she smelled like vanilla and something else he couldn't put his finger on. He lingered on the thought far too long and had to mentally shake off the effect she was having on him to get out his phone and dial Sheriff Winfield's cell.

"Evening, Agent Reed," Winfield said.

"I have a Sierra Byrd here in Eddie Barnes's office. She claims you know her."

She cleared her throat, likely over the word "claims," but Reed kept his focus on his call.

"I know *of* her," Winfield said. "But we've never met. Our former sheriff works with her and speaks highly of her."

That was a start. "You aware of Eddie having a kid?"

"No, and our investigation didn't turn that up."

Reed expected Winfield to ask what that had to do with Sierra, but he didn't.

"Give me the cell number for Jenkins so I can confirm her ID with him," Reed said.

A long silence filled the phone. "Doesn't she have her license?"

Yeah, but Reed wasn't ready to admit the first lead he had in this investigation in weeks really might not be a lead at all. "I need a character reference."

"Okay." Winfield gave Reed the guy's cell number, and he memorized it.

"What are you doing at Barnes's office anyway?" Winfield asked. "New evidence?"

Reed didn't need to explain his actions, but he'd developed a strong working relationship with this sheriff and wanted to keep that relationship going. "I had some free time this weekend and came by to interview the locals again. See if they learned anything new on Barnes. I noticed movement inside Barnes's office and decided to check it out."

"I'm assuming if there was anything new I'd have heard about it, but good luck with the interviews." The call abruptly ended.

Reed snapped a picture of Sierra as she glared at him, her mouth puckered. He made the call to the former sheriff.

"Blake Jenkins," he answered, his tone sharp and all business.

"This is FBI Special Agent Reed Rice. Sheriff Winfield gave me your number."

"How can I help you, Agent Reed?" he asked, his tone now cautious.

"I'm in Seaview Cove working a missing person's investigation and have a woman here who claims to be Sierra Byrd. I need you to confirm her ID and vouch for her."

"Sierra?" His surprise left Reed wondering even more about the woman. "She's our trace evidence expert. What's she doing there?"

He wouldn't answer that or share any other details until he was positive of her ID—and probably not even then. "I'm sending her picture your way. Mind checking it and confirming it's your expert?"

"Glad to."

Reed sent the picture and ignored the way she continued to glare at him as he waited for it to go through.

"Yeah, that's Sierra," Jenkins said readily. "Not sure why you have her cuffed, but she doesn't look too happy with you."

Reed ignored the last part of Jenkins's comment. "She ever tell you that Eddie Barnes is her biological father?"

"No, but then I've only worked here around six months and don't know all the partners' personal details."

"Thanks for your help."

"Is she under arrest?" Blake asked. "Does she need a lawyer?"

"I'll release her the minute we get off the phone."

"Tell her to call me once you set her free."

"Will do." Reed hung up and shoved his phone into the pocket of his suit jacket. He started for her, and she came to her feet.

She ran her gaze over him from head to toe, mimicking the way he'd given her the once-over. When her gaze locked back on his face, her expression said she found him wanting, and heaven help him, that bothered him almost as much as cuffing a woman who hadn't really done anything to deserve being shackled.

~

The fed was tall. Six foot two, Sierra figured, and wore what looked like a custom black suit that fit him very well. Broad shoulders tapered to a narrow waist. A ruby red tie circled the neck of his white dress shirt and made his black hair and swarthy coloring look even darker. But it was his eyes she couldn't stop looking at. Brown almost onyx. Dark and dangerous. Long lashes. Mesmerizing.

He held up his handcuff key. "If you'll turn around, I'll remove the cuffs."

She wanted to snap at him, but she wanted the cuffs off more, so she clamped her mouth closed and turned. She also wanted to punch the guy like she often socked her brothers in the arm, but she would never do that. The agent had simply done his job. Found someone he didn't know in the office of the man he was seeking for embezzlement.

"You're angry," he said, his touch gentle as he removed the metal circling her wrists.

"You think?" She rubbed her wrists and turned to stare up at him.

"Just doing my job," he stated, but his expression held remorse.

"I know, but that doesn't mean it doesn't make me mad."

He gestured at the chairs. "Let's sit down and discuss your connection to Eddie."

She wanted to thumb her nose at him and walk out, but she knew he could arrest her for failing to cooperate in his investigation. Anyway, she wanted Eddie found—no matter what he'd done.

She took a seat in the same white vinyl chair with silver arms meant to look stylish and contemporary. She waited for the agent to sit next to her, but he propped a shoulder on the wall and crossed his ankles. Right. He was trying to act relaxed to make her relax, too. She'd seen it a hundred times by detectives and agents on crime scenes, and she wouldn't fall for it. Besides, the intensity in his gaze was a dead give-away to his real feelings.

"So, Ms. Byrd." He paused and fastened those dark eyes on hers.

"It's Sierra."

He gave a clipped nod. "So, Sierra, you just found out today that Barnes is your father?"

She didn't miss the fact that he didn't return the favor and tell her to call him Reed instead of Agent Rice. "That's right, *Agent Rice.*"

"No need to be so formal," he said, his mouth inching up at the corners. "You can call me Reed if you want."

She didn't want to call him anything. She wanted him to leave her alone. "My father—at least the man I have known all my life as my father—needs a kidney transplant. I wanted to donate one, so I got tested. Today I found out that his blood type rules him out from being my father. I confronted my parents. My mom admitted she got pregnant by Eddie when she lived here. He didn't want to be a father. I guess he was a real player."

Reed looked sorry for her. "After investigating him for a month, I would concur with that."

"So he hasn't changed?"

"Doesn't seem like it." Reed tilted his head. "I would think as a scientist you would've wanted DNA confirmation that he was your father before making the long trip out here."

She resisted sighing over her hasty decision. "Yeah, you'd think that, but when my mom told me, I kinda lost it and hopped in the car. I don't know what I expected to happen, but I would've eventually asked for a DNA test."

"We'll be needing one," he stated matter-of-factly.

Of course they would. Law enforcement officers didn't take anyone's word for anything. She should know that. As a crime scene investigator, she spent a lot of time in their company. "I assume you have Eddie's DNA on file."

"We do."

"Mine's on file at Veritas for elimination purposes." She didn't have to explain to an agent that forensic labs kept workers' DNA profiles and fingerprints on file for comparison purposes, allowing them to be sure they hadn't contaminated the evidence they processed. "If you get his DNA profile to me, I can have our DNA expert compare them."

He snorted. "Right. Like your people would do an impartial analysis."

"I assure you we are all impartial, and our DNA expert will give you a legit analysis."

"I'll still want Quantico to do the analysis."

Of course. FBI agents were territorial about their forensics. And they were also biased toward their main lab in Quantico where nearly all of their evidence was processed. Not that Sierra thought their lab was subpar. She was impressed with their state-of-the-art facility, but the partners at Veritas could do everything they could and more. This guy wouldn't care though, so no point in arguing.

"If you give me your email address, I'll have Emory send the profile to you," she offered.

He nodded. "I'll also need your parents' contact information."

She pictured her dad and the way she left him. How she left her mom. Both in pain that she wished she could somehow take away. "I'd hate to have my dad disturbed when he's so sick."

"I'll be brief."

Another thing that arguing wouldn't change. She grabbed a notepad and pen from the desk and wrote down their names, address, and phone number. She jotted down the hospital name, too, and held it out to him, making him step away from his comfy wall position to come get it.

He didn't seem the least bit bothered by her behavior and confidently strode toward her, his walk more of a swagger than anything.

He took the paper, touching her fingers, and she felt a warm rush of attraction. Seriously. The guy cuffs her, irritates her, and what? She's attracted to him. Unbelievable.

He, on the other hand, didn't seem to notice they even touched. He simply stared at the paper. "I'll need your contact information as well."

She reached into the front pocket of her backpack and gave him her business card.

"Home address, too."

"The same. Our labs are in one tower. Condos in the other."

When most people learned that she lived on the same property as her work they said something about taking work home with her, but he didn't comment, just pocketed her card and the paper.

"Are we done here?" she asked.

"You're free to go." He stepped back.

His dismissive behavior got to her, and she finally snapped. "You'd like that, wouldn't you? But I'm not going anywhere except to my car to get my kit."

"Your what?"

"Forensic kit. I intend to find Eddie, and I'm going to process this place and his cottage." She crossed her arms. "After all, I have no proof he took off with the money. For all I know, he was abducted."

Reed scoffed. "Trust me. Eddie took off on his own, and the county forensic techs already processed both places."

County. He used them? Good news really. They might not have been as thorough as an FBI Evidence Recovery Team, and she had a better chance of finding something.

She touched the black powder on the desk. "Obviously the place has been processed."

"And, the locals will have already found everything of value," he added.

"Everything? I doubt it. Regardless, I know you're not planning to share your evidence with me, and I'll need to collect my own."

He arched an eyebrow, the first real sign that she'd gotten to him. "I can't have you interfering in my investigation, Sierra."

His no-nonsense tone might scare off some people, but not her. "I didn't see a seal on this door or one at his cottage. Means you're done with these locations, and as his daughter, I can do whatever I want on his properties."

"Technically this isn't his property."

She had to give him credit for his tenacity, but it also frustrated her. "I'm sure I can get Mayor Parks to give me a key."

He ran his gaze over her, starting at her face then running slowly down her body and back to her face where his gaze held tight, a hint of sarcasm in his expression. "Yeah, I don't doubt you can charm him."

She wouldn't let his comment bait her. She knew when to leave something alone. This was one of those times. "If you'll excuse me, I'll go grab my kit."

He planted his feet as if making himself appear intimidating might stop her from leaving. He was a big obstacle to get around, but she could force her way past him if needed.

She took a step.

"You carry that kit with you all the time?" he asked.

"I get called out at all hours of the day, and I'm not always at the lab with access to our crime scene van." She thought about leaving it at that, but then decided if she shared her intent to fully pursue finding Eddie, the agent would leave her alone. "You should know after a quick phone call to my lab assistant, Chad will be on the road heading here."

His eyes narrowed and were now more black than brown.

"In fact, I'll call in the entire team," she added without really thinking it through. "A quick phone call and they'll be in the air soon."

He ran a hand over his tie to straighten it, but it didn't need straightening. Maybe a sign that she was getting to him more than she first thought.

"Air?" he asked. "You own a helicopter?"

"We have contacts who make their aircraft available to us at a moment's notice." At least she hoped their contacts had a helicopter available. First, she would call Gage Blackwell who owned Blackwell Tactical. He'd always helped them in the past. She only hoped he would do it again. If not, she'd find someone else.

Reed lifted his mouth in a wry smile of acceptance. "Okay. So you're going to do what you're going to do, and without taking you to court I can't stop you. But I can watch your every move."

She imagined this suit standing over her as she processed both places, and she could honestly say as much as she was still irritated with him, he had this male magnetism that she found attractive, and his presence would distract her. "Is that really necessary?"

"Necessary, no." His voice was hard. Resolute. "But when you get to know me, you'll learn I go beyond necessary to get the job done. And I *will* get the job done here, Sierra. I *will* find Eddie Barnes, and when I do, he *will* be headed to prison for embezzlement."

3

Reed watched Sierra make her calls. She turned her back to him as if that meant he couldn't hear her, but Barnes's office was way too small to hold a private conversation. She said she was calling someone named Gage Blackwell to request the use of his helo, and after getting a positive response from the guy, she moved on to call someone named Maya. He pulled up the Veritas Center's webpage on his phone and saw Maya was a partner.

"Here's a shocker," Sierra said into her phone as she pivoted and started pacing. "You know how I got tested to donate a kidney for Dad? Well I'm not a match because he's not my dad."

Reed heard Maya's exclamation of surprise all the way across the room.

"I know, right? Shocking." Sierra paused to listen, nibbling on a full bottom lip as she did. "I'm doing better, but it'll take some time before anything feels right again." She massaged her neck.

She was truly suffering, and Reed didn't like seeing her in such a state. Not one bit. A woman experiencing any type of suffering was his Achilles' heel. It made him focus on helping the woman at all costs and try to do something to stop their suffering. Problem was, in his line of work, he rarely could. But then he could be all wrong here. This phone call could be an act for his benefit. A way to mislead him and get her way. Sierra was clearly strong-willed enough for that. But would she lie to her partner? Something told him she wouldn't.

"Yeah," she said. "Gage is sending Riley to pick everyone up."

There was that Gage name again. Reed left the Veritas website to look up Gage Blackwell. A link to Blackwell Tactical's website came up, and he tapped on it. Located in Cold Harbor, the company was a private investigation and protection company owned by Gage Blackwell. They also trained law enforcement. All team members were former military or law enforcement who couldn't continue their service due to on-the-job injuries. Blackwell, a former SEAL, hired them to work at his company doing similar work.

Reed had to respect the man and his dedication to these men and woman. Reed scrolled down their class listing. He was impressed at the depth of their offerings, and he would have appreciated this type of training when he'd signed on as a Washington County Deputy right out of college. Reed suspected he would like Blackwell if he ever met him.

Sierra turned to look at Reed. He wanted to keep reviewing the website, but her stance grabbed his attention. She was a confident woman. Confident in herself. Confident in her work. And Reed liked that. Took a confident person to stand up to an FBI agent, much less come back from being shackled by one. Couple her feistiness with her beauty, and his thoughts traveled as far from Eddie Barnes as they could possibly go.

"And will you please have Emory bring my DNA

profile?" she said into her phone. "Agent Reed is refusing to give us access to Eddie's profile."

She ran a hand through golden-blond hair with streaks of lighter blond. He had no idea if they were natural or from a salon, but her hair looked thick and silky soft.

"Right, I know," she continued speaking into her phone. "Eddie's DNA has to be all over this place and his house, but it'll still take twenty-four or more hours to process before we have a profile for comparison. If I can confirm Eddie's my biological father sooner, I'm all for that." A pause and another nibble on her lower lip. "Okay, see you soon."

She shoved her phone into her pocket. He noted a sheen of moisture in her eyes, but she batted those amazing lashes and cleared the tears away as she firmed her shoulders. "Prepare to be descended upon. My team's on the way, as is my assistant, Chad, with our forensic van."

He held her gaze. "Not sure why you need your entire team to process forensics."

Her shoulders went up into a rigid line, but he didn't know why. He wasn't baiting her. Just speaking his mind.

"We're not stopping with forensics," she said, a determined expression tightening her face. "Four weeks have already passed since Eddie was last seen, and we both know that if he didn't disappear on his own, each minute counts. So I can't afford to waste a moment and will need additional help as we launch a full-fledged investigation of our own."

"He took off on his own, all right," Reed said. "We have zero evidence to prove he met with foul play."

"I couldn't possibly know that since you won't share your information. If I want to get up to speed on finding Eddie, what's my alternative other than beginning my own investigation?"

Usually he didn't care what others thought when he withheld information, but she was getting under his skin, and he didn't like how she was making him seem like the bad guy here. "It's not that I won't share. *I can't*. It's an ongoing investigation."

"Whatever." She gathered up her thick hair into a ponytail and secured it with a holder from her backpack. "Just one question. If finding Eddie is so important to you, why didn't you call in one of your crack Evidence Recovery Teams to process this scene?"

"The locals got here first," he said which was the truth, but it felt like a lie to save his pride, so he added, "And even if they hadn't, the teams are all working much bigger investigations." That last bit still stuck in Reed's craw.

He expected a smirk from her, but he was glad to see a single nod. "Exactly the type of situation Veritas is often called in to handle. I'm going to get that kit from my car now."

She didn't seize an opportunity to make him feel like a loser, and his respect for her climbed the ladder. She stepped out the door and went to the Honda. He followed her to offer his help in carrying her things. He figured it might help change their antagonistic start and maybe get them off on a better footing. She stood by her trunk filled with plastic totes neatly labeled. A large portable case looking like a giant fishing tackle box sat closest to her, and she pulled it out.

"Can I carry anything?" he asked.

She lifted her gaze to his face. "What's with the helpful act?"

"It's not an act. I'm a genuinely helpful guy."

She didn't seem to buy his response, but pointed at a blue tote labeled Basics. "I need that one."

He lifted it out, and she slammed her trunk. She marched back inside, and he had to admit it was no hardship to watch the sway of her curvy hips.

30

She set her case by the door, and he put the tote on the floor next to it. She opened the tub to pull out white coveralls. After ripping open the package, she shimmied her shapely body into the suit then put on blue booties over her bright white sneakers and got out gloves.

If she were working for him, he would appreciate her thoroughness, but now it meant he'd be here longer when he wanted to be interviewing the locals instead. "Not sure why you need booties when this place has already been contaminated by us."

"No point in making it worse." She handed him a pair of booties and gloves. "If you'd be so kind not to add to the situation."

He really didn't see the point, but then he didn't see the point of her search. Still, no sense in antagonizing her any further. He slipped on the booties, and before he put on the gloves, he took off his suit coat, loosened his tie, and unbuttoned his shirt's top button. When he looked up, he found her standing like a statue staring at him.

"Something wrong?" he asked.

She blinked, but not before he caught the look in her eyes that said she was attracted to him. She could blink all she wanted, but it wouldn't hide that interest.

She swallowed, drawing his attention to her slender neck above the unshapely coveralls. "Looks like you're getting comfy."

"This will take some time, right?" he asked.

She nodded.

"Then I'll be here for a while and might as well be comfortable." That earned him a frown. "Do you honestly think you'll find something?"

"Yes," she said with unwavering confidence.

He liked her continued confidence, but he had to wonder if it was misplaced here. "So you think your skills are better than the entire forensic team who did the original work?"

"Without question." She held up a hand before he could respond. "I'm not being conceited. I just have more experience and a different approach to evidence collection than most forensic scientists."

"How's that?" he asked, honestly interested now.

"Most forensic scientists are just scientists. They don't go beyond the science to learn about the victim or suspect. I find getting into his or her head provides additional direction for my search, and I often come away with leads that are missed by others."

Interesting. "What's your background?"

"I have a BA in forensic science and master's in criminology. Plus, I worked three years for the LAPD in their forensic science division and five years at Veritas."

Okay. He was officially impressed now. "The crazies come out in Los Angeles. You must've seen some interesting crime scenes there."

She nodded and turned to her tote where she removed a camera. "But to be clear, processing a scene after someone else had done so will limit the evidence I can collect. Most of the trace evidence will have already been collected. Same is true of fingerprints. Once a tech lifts them they're removed unless they're fumed on scene."

"Fumed?"

"It's done to expose older prints. You put the nonporous item inside an airtight chamber, in this case a portable one, then add cyanoacrylate—basically Super Glue—and water. The fumes fix the print on the item and make it visible. These prints can be lifted many times."

"Interesting."

"Mind stepping behind me so I can take scene photos."

"Again, what's the point? It's not in the condition we

found it in. We've moved and rifled through everything in here."

"It will serve as reference later on if I have a question."

He moved behind her, and she started firing off pictures in rapid succession. She headed into the back room turning on lights as she moved, and he followed. She snapped shot after shot of the large space with boxes and other items stacked on one side and a small kitchen with table and chairs on the other. She went to the bathroom and did the same thing.

She backed her way out, heading for the front door, taking additional shots.

Confused, he asked, "Didn't you just take pictures of this area?"

She nodded. "Capture the scene on the way in and on the way out. You don't miss a thing that way."

He'd never seen a forensic photographer shoot pictures on the way *out* of a scene, and he was beginning to think she might indeed find something today.

Back in the front room, she snapped pictures again, then hung the camera around her neck and took out a tripod that she set up by the exit. She mounted a light on it and plugged it in. The room was suddenly flooded with bright light.

"Seems odd that you didn't use that light for the pictures."

"It's better to take the scene photos in the existing light." She grabbed a sketchpad and started drawing the room, noting each item within view.

She pointed her pen at the large picture window. "Were the blinds up when you arrived on scene?"

He nodded. "But I'd have to check the reports to see if the locals found them that way."

She made a note on her pad. "Are you bored yet? Because if you are, you could take off."

"I'm good," he said and meant it, as he was enjoying watching her. He wondered if she knew that the tip of her tongue peeked out the side of her mouth when she sketched and it darted back in every time she looked up at the scene. Did she do the same thing when studying evidence? He couldn't wait to see.

She grabbed a magnifying glass and turned to the knob. She looked at it for a long time, changing angles, her tongue darting in and out.

"What are you looking for?" he asked.

"Patent prints."

"Patent? I usually hear the term latent."

"Patent simply means prints that are visible to the naked eyed. Latents are hidden prints. They're undetectable until brought out with a physical or chemical process designed to enhance print residue. Like this fingerprint powder." She tapped the lid of a small jar in her kit that held black powder.

She strapped a white mask over her mouth and nose. "Protection from the powder."

She didn't offer him one, so he had to assume he didn't need it.

She dumped a bit in a small tray and chose a wide brush to dip into the powder. She gently swirled the brush over the knob and sat back. "I'll need your prints for elimination purposes."

He could easily refuse her, but why? She didn't actually need him to cooperate. She could have a law enforcement contact search AFIS. As a law enforcement officer, the FBI's Automated Fingerprint Identification System would contain his prints, but she might actually find something useful here and having his prints right up front would make eliminating them easier for her.

"You want to take them here or should I email my print

card?" he asked, as she would know that all law enforcement officers were printed for such a situation.

"Card," she said without looking up.

He continued to watch her work and a sad vibe emanated from her. Was she thinking about hearing about her biological father for the first time? That would freak anyone out. Even a strong woman—like Sierra was proving to be. And Reed was adding to her anguish.

He didn't much like that thought. "Maybe we could work together on this investigation."

Her head shot up. "Work together as in you share everything that has happened in the investigation up to this point?"

"Well no, but—"

"But you thought I'd agree and give you access to my information." She shook her head and got a flashlight out of her kit. "Let me know when you're ready to make this a two-way street, and then I'll be glad to partner with you."

4

Sierra couldn't believe this agent's continued nerve—give me everything you've got while I hold out on you. Seriously. Someone needed to teach law enforcement officers to share. They were excellent at holding things close to the vest. A lot of the time they *had* to keep quiet. She got that. Even appreciated their ability to keep leads quiet from the general public. But she wasn't the general public. She was a partner in their investigations. Sadly, even when it would benefit them to get approval to read her in on their case files, they often didn't.

No point in even thinking about that. Not when she had work to do to keep her mind occupied. She dropped to her knees and shone her flashlight on the doorknob.

She lifted her camera and snapped several shots of the fingerprints she'd developed. Might just be Mayor Parks's prints from when he let her into the office, but it was a start. She took her camera and shot several pictures of the knob before cutting off a strip of tape.

Reed stepped closer. "I've seen techs use wide tape like that as well as plain Scotch tape. Why use different tapes?"

Did he plan to question her every move? If so, it would

be a long night. Still, she liked to educate LEOs on the forensics process when she could. "Polyethylene tape like this works well on multi-curved surfaces because it stretches and conforms to the shape without distorting the print. Scotch tape is often used for soot removal as it's less likely to tear, it's more flexible, and has better surface cohesion than this tape. But it's also often not large enough to lift an entire print."

She pressed the tape over each print and fixed them to individual fingerprint cards. She quickly filled in the information on the card regarding the scene and where she lifted the prints, along with noting them on her sketch. She placed them in a divided section of her kit.

Each time she moved she was aware of the man standing over her. He was imposing, seeming to take up the entire space, and she couldn't tune him out.

She got up and met his gaze. "If you're not going to leave, you might as well bring a chair over here and make yourself comfortable. This will take a while."

"I'm good," he said.

She pinned him with a sharp gaze. At least she hoped she had, but if so, he didn't react at all. "Well, I'm not good with you lurking over me and studying my every move. So give me a break and take a seat."

He didn't move.

She marched across the room, grabbed the chair, and set it in front of him. "Sit."

A wide grin crossed his handsome face.

"What?" She planted her hands on her hips and stared at him.

"You're cute when you get tough." His grin widened.

She wanted to shout at him, but she couldn't seem to muster any anger at his comment. Not when his grin made her stomach flutter.

"I'm sorry," he said. "That wasn't very professional."

He dropped into the chair, but his focus remained locked on her, and she had to drag her attention back to her work. She would spend hours thoroughly processing this place, and then the rest of the night at the cottage. The work alone would tire her out, but this man's study? That would mentally exhaust her. For now, she would focus on the work until she figured out how to get rid of him.

She grabbed her magnifying glass, evidence markers, and her sketch, and went to the corner—as far from him as possible. She would cover every inch of this place before she was done, and she *would* forget he was here.

You can do it. He's just a guy.

Yeah, a guy who piqued her interest when none had in over a year. Not since she broke up with her last boyfriend. He wanted to get married, but to her, marriage meant smothering her independence like her parents and brothers often did. She wouldn't give up her independence for any man.

Remember that and having him around will be easier.

She dropped to the floor and collected soil samples. She bent closer and discovered a hair wedged in a floorboard. *Perfect*. It could provide DNA and they could run it through CODIS—Combined DNA Index System managed by the FBI. The tech probably thought they couldn't get it out with root and follicular tissue intact and left it behind. Which also told her if that was the case, that they might have retrieved other hairs of similar color. Or with very little of the hair protruding above the boards, they simply could've missed it.

She took out a plastic tweezer, and after grasping the end of the hair, she patiently worked the entire strand free with a bamboo skewer and bagged it. She held the strand up to the light and believed it to be ordinary brown in color. Eddie's?

She logged the find on her drawing and looked over her shoulder at Reed. "Do you have a picture of Eddie without a cap on?"

"I do."

"Can I see it?"

"Don't see why not." He got up and came to squat behind her. She swiveled, coming face-to-face with him, her knee bumping his leg. She felt oddly nervous about touching him. Sure, he slapped cuffs on her wrists and removed them, but touching him like this? That was a whole different thing. She scooted back. That earned her a cocked head and more intense study.

"The picture." She pointed at his phone.

He held out the phone, but kept his focus pinned to her.

She didn't care at the moment. Not when another picture of her biological father was right in front of her. She could hardly process the fact that she was using that term in relationship to herself. Crazy. Totally crazy.

She studied the man who looked to be about the same age as the picture on the wall, his skin tan and coarse from years of sun exposure, but the skin around his eyes was whiter likely from sunglasses. He had a head of thick, shaggy surfer-blond hair with hints of gray. Her assessment seemed apropos as he looked more like a surfer than a businessman.

"Your mouth resembles his," Reed said.

She didn't like him focusing on her mouth and turned back to her findings. "Thanks. You can go back to your chair now."

She tucked the hair sample into her tote and felt a sense of vindication as this hair wasn't from Eddie's head and could be an important lead. She finished searching the floor and stood to look at the desk.

A nine-inch whale figurine was one of the few things remaining on the dusty desk. If Eddie had been taken forcefully, the solid metal whale was the perfect item to knock him over the head. She shone her light on it, but as she suspected, it didn't reflect any prints or blood. If it did, the techs would have taken it. But that didn't deter her. Careful not to smudge any unseen prints, she slid it into a paper bag.

"Okay, tell me why you're taking that," Reed demanded.

"Just a gut feel."

"For what?"

"Maybe it was used to hit Eddie over the head."

"No blood or the techs would've found it."

"Unless the person doing the hitting cleaned the whale. Then any blood residue would be so minuscule that it couldn't be seen without additional testing."

He looked skeptical.

"And no offense to the local techs, but your case theory that Eddie took off on his own was likely communicated to the techs. They could've had a bias as they processed this space. Why look for blood in your scenario?"

He opened his mouth as if to shoot down her point, but then snapped it closed. Could he actually be keeping an open mind here? Not that it mattered, except she liked the fact that he might be considering her theory, too.

She continued searching the desk and developed a number of prints before combing through the drawers. She found an autographed baseball, golf tees, several matchbooks from local bars, and a stack of golf score cards that were filled in. She flipped through the dated cards. Eddie had played every day until the twelfth of August, about four weeks ago. About the time he disappeared.

She looked up at Reed. "Who was the last person to see Eddie and when?"

"Mayor Parks actually. August twelfth. Here in Eddie's office late in the afternoon around five."

The same day as the final round of golf. Could Eddie have argued with his golf partner and it carried over to later in the day after the mayor had left the office? She snapped a picture of that card and bagged all of them. Eddie had identified his golfing partners by initials only. She would have Nick Thorn, the team's cyber expert, try to match the initials to names, focusing on the person who played the last round with Eddie.

In the bottom drawer she found a bottle of whiskey and two glasses. She took them all out and was surprised to see latents still on the items where fingerprint dust coated them. The only explanation was that there were duplicate prints on the items and the techs only lifted a few of them. She would never routinely leave any prints behind, but in a public space like this there would be a huge catalogue of prints to review. Maybe the techs were lazy and didn't want to do all the work.

She lifted several good prints, then swabbed the bottle and glasses for DNA and bagged them. Another drawer held snacks and yet another was filled with paper plates, napkins, plastic silverware, and condiments.

She found zero paperwork or files in any of the drawers that would indicate Eddie actually worked at this desk. "I'm assuming you took Eddie's computer into evidence."

"We did."

"Any way I can get an image of the hard drive?" Law enforcement routinely made copies of hard drives to preserve the computer's integrity.

"No."

"Of course not," she snapped and instantly regretted her outburst.

He didn't say a word, but his jaw tightened.

She turned back to her work and finished the desk area, not recovering anything else of interest. She found a pair of athletic shoes under the desk and bagged them.

"What's the point in taking the shoes?" Reed asked. "Our techs would've already ruled them out as being unimportant."

"How could they? Without taking them to a lab they could only have considered the loosely held particles on the shoes."

"Explain," he said, but it was more like a demand.

She looked at him and tried not to glare at his continued demands. "There are three different categories of particles found on a shoe—loosely, moderately, and tightly held. The loosely held particles are like they sound, particles that will fall off quite easily, and that's where techs often focus. But if you really want to know where a person has been, you need to look at the recessed surfaces of the shoes. These areas hold a mixture of particles arising from activity before, during, and after a crime—or in this case, a disappearance. Examining this area allows me to develop a more sophisticated profile of where a shoe has been."

"And that can only be done in a lab?"

"I suppose a tech could do it on scene, but they would have to own expensive portable equipment, which I know a rural county agency wouldn't have the money for."

He gave a clipped nod, a hint of admiration in his expression.

Her shoulders rose of their own accord making her a prideful fool. Something she never wanted to be. Yeah, she was good at her job. Not because she wanted people to think highly of her, but because she wanted to find the truth.

What was the truth here? The truth of Eddie Barnes? He didn't seem to be a hard worker or there would be more evidence of his work in his desk drawers, not just food and sports-related items. Even his pictures on the wall were all about sports.

"Does Eddie have a business manager?" she asked Reed.

"No. It's a one-man operation. He does have an accountant in Portland."

"Couldn't the accountant have taken the money?"

Reed shook his head. "I'm not at liberty to discuss the details, but there's no evidence to suggest that—or to suggest Eddie was abducted."

Which was why no one was seriously considering that angle, and she had to. If he'd been hit over the head with the whale, blood could have sprayed on the wall.

"How tall is Eddie?" she asked.

"Five-eleven."

She was an inch shorter, and that would place the spatter around and above her eye level. She went to her kit, dropped BLUESTAR tablets into a spray bottle with water, and swirled the liquid to mix it.

"What's that?" Reed asked.

"It's a blood reagent like luminol, which I'm sure you've heard of." She set the bottle on the desk and went to close the blinds.

"But you're not using luminol?"

She shook her head. "It can alter DNA, but BLUESTAR claims it won't. Plus with the window in the door, I can't eliminate all ambient light, and BLUESTAR doesn't need one hundred percent darkness to display the stain."

He gave an impressed nod again, and she worked hard not to let it puff up her pride.

She ripped off her gloves. "I need to grab another tripod from the car while this mixes. Be right back."

She eased past him to step outside. She took a moment to inhale the fishy ocean air and blow out the tension she'd been feeling under this man's focused attention. He'd kept his gaze trained on her, never seeming bored or acting like his mind was wandering. That kind of attention to detail was the hallmark of a strong forensic tech and strong law enforcement officer. Maybe he was good at his job, even if he seemed to be unwilling to think Eddie was abducted. With no evidence pointing that way, she could see how he would come to and hold that conclusion as fact. She didn't like it, but she could understand it.

She grabbed her tripod, and as she closed the trunk, she noticed security cameras on several businesses across the street. Reed would already have asked the owners for any video feed catching this side of the road, he wouldn't share with her. She made a mental note to have her teammates talk to those shop owners. She carried the tripod inside and mounted her camera making sure to leave the shutter wide open to catch any luminescence of blood.

Eddie could've been struck on either side of the desk. If on the far side she might find blood on the wall. If on the closer side, blood would have sprayed onto the closed blinds.

She set her camera facing the blinds, put on a fresh pair of gloves, and sprayed the BLUESTAR mixture. A flashing hot release of white light appeared and disappeared rapidly, leaving only a blue glow.

"I knew it." She hurried behind her camera and took pictures of the glow before it disappeared—typically in thirty seconds or so with reagents.

"What?" Reed asked.

"Blood, but cleaned up with bleach. That's what's causing the white flashing light."

Reed crossed over to her and stared at the blinds as if he

was seeing the blood for the first time. "Could've been from another incident, right?"

She looked at him. "Didn't the forensic team find this?"

He clenched his jaw and shook his head. "There was nothing in the forensics report about blood, but they could have checked for it and didn't find any."

"If that's true, then this could have occurred after the techs processed the place."

"You're saying Barnes came back here at a later date and no one saw him?"

"It's possible, right?"

"Yes."

"It could also explain the hair I found on the floor. That the techs were thorough and didn't miss it."

Reed didn't say anything else but went back to his seat and started typing on his phone.

She decided to spray the floor and found more cleaned-up blood. She sprayed the wall, but with the distance from the window she didn't expect to find anything, and she didn't. She resprayed all areas where she located blood and snapped photos, then collected several samples before turning the lights back on.

Worried that Eddie had been hurt, she felt a new sense of urgency and grabbed her tote to move to the back room. Reed came along behind her, carrying the chair with the bin sitting on the seat. He set the bin by her bag and straddled the chair, resting his arms on the back and watching her with those bottomless brown eyes. She ignored him, grabbed her infrared light, and turned off the overhead light. She was glad for the dark again as she didn't have to see him watching her.

Hoping to locate prints, she shone the light over the door and frame.

"Why are you using infrared light?" he asked. "I know the techs used ultraviolet when they processed the place."

She wanted to sigh at the continued questions but kept her focus on the work. "Did they process the scene shortly after he disappeared?"

"Yeah, three days after he was last seen."

"Makes sense then. Prints change over time and the type of light that will best display them changes with it. Infrared is best for detecting long duration latent prints."

"I've never sat and watched our techs like this before," he said. "But I'm learning a lot from you, and have to say I'll be more thankful for our techs in the future."

"Glad I could help with that." She really was, even if it meant her every move being scrutinized.

She recovered several prints and headed to the kitchen area where two dirty glasses sat in the sink. She could swab them here or take them to Emory. Sierra bagged them, expecting Reed to ask why, but he didn't. She glanced back at him, and he was looking at his phone.

She let her gaze linger, admiring the planes of his face and his intense focus in the glow from the screen's bright light. She might find him attractive, but she already knew he would be a controlling partner. Probably not intentionally, but he would want to be in charge in a relationship. She had no doubts about that. Even if he was the first guy in a long time who caught her interest, she could never be with a guy like him. Never in a million years.

His phone chimed. "County CSI *did* check for blood but found none."

"So if this is Eddie's blood, he came back."

"Even more of a reason to believe he took off on his own."

Sierra thought about it. "Maybe he was afraid for his life

and went into hiding. For some reason, he had to come back to retrieve something and was hit over the head."

"We don't know it's Barnes's blood, do we? He might be the attacker."

She couldn't dispute that. Not at all. Not without DNA or blood type matches. "DNA will tell us that. And also once I'm back at the lab I can use Raman spectroscopy to accurately date the blood stains. Provided they're less than two years old."

"You can date blood?"

"Yes."

He shook his head, clearly impressed, and Sierra hated to admit that it made her feel special.

"Sierra," Maya's voice came from the other room.

Sierra felt like jumping for joy at the arrival of her team, but she calmly set down her light and left the room. Reed cast her a questioning look, but she didn't feel like explaining. He would encounter the full force of her partners' intensity in a minute. She honestly felt sorry for him. They knew he'd cuffed her, and if he thought she'd been difficult, the full force of the Veritas team would challenge even this strong law enforcement officer's resilience.

5

After cuffing Sierra and refusing to share much information on the investigation, Reed didn't expect the Veritas partners to open their arms to him as they stood on the sidewalk outside Eddie's office. But the instant dislike emanating from most faces? That he didn't expect. All three of the men were toned and clearly worked out, and they wore protective expressions—as a man, Reed totally got that. The three women had their gazes fixed on Sierra.

She rushed up to them. "Thank goodness it's Saturday and the lab's closed so you could all come."

"We're glad to be here," said the woman with curly black hair. She was wearing a feminine print blouse and dressy black slacks.

One of the dark-haired guys dressed in black tactical pants and an olive green long-sleeved combat shirt stepped forward. He wore a sidearm as did the redheaded guy. He held out his hand. "Blake Jenkins."

Reed shook, not at all surprised at Jenkins's firm grip. "The former sheriff."

"That's right," he said. "Now investigator at Veritas. Mind telling me your role here?"

"Lead agent investigating Eddie Barnes's embezzlement of a quarter of a million dollars of his clients' money."

Jenkins's expression didn't reveal anything. "Any local law enforcement involved?"

Reed snorted. "C'mon, Jenkins. You've already called Sheriff Winfield, and I wouldn't be surprised if you don't already have his report in hand. No need to play it cool. Just ask what you want to know, and I'll give it to you straight."

Jenkins eyed him. "I'd like a copy of your case file."

"Not happening." Reed widened his stance. "Anything else?"

The redheaded male stepped forward. He was dressed very much like Jenkins but his pants were khaki colored and his shirt navy blue. He offered his hand. "Grady Houston. Team ballistics, firearms, and explosives expert. It'd go a lot easier for all of us if we're more civil."

Right. Like *he* was the one with the attitude. "I didn't think I *wasn't* being civil, but I wouldn't mind if you all toned down the evil eye you're giving me."

The woman with red hair and glasses crossed her arms. "You cuffed Sierra."

"Just doing my job, Ms.—"

"Steele. Emory Steele. DNA expert."

"You all know Sierra." Reed let his gaze travel over the group. "*You* know her character, but she's a stranger to me. She was inside the office with the lights out when I arrived. I'd never seen her before and had to assume she wasn't up to any good and might flee if I didn't restrain her."

"He's right," Sierra said, coming to his defense, surprising him. "It was all a misunderstanding. And he released me after checking me out."

"Just like you to let something like this go so quickly." The other man dressed in torn jeans and a T-shirt that said

49

Be nice to me, You might need tech support someday smiled at Sierra.

"And you are?" Reed asked.

"Nick Thorn. Cyber and computer expert."

"And I'm Kelsey Moore. Anthropology," the ultra-feminine woman who first greeted Sierra said.

The woman with blond hair and a no-nonsense vibe about her offered her hand. "I'm Maya Glass, toxicology and controlled substances. I'm also our managing partner."

"You're all well-respected in the law enforcement world," he said sincerely.

Sierra frowned like she didn't believe him, but there was nothing he could do to prove that he thought highly of their team.

She looked around the group. "I'm nearly done processing this place. While I finish I want you all to interview store personnel before the stores close for the night. And there are security cameras pointed this direction so ask about those, too. Then we can regroup and formulate a game plan."

"I've rented a house just outside of town for the night." Maya handed Sierra a piece of paper. "The address. We can meet there."

"Perfect." Sierra smiled at her partner.

"What about him?" Grady eyed Reed.

"He won't be coming with us," Sierra said firmly. "He's unable to share anything on his investigation, and we won't be partnering with him."

Reed hated that they all looked glad. He was thick-skinned, but when seven intelligent people like these team members were glad to be rid of him, it was hard not to take it personally. Still, he would never comment on that.

Emory handed a large envelope to Sierra. "Your DNA profile."

Sierra waved her hand. "Give it to Reed."

Emory frowned but shoved the envelope in his direction.

He took it and gestured at the door. "After you, Sierra."

"Oh, right," she said. "Agent Rice is dogging my every move here and will be joining me to process the house."

"I know that sounds bad, but I need to keep track of items she removes." Skeptical gazes said they didn't buy his response, but he didn't need them to.

He followed Sierra back inside. He took a picture of her DNA profile and emailed it to their DNA expert in Quantico along with Eddie's profile. Reed could see there were several matches between the alleles in the two profiles, but he wasn't an expert and couldn't make the determination of parentage. The expert promised to get back to him right away.

He sat back and watched as Sierra finished the rest of the place in two hours. He made a long list on his phone of the items she collected, and he would talk to the lead forensic tech assigned to the investigation on Monday to get his take on the findings.

His phone chimed, and he read the text from the DNA expert before looking up. "Your DNA is a match to Eddie."

She sighed, but her gaze remained wary. "Not that I thought my mom was lying, but it's good to have an official confirmation."

He couldn't even imagine how it felt to have your life rocked like this. And he'd been making things difficult for her. Not on purpose, but he still didn't like hurting her more when she was already stressed out. "I'll help you load your car."

"You don't have to."

He focused on her very expressive eyes. "We should bury the hatchet before we go to Eddie's cottage, or it'll be a very long night."

"I don't have anything against you, Agent Rice."

"Reed," he said getting mad that she was taking a step backward and making things more formal between them. "Did I do something other than cuff you and refuse to share about the investigation? Because this is starting to seem personal."

She didn't respond right away, but blew out a breath of air that lifted her bangs. "It's probably the stress of the day. It's not often you find out your dad isn't your dad."

"I can't even imagine that." He picked up the bin.

She grabbed the bag and stepped outside. "Are you close to your parents?"

"Actually, no. They died when I was eight. My sister, Malone, was six, and we went into foster care." He couldn't believe he shared something personal. He never did that at work.

"I'm so sorry."

He set the bin in the trunk and waved a hand as a gusty ocean breeze blew over them. "That was a long time ago and we were lucky. We stayed together and got amazing foster parents who cared for us until we were both through college."

She smiled at him, her bangs blowing in the strong wind. "You hear so many negative foster family stories that it's nice to hear a positive one."

He nodded. "What about you? You mentioned your parents but any siblings?"

"Five brothers, if you can believe it."

"Wow. That must've been interesting growing up."

"Yeah, if you think being smothered 'by overprotective guys and being pushed into a career that's safer than being a law enforcement officer is interesting." She shook her head. "I don't mean to sound bitter. It's just that even though I'm the oldest, my parents and brothers often don't take what I want into account. I get that they love me, but they need to love me a little bit less."

"I can understand how they feel. I'm very protective of Malone."

She watched him for a long moment. "But you have a reason to feel that way. After your parents died, it's only normal for you to want to take care of her."

"I did—still do," he said, even more shocked that he let this conversation continue.

She frowned and headed back inside, but he didn't know why she was frowning. Maybe she thought he was controlling like her brothers. And he was—on the job—and he didn't hide it. But being controlling on the job versus in his personal life were two different things. On the job he had to take control or people could get hurt. Even die. But he wasn't the same way with Malone. Sure, he wanted to protect her, but he didn't interfere in her life.

Not something he would share with a virtual stranger. He'd already said *way* more than he felt comfortable with on the job.

They finished loading her car, and she leaned against the trunk. "You might as well take off. I'll be meeting with my teammates for some time."

"But you're still planning on processing the cottage tonight."

"After the meeting."

"You're sure I can't sit in on your meeting?"

She eyed him. "Can you provide details about your investigation?"

"Sorry. The answer's still no."

"Then so is mine." She met and held his gaze. "I'm not trying to be difficult."

"Aren't you? What's the point in you withholding your

findings or plans from me? The only thing that sharing your information can do is help find your father faster."

She frowned, and her exquisite eyes narrowed. He wanted to press out the line between her eyebrows and find a way to make her smile. The thought shocked him, and he stepped back.

"You're right," she finally said. "I *am* being difficult. I know you can't share, but that doesn't mean I can't."

He watched her carefully, looking for any duplicitous motive. "And what about your teammates? They made it clear that they don't think I'm worthy of your help."

"They're acting like my brothers. Being overprotective. But unlike my brothers, they'll get over it and move on." She pushed off the trunk and held out her hand. "So you're welcome to attend our meeting, and I'll be glad to share any leads I find once I process everything I gather tonight."

He took her hand. The warmth of her touch and the genuine smile he'd been wanting to see directed his way sent a shock clean through him. He'd wanted her to give in. To work with him, but maybe that wasn't such a good idea. At least not if he didn't want to be distracted from finding Barnes by this very captivating woman.

6

Sierra stepped onto the wide rental house deck overlooking the ocean, the moon casting bright beams onto the waves pounding against the shore. The rhythmic swells were both soothing and unsettling at the same time. She'd always loved coming to the beach. But tonight the rushing water reminded her of her parents' duplicitous behavior. Even so, the scene gave her a peace that she couldn't explain.

"The ocean always reminds me of God's power," Reed said, coming up behind her.

She looked over her shoulder at him and studied the contours of his face in the shadowed light. His wide jaw looked firm and imposing. His cheeks high and attractive. But his eyes caught and held hers again. She only allowed them to touch her heart for a fraction of a moment before turning back to the ocean.

He stepped up beside her. He was too close for her comfort, but she wouldn't move away and alert him to the effect he had on her.

He leaned his elbows on the railing. "Who other than an all-powerful God could create such power that is also breathtaking?"

"Agreed," she said, thinking about God in her life. "When I was a kid, I felt closest to God in my mom's flower garden. The colors were so vibrant. Colors man couldn't replicate." Memories flooded over her. The scent of the flowers, the bright sunshine. She was surprised to find they didn't bring tears to her eyes. "I would sit there for hours. A favorite book. Alone. Just the way I liked it. Not a brother in sight. They were too macho to go near flowers, so it was my hiding place."

"Do you still like to read?"

She nodded. "Though these days it's more likely to be a forensic or crime magazine or journal. Not much time for reading for enjoyment. I still have to hide out from my brothers' interference in my life, though. But if they're trying to butt in where they don't belong, I just don't return their calls." She risked a glance at Reed and found him staring into the ocean, and she loved looking at his chiseled profile. "What about you? A reader?"

He gave a firm nod but didn't look at her. "I started as a kid, too. Used it to escape the fact that our parents died. Now, I'm like you. More professional reading than anything else."

"And your sister? Are you close?"

"Very." His emphatic response put a slice of concern in her heart.

Was he just close or did he like to boss her around like her brothers did?

He looked at her. "Any boyfriends in the picture?"

Why was he asking that?

"Sorry. You don't need to answer. I'm not one for personal discussions on the job. Guess the scenery is making me relax."

"No boyfriend," she said figuring it didn't hurt to answer

his question. "What about you? Anyone special in your life?"

"No girlfriend at the moment," he said. "But I want to get married and have a family someday, so I'm looking."

"Not me." She shifted her focus to the moon hanging full in the sky. "I've had enough of a big family butting into my every move, and I like being on my own."

He shook his head. "It's hard for me to understand that. After my parents died, all I wanted was a family. Sure, our foster parents were great, but we knew it was temporary. Ten plus years of temporary made me want exactly what you have."

"I get where you're coming from," she said, feeling bad for him. "But a big family would make me crazy and isn't what I see in my future."

"I was old enough when my parents died to remember what being a part of a permanent family was like. It's hard for me to understand why you're fighting to break away from yours. I mean, I get the recent issue concerning your biological dad, but otherwise." He lifted those broad shoulders in a shrug.

"I guess we agree to disagree here," she said, not sure why that thought made her sad.

She heard a commotion from inside and turned to look through the open patio door. "Grady and Maya finally got here. We can get started with our meeting."

He connected gazes with her for only a moment, just enough for her to see the longing in his eyes. She totally got why he wanted a family and it still hurt that he lost his, but if he had five bossy brothers like she did, she was sure he would understand her viewpoint.

He gestured for her to go ahead of him, and she entered the family room. He pulled the sliding door closed, and she glanced at her partners already facing the portable white-board that Blake had brought along. He stood next to it, marker in his hand.

Sierra took a seat next to Kelsey on a comfy sofa covered with a tropical print. To her dismay, Reed sat next to her, his knee touching hers for a moment before he jerked it away. Kelsey noticed his sudden movement and eyed Sierra, but she pointed her focus at Blake.

He was looking at Reed. "Since Agent Rice is here, can we assume he'll be providing investigative details."

Sierra opened her mouth to respond, but Reed beat her to it. "First, call me Reed. And second, I put in a call to my supervisor asking to read you in. Got his voicemail, so until I hear from him, I'll have to pass on that. But if I get the okay, I'll let you know."

Sierra gaped at him. "When did you do that?"

"On the way over here."

She nodded her thanks, but when he smiled—a sweet one that tipped one side of his mouth up higher than the other—she quickly focused on Blake. "Even though Reed can't share details with us, I offered to share our information as it could result in finding Eddie faster."

Blake gave a firm nod. "I assume you want me to coordinate this investigation."

"Please," Sierra replied. "Let's start with forming an investigative hypothesis. I know I'm biased, but I think we should look at this from two points of view. First, Eddie was abducted and didn't walk away on his own. And second—"

"He took off with his client's money and didn't look back," Reed interrupted.

"Yes, that," she said, irritated that he was so adamant even after she found blood in the office, but she hadn't proven anything to change his case theory. "I don't know a thing about Eddie, so what Reed said may be true, but I'd ask that everyone keep an open mind."

"We can do that," Blake said. "Right?"

Her teammates nodded.

"Thank you." She smiled at them. "When I processed his office I was considering both angles and collected evidence accordingly. I located blood on the blinds and floor that had been cleaned up with bleach. And, I also took a metal whale. The perfect size to bonk someone on the head with if you were trying to subdue them."

"Blood on it?" Maya asked.

"Not that I can see, but the attacker, if there was one, could've cleaned it, too. I'll have to examine it in the lab."

"Any prints on it?" Grady asked.

"Maybe," she replied. "Metal surfaces are challenging substrates to reliably obtain fingerprints from. And this one is textured, too. I didn't try to develop them on scene as I could've messed them up. But in the lab, I'll cast any prints or even use Time-of-Flight Secondary Ion Mass Spectrometry if I find prints on this piece."

"We're going to pretend we understood that." Nick grinned.

"Hey," she said. "It's not like we all don't have to pretend when you start into your computer speak."

"Touché." His smile widened.

She loved how Nick could keep things light under the most difficult circumstances. The others laughed and even Reed smiled.

She waited for everyone to settle down before continuing. "I can tell you that Eddie was an avid golfer and played daily. He had a stack of score cards in his desk, but they only contained the player's initials." She looked at Nick. "Can you compare the names of people interviewed tonight with the initials on the cards to see if we can figure out who Eddie regularly interacted with? We can also run the initials past Mayor Parks as he seems to know what's going on in his small town."

Nick nodded, and Blake jotted the information on the board along with Nick's name.

"I might be able to help put names to the initials," Reed offered.

She nodded briefly, when inside she was overjoyed at his offer to help.

"And put me down for doing a background check on Eddie," Nick said. "Including his financials."

Blake added that to the board, too. "Did you collect any additional evidence, Sierra?"

"Loads of fingerprints," she said. "I'll review them when we get back to the office. And Emory, I have DNA for you."

Nick shifted to look at Reed. "I assume you took the computer."

"We did. If I'm given the green light to read you all in, I'll be glad to provide a copy of the drive."

Nick nodded, but his expression was skeptical, and Reed took a sharp breath. Surprisingly, Sierra felt bad that Nick didn't trust Reed. She thought of Reed as trustworthy, though this early in the game she had nothing to base that on.

"I also took a pair of sneakers I found under the desk to analyze in the lab," Sierra said, moving them on. "Hopefully the particles on the shoes will give us a history of his recent whereabouts."

Blake quickly updated the board with the information they shared and added *Sheriff Case File* and his name. "Trent emailed me a report, but he couldn't share many details—not even with me. Still, tonight I'll review what I received."

"Any chance that includes calls made from Eddie's cell and business phone?" Sierra asked.

He shook his head.

Reed shifted and looked like he wanted to say something, then clamped down on his lips. Sierra knew his team had already reviewed the calls, and if he could share, it would save them time, but she had to be patient. "What about emails? Are those in Trent's file?"

Blake shook his head. "Like I said, Trent couldn't share."

Maya shot Reed a tight look. "How long have you been investigating Eddie?"

"Two months including the month that he's been missing."

Grady propped a leg on his knee. "How did he first come onto your radar?"

"One of Eddie's clients filled out a complaint form on our website. She didn't have proof of his embezzlement, but she got to talking with a friend who also listed her rental through Eddie's company, and they both thought he was charging them for services they didn't use."

"Didn't they try to confront him?" Emory asked.

Reed nodded. "Barnes said his accountant handled the financial part of the business and claimed he had no idea what they were talking about. He said he would look into it, but he never got back to them, no matter how many times they tried to follow up. So as soon as their contracts with his agency expired, they moved their properties to a new leasing agent and contacted us."

"Since when does the FBI look into such a small claim?" Blake asked.

"We do an initial investigation into all claims. Unfortunately a white-collar investigation can easily cost the Bureau $200,000 and up, so all of our offices have a loss threshold.

But we quickly learned Barnes's theft was an ongoing problem, and that in the end, it would likely exceed our threshold. And it did."

Sierra shifted to look at Reed. "And what about this accountant? Did you look into him?"

He nodded. "I can't go into detail, but we quickly cleared him."

"Does Eddie have any other partners?" Maya asked.

Reed shook his head.

"I'll be glad to confirm that," Nick offered.

Sierra was suddenly very thankful for her partners. She couldn't do this investigation without them.

"We should look into social media, too." Blake noted it on the board.

"Let me handle that," Kelsey said. "I don't have any other responsibilities here, and that's something I can do."

Nick looked at her. "I'm thankful for your help with my workload, but be sure you check both his business and personal social accounts. And if you come up empty, let me know and I'll take over."

She nodded, and her springy curls bounced. "I wanted to mention that the people I interviewed only had good things to say about Eddie. Well, at least until the FBI started questioning his honesty."

Reed grimaced, but didn't defend himself. Sierra was impressed that he didn't try to explain.

"I heard the same thing," Maya said. "And also that he was obsessed with golf and probably put more time into perfecting his game than managing his business. They also mentioned that his accountant kept things going for him."

"Ditto," Grady said. "And a few of them questioned whether the accountant might be behind the embezzlement. They said he wasn't a local, and they preferred to think he was the one who stole the money."

Blake scribbled that on the board and underlined it. "I'll be glad to set up an interview with him when we get back to town."

Nick scrubbed his hand over his bearded chin. "I heard people ask if Eddie was taking this money for some time, why doesn't his lifestyle show it," Nick said. "He lives in the small cottage fully paid for, and his car is ancient. He's a member of the local country club so he has unlimited golf, but of course, he has that membership fee."

"Getting Eddie's financials could clear that up," Sierra said.

Blake tapped the board. "Okay, what are we missing?"

Sierra wished Reed would offer something as he knew exactly what they were missing, but of course he didn't speak.

"Someone should interview Mayor Parks first thing in the morning," Sierra said. "I really want to do it, but I'll likely still be busy with the cottage."

"I'll talk to him," Blake offered.

With years of interview experience, he was the right person for that task, and she nodded her thanks. "Can you ask about Eddie's golf partners, too?"

"Will do." He jotted the information on the board.

Sierra's phone chimed. She glanced at the incoming text. "That's Chad. He's waiting at Eddie's cottage for me. I hope we can finish up processing the place by morning, but it could take longer."

Blake nodded. "The forensics you recovered are our best leads, and we should get back to the lab as soon as possible to get them going."

"Anyone mind driving my car back to Portland?" Sierra glanced at her partners. "I'd like to take the evidence back on the helicopter and get started on it right away."

"I don't have anything but the social media to check on and can do it," Kelsey offered.

Sierra smiled her thanks and quickly snapped a picture of the whiteboard then stood. "If anyone needs me, I'll be at Eddie's cottage. Hopefully the evidence that will lead us straight to him is just waiting for me to find it."

7

Reed had been to Barnes's cottage more times than he could count. Each visit he hoped to find something they'd missed, but he always struck out. Tonight, with the obviously talented Sierra on the hunt for evidence, he once again believed it was possible to locate a lead. But he knew they wouldn't find anything to take them straight to Barnes like she hoped for. If that kind of lead existed, he'd have already found it. But then, he trusted County's forensics team. He believed they'd done a thorough job. Turns out they might not have, and if they'd fallen short, that mistake was on him.

He continued to watch Sierra, finding her attention to detail even this late at night admirable. She moved through the small living room inch by inch while her assistant snapped pictures of her finds and noted them on their sketch.

Chad looked to be about their age with blond hair that was messy in the front and sleekly tamed down with some sort of gel in the back. He had one of those mustaches that was barely there as if he couldn't grow a thick one. He was of average build, and Reed had gotten a look at the guy's jeans and a dark denim shirt before he slipped on a coverall. He tended to smile a lot, and he also looked at Sierra like she was the best thing since the discovery of DNA. Question was, was it because he was in awe of her skills or just plain in awe of the woman? It would be hard to separate the two. At least Reed wasn't able to do that.

They worked in such synchronicity that it left this weird feeling in Reed's gut as he watched them. Jealousy, he thought, if he had to put a name to it. He liked how they communicated without speaking. How they moved as one. Something Reed thought he would find if he ever got married. At least that was how his parents' relationship worked. But Reed's jealousy had no foundation. Sierra made it perfectly clear to him that she didn't want the same thing that he did. His best bet was to stow any thoughts in that direction.

"Done here," she announced and worked her way down the hallway toward the bedroom.

Reed followed behind Chad and leaned against the wall until they moved on again and entered the bedroom. Sierra dropped to her knees and crawled over every inch of the room with her magnifying glass, stopping along the way to place evidence markers. Chad rushed over to take close-up shots. Then she lifted things Reed couldn't make out from a distance and dropped them in evidence bags. Maybe hairs or fibers. He didn't interrupt her to ask and hoped with their newfound partnership she would tell him when she finished.

She crawled into the large walk-in closet. He moved to a spot where he could see her every move. She sat staring at something on the floor.

"What is it?" Chad asked.

"Take a look for yourself." She handed him the magnifying glass and pointed at something Reed couldn't even see.

Chad shifted around looking at the item from several angles. "What's so exciting about a sliver of wood? He likely just tracked it in here."

She picked it up with the tweezers and took back the magnifying glass. "It's not *just* a sliver. It's tipped with blue paint."

"Matches the outside paint color," Chad said. "So what?"

She bagged it and shoved the bag into his hands as she stood. "This room looks like an addition." She split Barnes's hanging clothing in two, the hangers scraping over the metal bar in an irritating screech. "So, the back wall of this closet was once the exterior wall and it's wood. I'd venture to say there's a layer of blue paint under this white color."

Chad frowned. "Again, I ask, so what?"

Reed couldn't believe Chad's lack of understanding. Maybe the reason he was still an assistant at his age.

Reed stood and joined them. "You're thinking there might be a false wall that opens and the sliver is from that."

She spun around, a satisfied gleam in her eyes, and she nodded.

"Oh-h-h," Chad said.

Sierra started running her hands over the wall. Reed wasn't about to be left out on a strong lead, so he brushed past Chad and entered the closet.

"Hey," Chad grumbled.

Reed ignored him and ran his gloved hands over the wall. He'd covered nearly the entire right side when Sierra's hands hit something and a small door swung open.

"Bingo!" She glanced at him, a radiant smile on her face.

Reed was excited about the lead, sure he was, but her thousand-watt smile directed at him was breathtaking. He grinned back at her and didn't care if Chad was witnessing his interest in her.

She, on the other hand, didn't seem to care about his response but swung her gaze back to the wall. She reached inside and came out holding a handgun. She quickly pointed it away from everyone, removed the magazine, and looked down the chamber. She also swept the chamber with her finger. Reed knew she was following proper protocol to make sure there wasn't a round chambered. She handled the gun like a pro, and he wondered if she was a shooter, but now wasn't the time to ask.

"It's a Glock 9mm," she said.

"One of the most common guns out there," Reed said, but still impressed that she could recognize the caliber.

"Why would Eddie need a gun?" She frowned. "And if he took off, why wouldn't he take it with him?"

"Great question," Reed said.

She handed the gun and magazine to Chad. "Bag and log it, please."

"Aren't you going to print it first?" Reed asked.

She shook her head. "I'll get better prints in the lab."

"I'll be glad to run the serial number to see if it's been used in other crimes."

She nodded and reached into the cubbyhole again. Her hand came out with a manila envelope. She opened it and pulled out pictures. Her mouth fell open.

Reed didn't like the shock darkening her expression, and he eased over to get a look at the top picture. It was of her, taken recently, if he was right. She started flipping through the photos, and they all included her, going back through time all the way to her toddler days.

She looked up at Reed and swallowed hard. "He's been watching me for years."

Reed didn't think it was done in a creepy stalker way but

as a dad interested in seeing his daughter grow up. "He followed your progress in life."

"Yeah," she said sounding dumbfounded. She shoved the envelope and pictures into Reed's hands and went back to the hole in the wall.

He couldn't believe she put that connection aside so quickly, but maybe she wasn't ready to process such a personal response from Barnes.

She pulled out programs from milestone events in her life and printed articles documenting her successes as a forensic scientist.

"He might not have wanted to be a dad, but he's clearly proud of you," Reed said.

She didn't respond except to shove those items into his hands and return to the hole in the wall. This time she brought out a large green journal and a stack of cash. Eyes wide, she opened the journal, revealing ledger pages. Barnes had recorded large sums of money and assigned them to different account numbers but he hadn't included names or other identifying information.

She stared at the pages and shook the cash in her other hand. "What in the world is this all about?"

Reed had the same question. What in the world was Eddie Barnes up to with hiding these items, and did they have anything to do with his embezzlement and disappearance? A question Reed would find the answer to no matter where it led.

~

"You can't be serious." Sierra stared at Reed and crossed her arms, trying to make herself seem larger and in charge as she stood by her car in the dusky shadows near Eddie's cottage. "I'm not giving these things to you. I located the evidence in my father's house, and I will retain them in my possession."

"I get that, but it's still evidence in my investigation."

"You don't know that there's a connection." She tugged her light jacket closed to keep the sharp ocean breeze out, but there was nothing she could do about the damp fog that wafted in and chilled her to the bone.

"But I also don't know there's not one."

"No." She resisted stomping her foot and slammed the trunk instead. "I'm not letting you take it."

"Sierra." His warning gaze was unsettling but she shoved her keys into her pocket and ignored him. "I could arrest you for impeding an investigation."

"How am I impeding it? You're more than welcome to come to the lab with me so you're there to see everything I turn up. And after I process the ledger for DNA and prints, I'll make copies for both of us."

"And what about when this goes to court and the defense attorney raises the question of why you took possession of this evidence, perhaps calling it into question?"

"We work for law enforcement all the time, and we *do* know how to handle evidence, you know." She crossed her arms. "We can each testify that we were both on scene and vouch for the chain of custody."

"I don't know."

Sierra remembered when Emory was involved with Blake in an investigation into her missing sister, and she'd gotten him to hire Veritas so they could both work the case. That could solve Sierra's problem, too. "You can always hire our agency. We would turn around the information faster than your lab in Quantico and our quality is equal to theirs or better."

"I don't know," he said again and bit his lip.

This was the only time she'd seen him the least bit indecisive, and she knew she'd made progress. "Call your supervisor."

"He won't likely approve paying your lab for this investigation."

"Then we'll work for you for a dollar. Surely, he'll authorize that."

He watched her for a long moment, clearly suspicious of her motives. "Why would you do that?"

"Because I have a lot at stake here in finding Eddie."

"And your partners will agree to this?"

"Of course. We're like family."

His eyebrow rose, narrowing one eye and reminding her of a pirate in the thick fog. "Thought you didn't like being part of a big family."

"This is different. We look out for each other, but know when to back off."

"That's how a lot of families work."

She didn't like how he was avoiding the issue at hand. "Let's stay on task here. Will you call your boss?"

He didn't respond.

"It's either that or arrest me, because I'm not giving up this evidence." She held out her hands so he could clamp on handcuffs if he so desired.

He took a long breath and let it out. "Fine. I'll call, but don't expect him to say yes."

"Why would he say no? There's no downside here at all."

He got out his phone and stepped out of earshot. She hoped he sold the upside to this offered deal. If he sounded skeptical, his boss could pick up on that and say no.

She went back into the cottage and helped Chad load their supplies into the van. They'd worked together for three years, and he was a top-notch lab assistant who was clamoring to be more than an assistant running tests in the lab and assisting at select crime scenes. He was ready to handle some things on his own, but she didn't think he was ready to take on a complete investigation by himself. Still, he was dedicated and a valued member of the Veritas staff, and she appreciated his help.

Each time they stepped outside, she checked on Reed, and he was still on the phone. He'd clamped his hand on the back of his neck. Not a good sign.

"I'm off," Chad said, taking her attention. "You gonna be okay alone with this guy?"

She glanced at Reed still on the phone, and it was no hardship to look at his broad shoulders in his fitted shirt. She wondered what he would look like in casual attire and what he might choose to wear.

"Sierra?" Chad asked.

"You go. I'll be fine." But would she? Not standing out here gawking at this fine-looking man. If they were to work together for days on end, how could she keep her thoughts on business?

She waved goodbye to Chad and went back into the cottage to look around. This time not as an investigator, but as a daughter. She brushed a hand over her bangs to settle them in place after being blown outside and removed her jacket. The place smelled faintly of bleach, and she'd first thought someone had cleaned up blood, but there was no sign of it. Just a sparkling clean kitchen and bathroom.

The décor had a decidedly feminine touch. The furniture was well-worn, and she suspected he'd never changed the place after his parents died. The only thing that looked newer at all was a flat-screen television mounted over a large wood-burning fireplace. The cottage confirmed what the shopkeepers had said about him not overtly spending money.

His kitchen counters were dingy brown Formica and worn, his appliances old. His refrigerator held little more than condiments and bottled water. In his freezer she found Vodka, ice cream, and ice cubes. It was like he hardly lived here. Maybe if he golfed every day at his club, he also ate there.

The front door opened, and Reed entered. The moment they'd arrived at the cottage, he'd rolled up his sleeves, revealing tanned arms. She looked at her own arms. Pale. She didn't do much outdoors except jog or go to the beach sometimes, and she only ran outside when she got up extra early in the summer. Definitely not in their rainy winters. She typically ran on the indoor gym track when she went to work out. But it made her wonder what he liked to do outside. Definitely something else they didn't have in common.

She looked at his face, trying to get a read on what his supervisor said, but he hid his emotions well.

"Well?" she asked.

"He agreed on both counts."

"Both?" she asked, confused.

"Your team can be read in on the investigation, and if you'll forward a contract to him, he'll sign it and get a check cut for the dollar."

She wanted to shout in victory, but at his frown, she held back. "Why don't you sound happy about it?"

"Honestly?" His eyes bored into hers.

"Yeah."

"I like to be in charge and don't like the way you're horning in on my investigation." He curled his fingers into tight fists. "But I like the thought of arresting you even less, so we'll do this your way."

Yeah, she'd thought he would have a hard time with letting go. Just like her brothers. Though their actions were motivated by love. What Reed's actions were motivated by

73

she didn't know. Other than consideration at the moment, as he said he wouldn't want to arrest her.

"But I'll be coming back on that helo with you and the evidence," he added. "And I'll be with you every hour you're working."

She crossed her arms. "I work long days. *Very* long. And with this being about my father, they'll be longer."

He put his fists on his hips. "I can handle it."

She lifted her chin. "You're going to be bored out of your mind sitting in my lab while I work."

He loosened his arms and shrugged. "Might learn a thing or two and appreciate our ERTs even more. Plus, I have work I can do from your lab."

She kept her arms crossed. "You'll have to promise not to distract me."

"I promise."

Right, like he could promise that when all he had to do was step into view to distract her. But he didn't know that.

"Then let's head out to the heliport and get this evidence loaded in the chopper." She started for the door.

He took hold of her arm. "One thing before we go."

"Yeah?"

"Promise me you won't do anything on this investigation without me knowing about it."

She shook her head. "I don't know if I can promise that. What if you're not around and a lead comes in? It might be critical, and I can't wait for you to show up."

"No worries there. I won't be leaving your sight except to shower and change." He firmed his stance. "And if I could find a way to do that at your lab, then I'd do that there, too."

She thought about him heading for a shower, and she couldn't believe her mind went to such a personal place. Heat climbed her neck and consumed her face. She rushed from the cottage before he caught a look at her blushing face and asked about it.

Having him at her side for the unforeseeable future? That she couldn't imagine. But now he could share what he knew about Eddie and help her locate her biological father. For that, she would put up with her unpredictable emotions.

8

Carrying his go bag containing law enforcement essentials from his SUV, Reed boarded the helicopter, and after weighing his options, he took a seat next to Sierra. Emory, Blake, and Grady sat across from them, and Nick and Maya were settled in comfy seats on the other side of Sierra. Blake put his arm around Emory, and she rested her head on his shoulder. Reed had noticed her engagement ring and figured they were a couple. Kelsey was the only other team member wearing a ring on her left hand. He assumed the others weren't married, but the guys could be engaged, as there were no man rings for such an occasion.

"Headset's behind you," Sierra said, settling one on her freshly washed hair.

He reached back, his leg brushing hers, and he was even more aware of her. He wanted to get married and start a family soon, so maybe thinking about that a lot lately was the reason she was getting under his skin so much.

"What did Mayor Parks have to say?" Sierra asked Blake.

"A lot, but not much of it was helpful," he replied. "He did say that he didn't believe Eddie embezzled from his clients."

"He say why?" Grady asked.

"Eddie's had the same clients for years. Since his dad ran the business. Parks figured they wouldn't stay with Eddie if they weren't happy."

"Doesn't mean anything," Reed said. "They've been with him so long they might not know the amount of money they're losing out on and how much income they could be making."

"Parks said Eddie's occupancy rates were some of the highest in the area," Blake said.

"Doesn't mean they generated the best revenue, though," Reed said.

"Did Parks have any idea where Eddie might have gone?" Sierra asked.

Blake shook his head. "He said Eddie rarely left town except to go to Portland. He went there a couple times a year."

"He could've made those trips to take pictures of Sierra." Reed explained about the photos and articles they'd found in Barnes's closet.

"That must have been a pleasant surprise." Emory smiled at Sierra.

She nodded. "After I got over the creep factor of being watched."

"There would be that." Maya looked at Sierra. "But still, he was interested in your life."

Sierra's eyes glistened with tears, and she clamped a hand over her mouth to stifle a sob. Reed started to reach for her hand, but stopped. He was on the job. Hand-holding was far too personal for a work relationship, and he surely wouldn't hold her hand with her partners watching his every move.

"We're cleared for takeoff," the pilot they'd called Riley

said. If he was an example of the people Gage Blackwell hired, the man found professional and sharp workers.

Reed sat back and enjoyed the feeling of weightlessness as the helicopter whirred smoothly up into the dark night. The town was soon just twinkling lights below, and then clouds wrapped around them and left nothing to see out the window.

Blake took out his small investigator's notebook and held it out to Sierra. "The top three guys Eddie golfed with, including the last guy who saw him. I'll follow up by calling them, and if I think they need interviewing, I'll come back here tomorrow."

Sierra took a long breath and nodded. Reed was impressed with the way Blake returned Sierra's focus to the investigation.

"Let me get a picture of the names." She took out her phone and snapped the shot.

Nick leaned across Sierra to eye Reed. "Maybe now would be a good time for you to read us in on your investigation."

Was Nick just another partner wanting to keep Sierra's mind occupied or was it more? They proved their willingness to support one another, so Reed thought Nick could be acting in her best interest, too. Regardless of the reason for the guy's comment, Reed was happy to oblige. "I called a fellow agent who's going to meet me at the lab when we arrive with copies of my case book. I think it's easier if you all read the file, and then ask any questions you might have."

"That will give us the facts," Blake said. "But then we'll want your take on the details as I know that won't be in your official file."

Reed was beginning to see Blake was a strong investigator with plenty of experience. Including knowing that law enforcement officers didn't record theories and supposition in official records.

Nick skimmed his gaze over Reed. "Will the information you turn over include an image of his hard drive?"

Reed shook his head. "It *will* include a report from our techs, but I'll see what I can do about getting that drive for you."

Nick still looked skeptical about Reed following through. His continued doubt in Reed's integrity made Reed determined to prove Nick wrong.

Reed got out his phone and set a calendar reminder to ask about Eddie's hard drive tomorrow when the techs were back in the office. He shoved his phone back into his pocket and looked up to find Blake watching him.

Blake squinted. "Did you find anything on Eddie's phone records that we should know about?"

"Yes and no," Reed replied. "All numbers except one were legit and we ruled them out. One number that Barnes called tracked back to a burner phone. We know he called the number on a regular basis and also on the afternoon he was last seen. We requested the burner's call log from the phone company to review other calls made from that phone, but Barnes's number was the only one listed."

Grady rubbed his jaw. "So the owner of the phone used it exclusively for Eddie, but Eddie didn't feel a need to use a burner in return."

Reed nodded. "Makes me believe the burner owner has something to lose. Barnes not so much. I personally think he used it to make his travel arrangements."

Nick made eye contact again. "I assume you checked his banking records to look for any tickets he might have purchased."

Reed nodded. "Nothing. And we also checked flight manifests along with bus and train tickets. But after he moved the money to an offshore account, he could've used that money or cash to buy a ticket under an assumed identity."

Sierra sighed and looked at him. "And yet, he not only left his gun behind, but the stack of cash, too. I find that odd."

Reed turned to face her. "He could buy a gun anywhere, and he had plenty of money."

"A quarter of a million bucks in my account or not, I wouldn't leave ten grand behind," Grady said emphatically. "And I sure wouldn't leave my piece behind."

"Yeah, but that's because you're a former Marine Scout Sniper and live for guns," Sierra said, sounding like she didn't understand his infatuation with weapons.

"Never a former Marine," Grady said adamantly. "Once a Marine, always a Marine."

"I wouldn't leave my weapon behind either," Nick said.

"But you're former army," Emory said.

"Then let me weigh in." Maya patted her handbag. "No military service, but I wouldn't leave home without my Walther PK."

Reed was surprised she carried as not a lot of women did, and he wondered who else in the group did, but before he could ask Blake started speaking.

"Let's assume Eddie *would* take his Glock if given the chance." Blake shifted to look at Reed. "I can't imagine having that much money, but I don't think I'd leave a size-able sum behind when I might need cash to move around. And let's not forget that ledger. It could be the key to finding Barnes."

"I totally agree with Blake." Emory patted his knee. "And it says to me that Sierra's theory that Eddie didn't leave of his own volition is a valid one that we need to explore."

Sierra looked at Reed. "Will we find anything at all in your report about the possibility of Eddie being abducted?"

He shook his head, but hated her disappointed look. "I know you want your father to be innocent. That everyone here wants to support you. I get that and honestly wished I could get on board with the theory, too, but even with the recovered blood and these two items, all the other evidence points to Barnes taking the money and running. Including his vehicle disappearing along with him. So you should also consider that Barnes wasn't wounded in his office, but that he hurt someone else."

Sierra frowned. "I guess I'm doing exactly what I accused you of doing. Setting a case theory and then trying to prove it."

He was impressed that she could admit that. "Hey, I'm glad to have you prove me wrong." He smiled at her. "If you can."

She arched a delicate eyebrow. "Is that a challenge?"

He nodded.

"Oh, man." Grady huffed a sharp breath. "You really stepped in it now."

Grady gave Sierra an exaggerated look of horror, and when she rolled her eyes, he laughed. The others joined in.

Reed felt like the odd man out again, and he didn't like it, but even wanting to know what was going on, he kept his mouth shut and waited out the laughter.

Maya smiled at Sierra. "Sierra is the most competitive woman you could ever meet. Issue her a challenge and you're bound to lose."

Reed looked at her. "Is that so?"

She shrugged, and a sweet innocent smile beamed back at him.

"Don't believe her innocent act for one minute," Maya said. "She's going to give you a run for your money."

He met and held Sierra's gaze. "I don't like to lose either."

Emory clapped her hands and smiled in delight. "Things are starting to get interesting here."

"Remember," Maya added. "Sierra has all of us to help her win."

Reed liked their comradery, but he didn't like it pointed at him like a weapon. "We should keep our focus on the investigation."

Sierra's eyebrow went up higher, and he felt like she was calling him out on moving on, but he didn't care. It was six against one here, and he would never come out on top of any argument.

"The ledger might be a strong lead," Reed said. "Sierra can process it, and we can all review the details, but from my quick look at the book, we'll need a forensic accountant to compare it to Barnes's other records. That could take some time."

"Or not," Blake said. "I have someone I can call in." He looked around the group. "He's not cheap, and we'll have to eat the cost, but he'll turn things around fast."

"Of course we'll do it," Maya said. "If it finds Eddie for Sierra, then every dollar spent is worth it."

The others enthusiastically nodded their agreement.

"Then I'll give him a call when we land." Blake shifted his focus to Reed. "We'll need Barnes's financial records."

Reed nodded. "I can get them to you tomorrow when our analysts are in the office."

Grady yawned and stretched. "Now that we got that settled, we should grab some sleep. We need to hit the ground running the minute we land."

The partners mumbled their agreement and settled back, eyes closing. Reed looked at Sierra, and she'd rested her head on the wall, her long lashes laying against her skin.

Reed closed his eyes, too, and listened to the *whomp, whomp, whomp* of the helicopter's blades, hoping the rhythm would help him relax.

But try as he might, sleep wouldn't come. He was about to open his eyes when Sierra's head came to rest on his shoulder, her soft hair brushing against his cheek. He took a long breath, inhaling her fresh scent and was even more thankful that the team had given him time to shower and change at their rental place after their all-nighter.

He loved the feel of her—the closeness—but she would be mortified if she knew what was happening. She shifted even closer, snuggling in. He loved the way her touch lit a fire inside of him that he hadn't found with other women, and if he was truthful with himself, he totally wanted to ask this woman out on a date.

She intrigued him in so many ways. Her looks for sure, but it was more than that. She was confident, and yet, humble. Talented, and yet, unassuming. Gorgeous and totally unaware of it. He wanted to delve into her life and find out everything about her. Like what made her so competitive. Could be from having so many brothers. With the way she stood up to him in Barnes's office, he could totally imagine her holding her own with all of those brothers.

Was that why he was so interested in her? She stood up to him when people often shrank back under an FBI agent's questioning. Or *was* it just her looks, and he wanted to think it was more? She was pretty, that was for sure. More than pretty, but he'd dated beautiful women before, and when they didn't connect, he had no problem saying goodbye. Maybe it was because she told him she didn't want to date, didn't want a husband or family, and he took it as another challenge.

Yeah. That was likely it. He liked a good challenge, and

when one was presented in such an amazing package, it was hard to refuse.

He opened his eyes to look at her. To get a better sense of his feelings. He found Grady watching him. Grady didn't look away but gave a pointed look at Sierra. Reed lifted his hands in a *What are you going to do* question. Grady's mouth tightened, but Sierra shifted on his shoulder, and his attention went back to her, his thoughts still on Grady's response.

Sierra said her teammates were like family, but they knew when to back down. That wasn't the vibe he got from Grady. Nah, the guy's warning said, "Mess with Sierra and you'll have *me* to deal with." Reed already knew that Grady was a worthy adversary. If he wasn't already fighting his interest in Sierra, he would start now. No way he'd come up against the former Scout Sniper without sustaining injuries he didn't need.

9

Reed shifted his go bag on his shoulder and cupped his briefcase handle then looked up at the Veritas Center. The buildings were super modern with glass everywhere and had a skybridge running between them that likely had a great view of the city of Portland. He could easily imagine standing on the bridge at sunset watching the city sink into darkness. Did Sierra do that? Or maybe she watched from her condo. He didn't know which floor her condo was located on. She might not have a view from there. Her comment about working long hours probably said she didn't spend a lot of time gazing out at the sunset or the stars.

He shrugged off his wayward thoughts and followed the team to the main entrance. A stocky security guard that Reed put in his early sixties and had a thick head of silver hair met them at the door. His name tag read *Pete Vincent*.

"Back so soon?" Vincent asked. "And I see you have a ton of evidence to process." He pointed a stubby finger at the cart loaded with equipment and evidence that Blake pulled into the lobby.

"Pete! What are you doing here during the day?" Sierra asked. "I thought you melted in the sunlight."

The man laughed, a full throaty chuckle of true enjoyment. "Traded shifts with Carlisle. His wife wanted him to go with her to a matinee ballet performance."

"Danny Carlisle at the ballet?" Maya wrinkled her nose. "I can't see that tough guy interested in it."

"Oh, he's not." Vincent grinned. "Which is why when he asked me to change, I said yes when he wanted me to say no."

Sierra's forehead furrowed. "I don't get it."

"I figured he should go on this date with his wife. The older you get, the more you realize it's not what you're doing with someone you love, it's being with them that's important."

Sierra squeezed Vincent's hand. "You old softie."

"That's me. A big old teddy bear." He rolled his eyes then looked at Reed and held out his hand. "You must be Agent Rice. I'm Pete."

"Call me Reed." He shook Pete's hand.

"I pegged you for a fed the minute I saw you," Pete said.

"How's that?" Reed lifted an eyebrow.

"You have the intensity of a law enforcement officer, but the suit and briefcase say fed."

Reed got that often with local LEOs. "Retired LEO, am I right?"

"Yep, PPB."

Reed nodded his understanding of the abbreviation for Portland Police Bureau. "Washington County Deputy for three years before joining the FBI."

Pete's gaze softened to approving. Reed wouldn't trade his years as a deputy for any reason, and as a bonus, it often made local law enforcement let go of their fed stigma, and he appreciated the change in Pete's attitude.

"Even if I wasn't super observant," Pete smirked, "another agent dropped off files for you and keys to a car that he left out front."

"Now that the two of you are done sizing each other up," Nick said, "mind if we get to work?"

"You go ahead." Pete waved a hand. "I'll need to get Agent Reed signed in, so whoever he belongs to stay behind."

"That would be me," Sierra said, but she didn't sound enthusiastic about her connection to him.

Still, Reed liked Pete's comment about belonging to her.

Blake looked at Sierra. "I'll distribute the evidence on my way up."

"Thanks," Sierra said.

At the time she'd packed up the evidence, Reed had thought her order seemed odd, but now he understood that she'd done so for ease of distribution among her colleagues.

The team trudged toward a door in the back of the large, coolly decorated lobby, and Reed took a look at the space. Leading to the second floor, a curving staircase with open risers seemed to float above a seating area with plush leather furniture. "Connecting Loved Ones Around the World" was painted in bright red letters circling a black globe on the wall above photos of smiling people. Must be their logo. And he also figured the lab helped reunite the people in the pictures through their DNA testing. Maybe through other tools as well.

He noticed a vanilla scent, but Reed couldn't find the source. Still, it was calming, and he assumed that was what the partners were going for.

Pete stopped at a curved reception desk and handed Reed an iPad. "Fill in the form and sign."

Sierra lingered by the desk.

"So he's your guest, huh?" Pete asked.

Reed looked up from the tablet and saw Sierra nod, but she didn't provide any details. In fact, she looked a bit irritated at having Reed here. He figured they'd worked all of that out, but maybe it bugged her to see him in her personal space. He didn't like the thought and quickly finished the form to move on.

Pete handed Reed a badge. "Wear it at all times, and you'll also need an escort while in the building."

Reed nodded.

Pete lifted two storage boxes to the counter. "Your files."

"Thanks." Reed set his briefcase on top of them and followed Sierra through the back doorway with print reader access only. The elevator had the same security.

He rested the boxes on a handrail in the elevator. "This place is locked down tight."

"With the evidence and DNA samples we keep here, we need to maintain top-of-the-line security." She punched the number four button. "Plus, we have a guard on premise because we need to protect ourselves at times. Clients or the people they match can get upset when their DNA results come back."

"I can see that. Kind of like how you felt when you found out about your dad."

"Exactly, except I internalize my stress while others lash out and can be dangerous." She curled her hands into tight fists, and he wished he hadn't upset her with his careless comment.

The elevator door opened, and they stepped into a brightly lit hallway. Windows in the wall overlooked a large lab. A sign at the door read Trace Evidence and Fingerprint Analysis. She pressed her fingers on the reader. "Nick and Blake are on the floor below. Emory's and Maya's labs are on two, Grady on one, and Kelsey has the basement."

He thought to ask for a tour but figured as she processed evidence they would visit the other labs. "And your condo? What floor are you on?"

Door in hand, she looked over her shoulder at him. "I'm not sure how that's relevant."

"It's not. Not really. But when I looked at the building I was thinking about the great view you all had from the bridge, but then if your condo is on a lower floor, not so much."

"I'm on five and so is Kelsey." She stepped into the lab and the lights above automatically turned on.

Of course they did. This team would have the best of the best and that meant automatic lighting that turned off when the sensors didn't detect motion.

A strong chemical smell greeted him as he took a look around the large room. One wall held lockers with secure locks much like other law enforcement offices and labs contained. Counters with upper and lower cabinets lined two walls with breaks in uppers every so often to house large equipment that he couldn't identify. He visited the Quantico lab in his FBI training, but that was five years ago, and he didn't remember half the details their tour guide had shared.

Six tall lab tables with stools sat in the middle of the room along with a few desks. Commercial refrigerators took up the other end wall, and next to them was a large stainless steel sink like you might see in a restaurant's kitchen.

She went to one of the tables and dropped her backpack and phone.

"Go ahead and set your boxes on a table," she said, as she slipped into a white lab coat with knitted cuffs. "Would you like some water?"

"Sure. That would be nice." He set the boxes and his

briefcase on the nearest table and dropped his go bag to the floor.

She grabbed a couple of bottles from a small refrigerator by her desk and handed one to him before cracking hers open and taking a long drink. "I'll start with processing the ledger so Chad can copy it when he returns."

Reed had to admit he was disappointed that he wouldn't be alone with her. "He'll be working today, too?"

She nodded. "Something I'm happy about, as it's a long and tedious task to log in all of this evidence and assign it to lockers for storage."

Now that he saw the size of her lab and the facility over-all, he could only begin to imagine the amount of evidence that passed through her lab. "Does every piece of trace evidence come through you at first?"

She shook her head. "We have lockers downstairs where officers can drop evidence off. And then we have clerks who empty the lockers, log in the evidence, and store it in a central room. Each morning we look at the inventory and ask for files to be delivered. At the end of the day we return all items we've finished working on."

"And do the files stay here until an investigation closes?"

"Depends on the investigation. If we're handling all of the evidence, it remains here. If not, it usually goes back to the agency. Today Chad will log everything in and lock it up here because our techs are off—he knows I'll want to work on all of this as soon as possible."

For some reason, her connection to Chad kept bothering Reed. "He knows that without you telling him?"

"We've worked together for years, so yeah, he can predict my actions pretty well." She stepped back and lifted her thick hair into a ponytail and used an elastic band from around her wrist to secure it. "This is going to take a while. You might want to have a seat."

He did his very best to ignore the slender column of her neck, but he wondered if her skin was as soft as it looked.

Focus, man.

She covered the table with white paper and opened one of the tubs that Blake had dropped off. She lifted out the journal, and after putting on latex gloves, she removed it from the bag and laid it on the paper.

He took a long pull on the water bottle. "Anything I can do to help?"

"I assume you have Eddie's prints in your report." She looked at him questioningly. "If so, it would be great if I had them for comparison."

He went to his boxes. "You analyze your own prints? You don't send them off?"

She looked up. "That's right. I'm fully trained in print examination."

"I have his prints in here." He grabbed a binder and started toward her.

She held up a hand. "Don't bring your files over here. I don't want you to contaminate the paper. Just pull out the print page and leave it there for now."

He stopped and set down the binder. She got out her camera and took several photos of the ledger before grabbing a packaged swab and ripping it open to reveal a plastic tube containing a swab. She ran the tip of the swab over the entire surface of the book.

He continued to watch her. "DNA?"

She nodded.

"Couldn't taking a sample like that from the entire book give you more than one person's DNA?"

"Yes, it's very likely we'll have a mixed sample." She put the swab into a plastic tube. "The person processing it has to separate out the samples and quantify them. That's one of the reasons it takes so long to run DNA."

He flipped through the binder, keeping an eye on the pages, but also glancing up at her. "But what about those instant DNA machines you hear about?"

"They're only approved for buccal cheek swabs where there's little chance of mixed DNA."

"Interesting."

She met his gaze as she capped the tube. "Emory can tell you far more than I can. Maybe you'd like to go hang out with her as she works, and she can explain the process."

He hated how enthusiastic she sounded about getting rid of him. "I'm good."

"Suit yourself," she said and labeled the tube. She bagged it, recorded it on a log, then crossed the room to one of those big machines.

Reed snapped the binder open to take out Barnes's prints and laid the page on the table before joining her. He peered over her shoulder at the hooded machine.

"It's a fingerprint powder station." She pointed to the stainless steel work surface that looked like a flat colander. "It has a downdraft to take fumes and particulates away."

She poured a small quantity of black powder in a tray and loaded her brush like she'd done at Barnes's office. As she swirled the brush over the ledger's cover, her tongue poked out of her mouth just like he expected, and he found the quirk endearing.

She revealed several nice prints, but continued to twirl the brush over them. "This eliminates as much powder as possible, allowing me to get the best ridge detail."

"It's amazing to see the prints appear," he said, admiring her work instead of her for once.

"It's one of my favorite things to see on the job. It provides instant affirmation." She took pictures of the prints, then lifted them with the wide tape and affixed them to cards that she filled out with the information of where she'd located them.

She flipped the book and followed the same procedure on the back and the spine. "Mind grabbing Eddie's prints now?"

"Glad to." He quickly got the page and handed it to her. She flipped on a lighted magnifying glass and studied the page, then gave the prints she lifted from the journal the same careful examination. "Level one details say these are all Eddie's prints."

He moved over to look at them. "You can tell that quickly?"

"He has tented arches in his prints and only about ten percent of the population have those arches." She held out the paper and pointed at the arch in the center of his print. It rose up in the middle like a bell curve. "I'll need to spend additional time looking at second level detail to officially confirm a match, but I want to get to the whale next."

She handed the paper back to him before returning the ledger to the table to bag it again.

The door opened, and Chad strolled into the room carrying a McDonald's bag. The room filled with a mouth-watering smell, and Sierra beamed a smile at her assistant who looked tired and cranky. He'd left town well before they all had, but he still must've only made the one stop at McDonald's to arrive back this soon.

"Perfect timing," she said. "I just finished the ledger, and you can copy it."

"I was hoping to scarf this down first." He held up his bag. "I brought extra fries for you."

"Be still my heart." She laughed and fanned her face. "And right now I want fries more than I want to see if there's blood on the whale."

She marched past Reed to join Chad. Surprised at her choice, Reed watched her.

"What?" She fired a grin at him that sent his pulse speeding. "My big weakness in life is McDonald's fries, and after my all-nighter, I feel like I deserve to splurge."

10

Reed didn't like how Chad was looking at Sierra as he scarfed down his burger—like he had a thing for her. She didn't seem to return the feelings at all. Not that it was any business of Reed's, but he'd have thought with her response to the fries that Chad had brought her diamonds.

She settled on a stool by the large box of fries that Chad placed on a napkin for her. He dropped several packets of ketchup next to it.

She looked over her shoulder at Reed. "Want some fries?"

He shook his head.

"Watching your figure?" She laughed.

A deep rumble came from Chad's chest, irritating Reed. Man, it bugged him to see her relax with this guy and then be so tense with him. His fault, he supposed. He'd set the tone right off the bat by cuffing her and refusing to give her any information on the investigation. He probably could've shared a few things, but with the way she set out to prove him wrong, he hadn't felt like cooperating.

And where did that get you?

Nowhere positive, that was for sure. He was attracted to

a woman who was barely tolerating him. He had to change —forget about the competition comments made in the helicopter and show her clearly that he wanted to help with the investigation, no matter where the evidence led.

"Maybe I *will* have some fries after all." He straddled a stool next to her and dipped one in her ketchup. He met her surprised gaze as he shoved it into his mouth.

She blinked as she chewed, her gaze remaining fixed on his.

In his peripheral view, he caught Chad frowning. Reed didn't want to irritate the guy, but he did want to get between him and Sierra. He let his jealousy take hold and grabbed another fry, smothered it in ketchup, and lifted it to her mouth.

Her eyes flashed open, but she took a bite of the fry, her gaze locked on his. He took the moment to transmit his interest and shove the rest of the fry into his mouth.

"So any luck with the evidence so far?" Chad asked.

She swallowed hard and looked very reluctant to change her focus, but she slowly swung her gaze to Chad.

Reed felt his shoulders lift over having finally connected with her, but then he had to ask himself why he'd done it. Did he want to pursue something with her even if she didn't want a future? At his age he needed to be thinking about having kids, and that meant not wasting time on a fling. Not that he thought she was a fling. Far from it. She was the keeping kind of woman.

"Reed, did you hear me?" she asked.

He shook his head. "Sorry, was lost in thought."

"I was wondering if you have Eddie's blood type in your paperwork."

"Not sure," he said. "But I can check."

He started to get up, but she put a hand on his to stop him. "Have some more fries and take a break with me first."

She didn't have to ask twice, because her touch sent fire racing through him.

"You never officially said that you're assigned to the Portland office," she said.

With Chad watching, Reed was grateful she'd brought him back down to earth. "I am."

She swallowed her bite. "And where are you from?"

"Portland. I was lucky to be assigned here last year. I hope I never have to leave."

"Hard to advance in the FBI if you don't move around, right?" Chad asked.

Reed nodded. "But I love my job just as it is, and there are some things that are more important than advancement."

"Like what?" Chad challenged.

"Like family." He looked at Sierra. "Stability. A wife. Kids."

She picked up a fry and looked at Chad. "Since you're engaged, Chad, you should agree with some of that."

Engaged. Perfect. Reed let out a quiet breath.

"I do." He took a large bite of his Big Mac and chewed. He took a long drink, then cleared his throat. "Um, you should know. Greta called things off last week."

Sierra grabbed Chad's hand. "Oh, Chad. I'm so sorry."

So was Reed, but for all the wrong reasons, and he didn't feel very good about himself at the way he responded.

Chad blew out a long breath and rubbed his forehead. "It wasn't right. We were both in love with the idea of getting married more than we were in love."

Reed nearly gawked at the guy who freely shared his feelings in front of a stranger. Reed would rather be shot on the spot than share his emotions with a strange guy.

"Anyway," he shook his head, "if she didn't call it off, I probably would have."

"Is there anything I can do?" Sierra asked.

"Give me tons of work to keep me busy." He half-smiled at her.

"No problem. But, I'm so sorry." She squeezed his hand. "Okay, any more of these fries, and I'll have to be watching *my* figure." She got up and smiled at Chad. "Finish eating and take a longer break. The ledger's on the table when you're ready."

Reed scarfed down two more fries then drained his water bottle and followed her to a different table. She followed the same procedure with clean paper then gathered several tubes filled with liquid and set them on the table. She put on gloves and took out the whale.

Reed settled on a stool across the table from her. "Okay, you gotta know I'm going to ask what that is."

She looked up at him and smiled her cute little crooked smile. She slid a protective sleeve up over the outside of the tube and broke an internal glass ampule. "This is called QuickCheck Bloodstain Green. It's used to test for blood. I mix the ampules in this vial, put a little water on the swab, and rub it over the whale. Then put a few drops of the QuickCheck on the swab, and if it turns green, we have blood."

She followed the procedures exactly as she shared, but as she lifted the tube of the QuickCheck, she paused and looked at him. He suspected she was teasing him by making him wait.

"Come on." He groaned, getting into her teasing spirit. "Add it and put me out of my misery."

She flashed that smile again and released a few drops on the tip. The swab instantly changed to green.

"Blood," he said, instantly sober. This information could change everything. Blood could indicate a crime had been committed. "You were right."

She started to pump a fist into the air, but then stopped and nodded.

He suspected she was holding herself back, and he not only appreciated her not trying to rub it in, but he dared hope she was doing it for him because she was starting to like him.

The thought was at once exciting and sobering, and he had to swallow hard. "So now what?"

"Now I take a sample of the blood and run it down to Emory."

Chad put something in one of the small refrigerators, tossed his food bag into the nearby trash can, and joined them at the table. "I'll take it for you, and start copying the ledger when I get back."

"Perfect." She wetted a swab and rubbed it over the whale again before putting it back into the tube. She filled out the label on the tube and added it to the log before handing it to Chad who rushed out.

"Now what?" he asked, feeling impatient now that she'd proven the possibility that Eddie had been hurt or that he'd hurt someone else.

"I'll date the blood found at Eddie's office." She went to sit behind a microscope that was connected to a small computer and monitor. She put a blood sample she recovered at the scene under the lens.

"How exactly does that work?"

"Raman uses scattered light—lasers—to characterize materials. It can be used for a solid, liquid, or gas sample when current biochemistry tests only handle one type of sample, and it's nondestructive. Most field tests today are presumptive, but Raman confirms the presence without any reagents or additional chemicals. A handheld device that did this would be ideal to have in the field, and researchers are working on developing a field device now. It will revolutionize forensics for agencies who can afford them."

"Which I'm assuming you can."

"Hopefully by the time they're released, yes. But before then, we're on the list to test the first prototypes."

She slid over to the monitor and read the data that looked like gibberish to him, but she sat back and looked satisfied. "Blood is three weeks old. That's why the techs didn't find it—they processed the office a week earlier."

Reed exhaled and let the thought settle in. "So Barnes returned to his office. It's a good thing you insisted on processing the place again."

She looked pleased with herself or pleased that he was acknowledging that she'd done the right thing.

"Now we need to know who the blood is from," Reed said. "Too bad DNA takes so long to process."

"Yeah, but you can be sure Emory will turn it around faster than any lab you could have sent it to." She printed the report and stood. "I'm moving on to prints."

She sat at a table and sorted through fingerprint cards. For the first time he found what she was doing not very interesting so he took out his phone and caught up on email.

The door lock clicked, and Chad entered the lab. Without a word, he grabbed the ledger and went to a copy machine on the far side of the room.

"Be sure to clean the machine first," Sierra warned.

She didn't look up but Reed saw Chad frown at her. This was the first sign that the guy didn't completely adore her. But Reed supposed being reminded of what sounded like a basic task in front of a visitor was like your mom telling you to wash your hands in front of your school buddies. Not that Reed experienced such a thing, and wished for the millionth time his mom was still alive to nag him.

He thought as he aged that these feelings would go away, but the opposite was true. The angst would unexpectedly hit him, often at the worst times. Like now. When he had reports to read.

He pulled them from his briefcase, but continued to take quick looks at Sierra as she worked, the tip of her tongue pretty much fixed at the corner of her mouth. She warned him that he might be bored, but as long as he had her to look at, he knew that wouldn't happen. Even when she spent the next few hours sorting and recording that huge stack of fingerprint cards.

She got up and lifted her arms overhead, stretching out her lean and firm body. She put on clean gloves, retrieved the whale, and took it over to the fingerprint table.

He trailed after her. "If your theory is right and the whale was cleaned with bleach, could prints survive?"

"Fingerprints are pretty fragile so very unlikely. But if this was a crime of opportunity, the person who cleaned up the blood may not have worn gloves and deposited their prints back on the whale as they cleaned."

"It's hard to imagine someone would be that dumb, but I've seen crazier things."

She sat, loaded her brush, and swirled it over the whale. She was so wrapped up in her work he doubted she even remembered he was standing over her shoulder.

He didn't like to be inside all day and hated all the time he had to spend in the office, but she seemed okay with it. "Do you ever get tired of working inside?"

"I get called out to crime scenes quite often, but even if I didn't, I wouldn't get tired of my job. I love it. Plus, I'm not much of an outdoors person."

"I get the loving your job part, but I'd rather be outside than sitting at desk all day. As a patrol deputy I was on the road all shift, but now I spend a lot of time in the office doing paperwork. An agent's job isn't as glamorous as you see on TV and in movies."

"They get things wrong a lot in those shows, don't they?" She paused and looked at the whale then swirled her brush over other areas.

"Yeah, especially when they portray agents as the bad guy who sweeps in and takes over crime scenes from locals. That rarely happens. More often than not we're invited to bring our many resources to the dance."

"Is that what happened with Eddie?" She glanced up at him.

He shook his head. "I'd already been investigating him and arrived on scene after Sheriff Winfield had started looking for Barnes. Winfield was glad to hand over that investigation."

She frowned. "He's still pretty green in his sheriff's role. If Blake was still sheriff I know that wouldn't have happened. He would have kept the case until it was resolved."

She held out the whale. "There. Three pretty latents."

He shook his head. "I thought for sure you would be wrong about the whale."

"When are you going to learn to stop doubting me?" She grinned and headed back to the other table.

She took out a tongue depressor, two tubes, and a finger-print card. "Since the surface of the whale is irregular, I'll mix up a silicon casting material for the prints."

On the card, she squeezed out a line of white goop the thickness of toothpaste from one tube and blue stuff from another and began mixing them together with a tongue depressor. When the blue was completely blended into the white, she scooped up the mix and smeared it over the prints.

"This will take about ten minutes to dry, and then I can

remove the silicon. The print will show black against the white putty, and I'll use digital photography to reverse the images. Then we can compare them to Eddie's other prints. If they're not a match, we'll run them through the database to search for a match."

He met her gaze. "I won't even ask if you think these will match Barnes, as I know what you'll say."

She tilted her head and held his gaze. "If only I could predict what you might say at any given time. But you, Agent Rice, continue to surprise me, and I never know what you might say or do next."

11

Sierra removed the cast from the whale and studied the prints under her magnifying glass. They didn't have Eddie's arches. Just what she wanted to find. She was tempted to pump a fist up in victory, but for some reason she was starting to really like Reed and didn't want to gloat. Especially in front of Chad who kept giving Reed the stink eye. She had no idea why Chad was acting that way as there had never been even a hint of anything personal between them, but she could see how Reed could be intimidating and make a fairly introverted guy like Chad shrink back.

She looked up at Reed. "Not a match to Eddie's prints."

"I can run the prints through AFIS for you. Unless you have access."

She shook her head. "Maya's working on getting us search permissions, but so far, our requests for access to the federal system and even regional databases have been rejected. It feels like that will change now that Blake's here and can use his influence."

"Well then I'm glad we're working together, and I can help."

"Thank you." She looked away to avoid transmitting any

signals that told him she was just glad he was nearby. "I'll get these prints prepared for the database, and after I log them, you can sign them out."

"If it's okay with you, I'll wait until the end of the day and stop at the office on my way home to run all the prints."

She nodded. "Assuming you plan to share the results."

He frowned. "I thought we were long past that." He honestly sounded hurt.

"I just needed to confirm." She smiled to make light of the sudden tension. "And thank you. That'll still be faster than getting one of our sources to run them."

He nodded, but his frown remained in place. "What next?"

"I need to transfer these prints to digital media." She grabbed her camera and snapped close-up pictures of the prints then uploaded them to her computer. "I'll put these on a flash drive for you once I'm done for the day."

He nodded and continued to watch her so closely she became self-conscious again.

"Now the gun," she said to cover her unease and hurried to a clean table, covered it with paper, and opened the bin she'd labeled as Cottage 1. She drew out the Glock and magazine and after taking photos and swabbing for DNA, she took them across the room to the fuming cabinet.

Of course Reed followed her, and she knew he would ask questions.

"It's a fuming cabinet," she said as she opened the door and hung the gun inside and ejected five bullets from the mag. She put them along with the mag inside the cabinet. "Magazine isn't full."

"I noticed that," was all he said when she was speculating as to where the other bullets might have gone. "You mentioned fuming at a crime scene but not this."

"Right," she said. "It can be done in both locations.

Usually onsite for items that can't be brought back to the lab, but otherwise it's usually done in the lab."

"And it's for old prints, right?"

"Yes, and prints that are difficult to recover." She got out the bottle of cyanoacrylate. "Fingerprints are made of sweat, amino acids, proteins, and fatty acids. Sweat evaporates relatively quickly while the other compounds remain for a longer period of time. Fingerprint powders adhere to sweat and without it, the powders have a difficult time adhering to the other compounds."

She placed drops of the cyanoacrylate into a disposable metal cup and set it in the cabinet. "The cyanoacrylate—Super Glue—fumes don't need the sweat to develop the fingerprint. That's why it's good for older prints. Also, prints are hard to lift from uneven surfaces and hard-to-dust surfaces such as bottles, knives, and guns. The Super Glue fixes the print and gives you multiple chances at lifting it."

"But you didn't do this with the whale."

"Even with multiple chances, I would likely have failed due to the extremely uneven surface. But casting can give me perfect prints every time."

"So why not cast all the time then?"

"Cost and sometimes ease. Like now, I can develop multiple items at one time." She poured water into the chamber's reservoir in the door and turned on the auto cycle humidify setting. "Water speeds up the process. The machine will automatically shut off and clear the fumes, and then we can look at the prints if there are any."

"And until then?" His stomach growled. Not surprising. They only had a few fries since breakfast.

She looked at him. "You're hungry."

"I could eat, but if you want to keep working, I'm right here with you."

"We could go up to my place. I could whip up an omelet."

"You sure you want to do that?"

"If feeding you means I can work later tonight, then yes. I want to do that. Just let me wash my hands first." She removed her gloves and crossed the room to the sink. As she scrubbed and watched the bubbles disappear down the drain, she was already regretting her impulsive decision to invite him into her personal space. But there was nothing to do about it now, and she had to make the best of her hasty decision.

She dried her hands and grabbed the DNA samples. "We can drop these off with Emory on the way." She glanced at Chad. "Be back soon. You want me to bring you an omelet?"

He shook his head. "I figured we'd be here late so I brought a wrap from McDonald's, but thanks."

She led the way to the stairwell and jogged down to Emory's lab. She wasn't present, but her assistant, Lara, stood behind a lab table. In her late twenties, she had neon-blue hair cut in an adorable pixie style, and she'd spiked the top. She looked up and smiled.

"More DNA evidence in the Barnes investigation," Sierra said and laid the log in front of Lara to sign.

Lara scribbled her name. "I'm taking off as soon as Emory comes back, but I'll make sure she gets this."

"Thanks," Sierra said, and despite Lara's questioning looks at Reed, Sierra left without introducing him.

She went straight to the elevator and once inside she punched the number six. "I'm on five but we have to cross over to the other tower. Only place to do that is the ground floor and skybridge on six. Since you mentioned the view, I thought you might like to take the skybridge. At this time of night, we should be able to catch an amazing sunset."

"Sounds good."

She met his gaze, but the space felt far too small for his larger-than-life presence, and she looked away. When the bell dinged, she hurried out and onto the bridge that swayed a bit under their footfalls. The sun was just dropping below the downtown buildings, and the sky was painted in striations of reds and oranges, a vibrant purple color filling the sky above them.

Reed stopped next to her and stared out the window. "Wow. Just wow. Amazing."

She took in his tough profile, and his nearly perfect shape outlined by his fitted shirt. She noticed the muscles in his forearms and imagined him turning to wrap them around her waist and kissing her.

"Amazing view is right," she said and decided she should actually look at it instead of him.

He planted his hands on the safety railing. "You must never get tired of this."

"I'd like to say I come up here a lot, but usually I'm still in my lab at this time of night."

He turned to look at her, his eyes alight with happiness that warmed her clear to her toes. "Then thank you for taking time to share it with me. And for cooking, too."

His compliment made her blush for some odd reason. To hide her reaction, she headed toward the stairwell. She rarely blushed, but something about him made her color easily. Knowing she never wanted to marry, she hadn't dated a lot. She would rather further her career than go on dates where it usually ended with the guys upset with her because she wouldn't make a commitment. So maybe that was it. Maybe she was just out of practice in interacting with men in a romantic way.

She led him down the steps and into her condo.

Had she left the place a disaster?

Not spending much time here, she didn't really have a chance to make a huge mess, but it wasn't exactly tidy. Journals lay on the coffee table and on the sectional covered in a nubby gray print. She grabbed them up and started to stack them on the glass coffee table covered with a layer of dust.

"You don't have to do that for me. I'm going to sit at your island and watch you work in the kitchen. Or help you, if you want me to."

She sighed and went into the adjoining kitchen.

"What's wrong?" He slid onto a stool and rested his forearms on the counter.

"You've been watching me all day. Nearly anyway." She planted her hands on the cool stone counter. "Aren't you tired of that?"

She expected him to say it had been boring, but he locked his gaze with hers, and she couldn't seem to look away from those intense brown eyes and his impossibly long eyelashes.

Which she should of course. For so many reasons, number one being that he was the bossy, controlling kind of guy she avoided at all costs.

"You must know by now that I find you very attractive," he said, his voice husky.

"Yeah, I might have caught that." She turned away to get orange juice, eggs, shredded cheese, and omelet fixings from the refrigerator that she kept ready for quick meals at the end of her long days.

"I've been getting the same feeling from you." He sounded unusually tentative.

Surprised, she glanced at him on her way to grabbing a frying pan. "You're a very good-looking man, Reed. I'm sure you know that."

"That's not what I meant at all."

She poured two glasses of orange juice. "I know."

"You're going to make me come right out and ask, huh?"

Her back to him, she cracked eggs in a bowl, started whipping them with a wire whisk, and took a quick look over her shoulder. "I'm attracted to you."

"But," he said, glass in hand. "There's a big but coming. I can already hear it."

"But I told you I don't want to get married and have a family."

"I'm pretty sure I haven't asked you, so we don't have to worry about that just yet." His tone was humorous, but she was too nervous with having him in her condo to laugh, so she worked on the omelets and made a few slices of toast in silence.

When she turned to serve him, she found him looking at his phone.

"Dig in," she said and sat two stools away from him so she didn't need to look at him.

He forked a bite. "What will you work on when we get back to the lab?"

She nearly sighed her thanks for the change in topic. "I'll finish up the gun and ammo first. Then get the serial number for you so you can check it. I'll finish up the prints for you, too."

"And then you're going to kick me out." He took a bite of the omelet and chewed. "And here I thought you worked late."

"I think we both will benefit from a good night's sleep tonight." And some time apart.

He studied her face, seeming to look for some hidden meaning. She needed a break from the intensity of this man's study, but even more from the way he seemed to be able to capture her interest without trying.

She took a bite of her omelet.

"This is good. Thanks again for making it." He paused his fork midair. "Do you cook often?"

"Me? No way." She laughed. "Omelets are my go-to meal after a long day. Or I scramble the eggs with the same fixings and put it in a tortilla. That's about all I can do, other than call for takeout."

"I like to cook," he said and took a big bite of the toast.

She gaped at him.

His eyes narrowed. "It's not *that* weird is it? Guys cook more often these days."

"I know, but *you*. I mean, I get this vibe of a super tough agent who lives for bringing in bad guys at all costs, even at the expense of a personal life. But here you sit on a Sunday night. *And* you cook!"

"I meant it at lunch today when I said there's more to life than a job." He polished off his toast in one giant bite.

She really shouldn't keep this personal conversation going, but she had to clarify. "You mean like family?"

He took a drink of the juice. "Yeah. Like yours, for example. I can imagine with five brothers, things get crazy when you all get together."

"Yeah," she said remembering the last time she'd gone to their Sunday family dinner, which was months ago. "I keep looking for silence in the middle of all of it."

"Something tells me if you were ever faced with silence on a permanent basis, you'd want the noise." His eyes darkened with anguish.

She had to sit on her free hand not to reach over and pat his. "I'm sorry. You must think I'm terrible. Wishing away what I have when you lost your parents at such a young age."

"Terrible, no. I just think you should appreciate it more."

"Maybe after I work through my Dad lying to me, I will."

They resumed eating, but in an uncomfortable silence

that she couldn't wait to escape. The minute she took her last bite, she grabbed her dirty dishes and took them to the dishwasher.

He brought over his plate just as she turned to retrieve them. She bumped straight into him. With his free hand, he grabbed her around the waist and pulled her against his firm body to steady her. She looked up into his eyes now warm brown and filled with the same emotions burning through her. She felt a strong pull of attraction deep in her stomach. She rose up on her tiptoes to kiss him. He set down his plate with a *clank*, bringing her back to reality. She'd completely lost herself in those amazing eyes and broke the hold to push away.

"We should get going." Gulping deep breaths, she set his plate in the dishwasher. She shoved the door closed and nearly fled from her condo before she lost all common sense and turned back to kiss him—as she still desperately wanted to do.

12

Sierra rushed into her lab as if someone was chasing her and almost shouted for joy at seeing Chad still working hard. "Oh, good, you're still here."

He looked up from bagging the ledger and gave her a funny look. "Just finished the copies."

"Perfect," she said, still breathless from her interaction with Reed or maybe from the race down here.

"I'll go put a copy in the locker for Blake so the forensic accountant can review it," Chad said, eyeing her as if he noticed her distress.

They worked together so often he likely did. She nearly shouted at him to stay, but nodded her understanding and forced out a smile.

He kept watching her. "And your prints are done fuming."

"Perfect," she said again, as that was the only word that came to mind, and she hurried over to the fuming cabinet.

"Wow." Reed's voice came from right behind her, and she jumped.

"Sorry. I didn't mean to startle you."

He had in more ways than one in less than five minutes.

"That's cool," he said, his tone softer and more intimate, making things even worse for her. "Three super clear prints on the gun's grip."

She couldn't seem to form any words so she snapped on gloves and took the Glock to her lighted magnifying glass. "They're all a match for Eddie's prints. Not unexpected." She grabbed the magazine and bullets and reviewed them, too. "None on the magazine or bullets."

"That's odd, right?"

She nodded. "He could have worn gloves when he loaded the magazine, but why?"

"My thoughts exactly." Reed took a long breath, and he was so close she felt him inhale the air.

"Maybe he bought it like this and whoever loaded the ammo didn't want to be tracked."

"Maybe. But I assume he was given the gun with a full magazine so where was it discharged?"

"We might not get that answer until we talk to Eddie when we find him."

"*If* we find him."

She wouldn't respond to that as she had to believe God wanted her to find her biological father. Otherwise, why had this all happened in the timeframe that it had? Had God put her here because Eddie needed her? Or maybe it was because she had to find him to get the answers she needed. Either way, she wouldn't stop looking until she located Eddie.

"I'll still need to enhance these prints with powder and lift them." At the print station, she completed the work while Reed watched. She couldn't seem to let go of their brief contact in her kitchen, and her hand trembled. Fortunately, she was swirling the brush so Reed probably didn't notice it, but she sure did.

"So that's it then?" he asked after she finished.

"Not quite." She took the Glock to the counter holding her microscope, disassembled the gun, and set the pieces on paper by her microscope.

"Wow, you field stripped that like a pro. You shoot?"

"Good grief, no. I see the terrible things guns do to people all the time, and I'm never going to own one."

Reed didn't speak so she looked at him and found disappointment in his expression.

"I know that you need to use a gun on the job, and I'm thankful you and other officers have them for protection. And to protect innocent civilians. So I'm not judging you. I just don't want them in my life."

It seemed like he wanted to argue, but she looked back at her magnifying glass to stop him. Pushier men than Reed had tried to get her to change her mind about firearms. Her father. Her brothers. Not only was her dad retired law enforcement, but all of her brothers followed in his footsteps and were currently LEOs. They tried to force her to learn to shoot for years, which of course, meant she took a complete opposite stance, and who knows, maybe that was her main reason for not owning a gun.

She checked each gun part under the microscope, but sadly, she didn't locate additional prints. She would fume them, too, just to be sure. She gathered them up and repeated the fuming process. "I'm going to go back to reviewing fingerprint cards while that processes."

"Guess I'll catch up on email then, as—no offense—but that's unbelievably boring." Reed chuckled.

She laughed and said, "Told you you'd be bored." Then she turned her back to him and got to work. Before long, the fuming chamber dinged, and she went back to it.

She opened the door and removed the spring guide. "Well, would you look at that?"

He strode over to her.

She held out the spring guide. "A partial on the tip."

"Eddie's?"

"I don't think so, but let me get a better look." She held it under the magnifying glass. "No arch. So not his."

"Means someone else handled this gun. With where the print is located, it could've happened during cleaning." Reed tipped his head and stared ahead. "What if the ledger and gun were left to implicate Barnes, and he didn't actually leave them behind himself?"

"Good possibility." She smiled. "And one I'm glad to hear you consider."

"I have no choice when you keep uncovering evidence that makes your theory viable." He didn't sound happy, but he also didn't sound mad, so she had to believe he might honestly be rethinking his opinion.

She checked the gun's other parts, looking inside the frame and at the barrel, but found nothing else. So she lifted the partial print and added it to the pile of prints that she would send with Reed. When she finished, she glanced at the clock to discover it was after ten. She pushed back from the table and lifted her arms overhead to stretch.

"You hit the gym a lot," he stated.

"Um...yeah."

"I could tell when we bumped into each other in the kitchen. You have abs of steel."

"I could say the same thing to you."

His eyebrow went up in that quirk she was coming to know was common for him.

"Strong core muscles help me do my job," she explained. "Never know what position I might find myself in at a crime scene."

"And we know it's all about that for you. The job I mean." He honestly sounded sad.

She didn't know if he was sad for her or him, but she wouldn't venture into that personal realm.

She handed him the note she'd written the Glock's serial number on. "Right now all I want is some sleep."

He packed the paper in his briefcase with other files he'd taken out while she worked. She handed over the cards and gave him the log to sign them out. He compared each card with the log and signed for each one. Though it took some time, she appreciated his thorough handling of evidence.

He put the cards in his briefcase and snapped the hinges closed. He grabbed his go bag. "Lead the way."

She walked him to the elevator, and they rode down to the lobby where Danny Carlisle was on duty.

"How was the ballet?" she asked the tall, solidly built guy with a buzz cut.

He rolled his eyes. "I think I might've died of boredom if my wife hadn't kept tapping me and pointing out her favorite parts. She was so excited to be there."

"So you had a nice time then," she said and chuckled.

"I honestly did. Good to get away from our kids for the day."

Reed handed his badge to Danny, and Sierra walked Reed out the door to the black SUV the agent had left for him.

"I'll see you in the morning." She tried to sound light-hearted and look anywhere but at his eyes and failed.

He held her gaze. "You promise you're going to bed and not back to work."

"I promise." She laughed. "I can barely keep my eyes open."

"And you won't start without me in the morning?"

"You don't trust me," she said feeling the sting of it.

"It's not that at all. I feel like I've gotten to know your

character today, and I doubt you could lie to me if you tried."

She opened her mouth to say she could, but she knew he was right. Lying wasn't something she was any good at. "So why do you need to dog my every move?"

"I need to see everything with my own eyes if I'm going to get my supervisor to trust in forensics that the official team missed."

"Ah, *he* doesn't trust us."

"Exactly. And you do have a vested interest in skewing the results. So watching you eliminates any question of conflict of interest."

"I don't like to think anyone would doubt my work when I do my very best to remain impartial in the lab, but I get that he might be suspicious."

"All he would have to do was spend a day with you and he'd know that about you." He smiled.

"Still, promise me you won't bring him with you in the morning." She grinned at him.

He laughed. "What time do you want to start?"

"Is six too early for you?"

He shook his head and reached out to tuck a strand of hair behind her ear. "Goodnight, Sierra. Sweet dreams."

A shiver started where his finger brushed her cheek and flooded over her body. She thought she might melt into a puddle right there in the parking lot.

He smiled, an intimate one, that made the shiver start all over again. Just when she thought he might kiss her, he turned and strode off.

She exhaled. Did he know the effect that look had on a woman? Likely.

They worked together—that was all. A statement she kept repeating all the way up to her condo, through her shower, and until she crawled into her bed and turned off the lights. Then his face replaced all thoughts, and she drifted off to sleep.

13

_____

Sierra struggled awake. Struggled to figure out where she was and make sense of her phone ringing from her night-stand. She saw Maya's name and that it was one-fifteen a.m. and quickly answered. "You have results for me?"

"No. A murder."

"What?" She shot up in bed.

"The Washington County Sheriff called me personally," Maya said. "Apparently, the victim is some big shot in the county and the sheriff wants quick and thorough results."

"Which means us, but I'm really swamped with looking for Eddie."

A strained silence stretched out.

"Go ahead." Sierra got up to get a glass of water. "Say whatever it is you're not saying."

Maya blew a breath through the phone. "You not taking this callout isn't in the lab's best interest. Not with our contract with the county coming due soon."

"But I..." Sierra didn't know what to do. She couldn't possibly manage a murder investigation and find Eddie at the same time.

"You could process the scene like the sheriff is expecting," Maya said. "And then have Chad do the lab work."

"I don't know."

"You keep saying he's ready to do more. Let him prove it."

"And what if he screws up, and we lose the contract?"

"I'll get Blake to check in with Chad on a regular basis, and you can too. Just to be sure he's on track."

Sierra let the idea settle in. She didn't like giving up control of part of an investigation much less the whole thing, but it was looking like she didn't have a choice. "It might work."

"Sure it will. I'll text you the address. Just get over there now, and we'll figure it all out tomorrow."

"Okay. Talk to you then." Sierra went to the bathroom to clean up and brush her teeth but didn't bother with makeup. She slipped into jogging pants and a T-shirt as she would be wearing a coverall on the scene anyway.

At the house located in a new and pricey subdivision on the outskirts of Washington County, she parked her van near the crime scene tape strung by the reporting deputy and opened the back door to slide into her coveralls. She hung her camera strap around her neck, picked up her kit, and slipped under the tape.

"Excuse me," a man called out from the sidewalk.

Startled, she spun to look at him. She'd been so focused on getting ready and inside the house that she missed seeing him. He stepped closer, and she took in his athletic pants and T-shirt, both black, on a buff body. Had he been out running at this time of night?

"Sorry to bother you." He smiled.

His smile might be meant to disarm her, but she knew to keep her guard up with any stranger approaching a crime scene, especially in the middle of the night. "Can I help you?"

"Something bad happened, didn't it?" A deep frown marred the very handsome face with wide jaw and deep-set eyes.

She wanted to tell him everything was okay and to go back home, but as Reed recently pointed out, she didn't lie very well. "I'm not at liberty to say."

"Sorry. It's just...I live next door." He jerked a thumb over his shoulder at the large two-story home on the next lot. "This is a quiet neighborhood...safe neighborhood, and I wanted to know if we need to be concerned about our safety. I'm former military, and I can sense danger in the area."

She noticed an Army Ranger tattoo on his forearm, and found it a bit odd that someone who served in that capacity was so concerned about safety. But then if he had a wife, which his wedding ring suggested, and kids, she could understand he would want to protect them.

But she wasn't the one to tell him about the murder. "I wish I could update you, but I only handle forensics, and it's not my place to share."

"I understand." He smiled. "Thanks for talking to me and not just blowing me off."

She nodded and smiled then stepped up the long walkway to the contemporary home with odd slanting rooflines. She found the door open and entered the large entryway with wood floors and pale gray walls covered in expensive artwork and a high ceiling holding a ginormous gold chandelier. The house smelled like tangy barbecue sauce as if someone had recently grilled dinner.

The responding deputy had his back to her but he spun, and she almost sighed when she realized it was her brother Brendan. She had to admit her younger brother looked handsome in his uniform. He'd inherited their father's chiseled good looks, and at around six feet tall was one of the shorter brothers. He worked out, and his posture was nearly perfect.

"Hey." He gave her a quick smile and handed her a clipboard to sign in. "I always figured we'd run into each other at a crime scene one day."

"Yeah, me, too," she said as she scribbled her name on the log, but wasn't as excited about seeing him here as he seemed to be with her. She worried that he might say something personal around other officers, and her reputation as a no-nonsense investigator might be shot.

She slipped into her booties and was glad to see Brendan was wearing a pair, too.

"This is a bad one, sis." He cast her a concerned look. "Maybe you want to sit it out, and we can get someone else out here."

She lifted her shoulders. "I'm a professional and can handle it."

"Always so stubborn." He watched her for a few more moments then spun. "Body's this way."

He headed into the family room, and she heard a television playing a mattress commercial in the next room, but she tuned it out to squat down by the body. The victim was lying face up with a violent slash on his neck and multiple stab wounds to his torso and chest.

"I told you it was bad," Brendan said.

"Yeah," she replied, but instead of thinking about hating to see this brutally murdered man, she honestly hated that her little brother had to see the results of a brutal attack. She started at the victim's head and counted the stab wounds as she moved down to his waist. Ten punctures in all. "Everything but the neck looks like it was inflicted postmortem."

"How can you tell?"

"Not much blood."

A swatch of blood was smeared across the floor but most of it pooled around his upper body. He could've been moved, accounting for the smeared blood. "You touch him or anything in here?"

He snorted. "I know what I'm doing, Sierra."

She'd like to think her brother wouldn't make a mistake after being on the job for five years, but he could've been spooked and forgotten all about his training and experience. "Who called this in?"

"His daughter. She's been trying to reach him for hours and finally came over to check on him." He tipped his head at an adjoining room. "She's waiting for the detective in there."

She heard the front door creak open, and whoever entered stopped at the door. A breeze rushed in after the person, and the enticing smell of warm cinnamon mixed with leather came along with it. Even before turning, she knew she would find Reed standing at the door.

She slowly got up, schooling her expression, and faced him.

He stood up from putting on booties from the box Brendan had left at the door and gaped at her for a moment. "What are you doing here?"

"I was going to ask you the same thing."

That eyebrow arched up as he grabbed the clipboard and signed in. "You don't know who this is, do you?"

"ME's not here so we haven't gotten an ID yet, but you obviously know him."

"It's Ira Caulfield. Barnes's accountant."

"His what?" She spun and looked at the man who'd lost his life to a very violent death. Did Reed think Eddie did this? Probably.

She heard Reed start across the room, but Brendan stepped in his path. "You are?"

"FBI Special Agent Reed Rice. I'll be partnering with your agency in finding the person responsible for killing Caulfield."

Sierra didn't have to look to know Reed's entitled tone would make Brendan bristle and he wouldn't back down and let Reed pass. She turned and the pair were engaged in a visual battle of wills.

Brendan glanced at her. "You know this agent and can vouch for his right to be here?"

She nodded but didn't introduce them as she didn't want Reed to know Brendan was her bother. Thankfully, he stepped back to let Reed pass.

"We can take if from here," she told Brendan.

He stood watching her for a minute like he wanted to argue and whisk her out of this gruesome scene, but he shook his head and strode to the door where he would meet with his sergeant when he arrived and then make sure everyone who arrived signed in.

"Glad to see the deputy is doing his job." Reed snapped on latex gloves.

The perfect opening for her to tell him Brendan was her brother. Instead, she kept her mouth shut and crouched down by Caulfield's body. Now that she knew who he was, before the ME took the body away, she wanted a closer look at the wound that had likely taken his life. She lifted her camera and zoomed into the wound that crossed his entire neck.

Reed squatted next to her, and now that her initial shock had faded, she noted his attire. At least what she could see without shifting to look up at him. He wore another custom suit, this one gray, his shirt was white, and his tie blue.

"What are you thinking?" he asked.

Um, that you smell great and that suit looks amazing on you. "Someone wanted him really dead."

"That's a vicious wound for sure. And that many stab wounds says this is very personal."

She tilted her head and looked at Caulfield from another angle. "Smear on the floor looks like he was trying to get away. Or get to something. Then the killer flipped him over and started stabbing."

"Maybe Caulfield was trying to get to the phone."

"Maybe. Or he was going after something else. A gun maybe."

"We should consider that in our search." Reed stood.

She took a breath and stood, too, refusing to look at him and get distracted when she needed to be sharp. "I'll need to get scene photos before the ME arrives."

"Have at it," Reed said.

She wanted to point out that she didn't need his permission when she'd been hired to do this job by the jurisdictional agency, but she didn't want to start something with him. Especially not with Brendan watching and listening. He'd chime in about her stubbornness, and that wouldn't go well for either of them.

She raised her camera to her eye again and started snapping pictures, making sure to get the body from all angles, and mentally marking the distance he lay from landmarks in the room so she could accurately sketch the scene. She also made a mental note to suggest to the partners that they hire a forensic photographer in the future. With the center gaining notice in law enforcement circles, they were getting called out to more and more crime scenes. She was doing both jobs along with processing the trace evidence, and it was getting difficult to do it all in a timely fashion.

The door opened again, and the ME bustled into the room. Dr. Albertson was slender, medium height with a short bob of gray hair and a wrinkled face. She looked at them both.

"Sierra." She smiled then held out her hand to Reed. "Good to see you again, Agent Rice."

"You two know each other?" Sierra asked.

"I posted a victim in one of his recent investigations." Dr. Albertson looked at the body. "Must be something big going down here if the bureau's involved."

"It's simply related to an ongoing investigation." Reed sounded like he was trying to downplay his involvement, but Sierra had no idea why he would do that.

"But it's your investigation?" Dr. Albertson asked.

"I'm not assuming jurisdiction at this point, but that could change."

"Got it." She snapped on gloves and went straight to Caulfield. "Well, now. This is a particularly nasty bit of work." She glanced at Sierra. "You get his photos yet?"

Sierra nodded.

Dr. Albertson looked at the body.

"Killer surprised him from behind," Sierra said without thinking. "And the wound suggests the killer didn't pull the head back, right?"

"Yes." Dr. Albertson nodded her approval at Sierra. "Not many CSIs would notice the lack of gaping wound suggests his head was forward when the wound was inflicted. And in my experience that means an experienced killer."

"Military?" Reed asked.

"Could very well be."

Sierra's alarm bells went off. She talked to that Army Ranger outside. Coincidence?

"And what about time of death?" Reed asked. "Hazard a guess?"

"It would be just that, a guess, but..." She reached for Caulfield's arm and lifted it. "Rigor has fully set in, so four hours at a minimum. I'll know more after we take his and the surrounding air temperature and can run our calculations."

Sierra looked at the arm. "He's wearing an Apple Watch. After we take an image of it we can look at it to see when his heartbeat stopped."

The ME looked up at Sierra and smiled. "Yes, of course."

Sierra was thankful Dr. Albertson had caught the case as many MEs could get snippy when offered suggestions or ideas.

The doctor removed the watch and handed it to Sierra. "I don't know how to work this, and I'm glad we have people like you who do."

"Actually, that will be Nick, but we'll get the time for you." Sierra took the device and dropped it into a plastic evidence bag.

"I want to attend the autopsy if possible," Reed said. "When do you think you'll get started on it?"

"Not today, I'm afraid. We're swamped. I'll call you when it's scheduled." She returned her attention to the body.

Sierra needed to get the other scene photos taken, but first she had to tell Reed about the Ranger. She tipped her head at the other side of the room, encouraging him to join her out of everyone's earshot. He took her hint and followed her.

"This might just be a coincidence, but I talked to an Army Ranger on my way in. He said he lived next door. The house on the south side. He seemed legit, and was concerned about the safety of the neighborhood, but you know how killers like to come back to a scene to watch. He could be the one who killed Caulfield."

She expected Reed would be happy for a lead, but he frowned.

"What's wrong?" she asked.

"I don't like that you might have run into a vicious killer.

He could've—"

"But he didn't." She tried not to get angry with his protective reaction instead of thinking about the investigative value of her sighting. "I saw him well enough to sit with an artist to have a sketch made."

He ran his gaze over her like he had to visually confirm she hadn't been harmed. "The blood on your legs."

"From kneeling by Caulfield." She gritted her teeth to keep from saying anything else and waited him out.

He blew out a breath. "Okay, I'll go check out the neighbors. If he doesn't live there we'll arrange for a sketch artist."

"No need to arrange. Kelsey can do it. She's often drawn reconstructive photos and has done witness directed sketches too."

"Perfect. So I'll head over to the neighbors, but I'm also going to call in ERT to process this scene with you."

He couldn't have found anything more upsetting to say to her. "You don't trust me?"

"No, it's not that at all. I want to give you help so we can do this faster."

Was he telling the truth? She searched his eyes and found them free of any duplicity. "Help or not, I'll still personally want to review the entire scene."

"Understood. Can you do that as you take photos and set priorities for the team?"

"As in—be in charge of them?"

"I don't think they'll take too kindly to that." He smiled. "But you can give me a list of things you want them to do, and I'll relay that to get them started."

She nodded, her mind racing over what she might be willing to let go of and allow someone else to process. She never had to do that before, and she didn't know if she could. Only time would tell how successfully she managed it.

14

Reed had hoped to interview the daughter who called in the murder, but if Sierra was right and the Ranger could be a suspect, he needed to act on that first. Under the moonlight beaming down from clear skies, he stepped toward the house next door and noted there wasn't a car in the driveway.

Not unusual. This was the kind of neighborhood where residents parked in their three-to-five-car garages, and Reed had noticed when he pulled up to Caulfield's place that there weren't any cars on the street or driveways. Only Caulfield's daughter's vehicle sat in his cobblestone driveway.

What *was* unusual was that the lights were out in this house, instantly raising Reed's suspicions. If this Ranger was as concerned as he told Sierra, Reed doubted the man would go to bed.

Reed pounded on the door with the side of his fist. The thud echoed through the peaceful neighborhood where residents would wake up to find out one of their own had been murdered.

The exterior light flashed on, momentarily blinding

Reed. He blinked a few times and raised his voice. "Agent Reed Rice. FBI. I have some questions for you."

A gray-haired man Reed put in his late sixties opened the door. He wore paisley pajamas and a brown robe. His hair was tousled and sleep still lingered in his eyes. "How can I help you, Agent?"

"And you are?"

"Michael Driscoll."

"Who all lives in your household, Mr. Driscoll?" Reed asked.

"My wife, LeAnn, and me." Driscoll looked over Reed's shoulder and frowned.

"Any children?"

"A daughter, but she lives in Washington. Nothing's happened to her has it?" Panic wedged its way into his tone.

Reed waved a hand. "No. No. I'm investigating an incident at Ira Caulfield's house. There was an Army Ranger standing out front who claimed to live here."

Driscoll shook his head. "No Ranger here. Or in the neighborhood for that matter. I'm in charge of the neighborhood social committee and make it a point to keep up with everyone."

"And you're positive no one new has moved in that you don't know?"

"Positive. I can get you a list of all the residents if you'd like."

"That would be great."

"Come on in, and I'll make a copy."

Reed stepped into the formal entryway that smelled like freshly baked bread and had soaring ceilings as a woman around Driscoll's age came down the stairs. Her short black hair with streaks of gray stuck out at odd angles, and she rubbed her eyes. LeAnn, Reed assumed.

Her gaze went to her husband. "Is everything okay?"

Driscoll nodded. "Something happened with Ira, and this is Agent Rice with the FBI. I'm getting him a residents list. Be right back." Driscoll disappeared into a room to the right.

LeAnn shot Reed a look. "Is Ira okay?"

Reed wanted to know more about Ira's death before he started asking questions that might lead her to think he'd been murdered. "I'm not able to discuss the incident quite yet. When was the last time you saw Ira?"

"Yesterday morning when he took the trash out to the curb."

"Good neighbor?"

"He has a girlfriend young enough to be his daughter," she said, her tone full of judgment. "They loved to hot tub all hours of the night and play their music loud enough to be heard above the tub. The sound carried over to our bedroom windows. But they knocked that off a few weeks ago, so yeah, he's a decent neighbor."

"Any idea why he stopped the parties?"

"We haven't seen the girlfriend lately and figured they broke up." She narrowed her gaze. "Not surprising. Never could understand what a pretty young girl would see in a man twice her age."

"Do you know this girlfriend's name?"

"We never met her in person, but Ira called her Tricia."

Reed committed the name to memory as Driscoll returned and handed Reed a stapled packet of paper. "This list is current as of yesterday morning."

"I appreciate it, Mr. Driscoll. Once I have a better idea of what we're looking at next door I might be back to ask additional questions."

Driscoll gave a firm nod. "We'll help in any way we can."

"Thank you." Reed departed, both buoyed by the fact that

the Ranger didn't live here and also distressed by it, because the guy had taken off. They likely had their murderer within reach, but now he was on the loose and free to kill again.

Reed stepped into Caulfield's door to find Detective Miller signing in with the deputy, and as Reed slipped on fresh booties he explained his interest in Caulfield's murder. Reed knew the detective from his time as a deputy, so when he took him to the side, it was easier to get a buy-in on their agencies working together, and the conversation was quick and to the point.

Reed started for the room where the daughter was waiting, but then ERT arrived and Reed had to find Sierra so they could hand out assignments. Then Nick stepped through the door.

He was wearing the same clothes as the last time Reed had seen him, and unlike most of the others working the scene, he didn't look tired at all. In fact, his eyes were alert, and he looked jazzed about something. "I'm here for the watch, computers, and cell phone."

"Phone hasn't been located, but the watch and computers are this way." Reed took him into a large office where Sierra had put the watch on her way through the house. The room had a separate exterior entrance in the front and custom built-ins on three of the walls. The back wall held a floor-to-ceiling sliding door that led to a small patio.

Nick gave a low whistle and headed straight for the desk. "Nice digs. Guess accounting paid off. Or not, I suppose, since Caulfield was murdered."

"I have a favor to ask," Reed said.

"What do you need?" Nick dropped into the expensive desk chair.

Reed held out the resident list. "This is a list of names of everyone in the neighborhood. I need to know if any of the men are Army Rangers or former Rangers."

"Sure, man. We can run that quick enough."

"How quick?"

"Could have something for you first thing in the morning."

"Excellent." Reed gave him the list. "I'd like a copy of this back."

Nick pulled a device out of his case. "Portable scanner. I'll scan it, and you can have it back right now."

Reed could get used to having his every need met this quickly. If he gave the list to an analyst at his office, days might pass before they got to it. "You always have this kind of turnaround for your clients?"

"I wish. Though we're still faster than most law enforcement labs." Nick fed the pages through the scanner and gave them back to Reed. "If there's nothing else, I'll get the watch along with this machine and the laptop taken into evidence."

"Have at it and thanks." Reed left the room and headed straight for the study to interview Caulfield's daughter.

She was seated on the sofa staring ahead, her eyes glazed and vacant. She wore jeans and a zipped-up brown leather jacket. Her nose resembled her father's narrow nose, but her hair was blond and long enough to sit on. Someone had thankfully turned off the television, and it was no longer blaring in the background.

"Ms. Caulfield, I'm Special Agent Reed Rice with the FBI," he said as he approached and caught a whiff of her cloyingly flowery perfume. "I'm very sorry for your loss."

"FBI?" Her thin eyebrows rose over swollen and red eyes. "What's the FBI doing here?"

Reed sat on the sofa a few feet from her. "We've been

investigating one of your father's clients. An Eddie Barnes. Do you know him?"

She shook her head. "Dad never mixed business with home life and didn't talk about his clients." She clutched her hands together and looked out the door. "Someone stabbed him, right? I mean all the blood and his shirt. The holes."

"We'll have to wait on the medical examiner's findings," Reed sidestepped to keep her focus off the horrific way her father died. "When was the last time you spoke to your dad?"

She looked up at the ceiling and tapped her chin. "I guess last week. He came over for dinner on Friday with me and my brother. We texted throughout the week, but never talked."

Reed got out a notepad and pen from his jacket pocket. "Do you usually communicate through texts?"

"Most of the time."

"And why did you call him tonight?"

"I texted him a few times after dinner, and he didn't reply. He has a heart condition, so I finally got worried and called. When he didn't answer, I called my brother, and he said if I was worried to come check on Dad."

"Is it normal for your father to be awake at this time of night?"

She nodded. "We're a family of night owls. All of us. Even Mom was."

"Was?"

"Breast cancer took her from us fourteen years ago."

"I'm sorry for your loss," Reed said, feeling worse now that he knew she'd lost both parents. "Can you think of anyone who might want to harm your father?"

She shook her head and started crying. "He is—was—a great guy. Everyone loved him. Well, I mean in his personal life. Like I said, I don't know anything about his business."

"He has quite an extensive office here, but did he also have a separate office?"

She dabbed a tissue at her eyes. "Just here."

"How about your father's attitude? Has he been himself lately? Worried? Distracted?"

"He seemed normal, but then I haven't seen him as much as usual. He has—had—this new girlfriend." She frowned. "We do family dinners every Friday night, but he bailed most every night for the last few months to be with *her*."

"Sounds like you didn't like her," Reed said wondering if it was the age difference.

"Never met her, or even talked to her, but I didn't like that she took all of dad's time."

Reed would circle back on that. "Were these dinners held here or at your place?"

"My house. Dad isn't—wasn't—much of a cook. In fact, I don't know the last time I was over here." She frowned. "When mom was alive we spent a lot of time here, but since then, not so much."

"Tell me about the girlfriend. Do you know her name?"

"Dad called her Tricia, but like I said, I've never met her. My brother either." She shook her head. "We kept telling him to bring her to dinner, but he just clammed up and said no."

"Do you have any idea why?"

She shrugged. "My brother and I figured she was too young for him and she was just after his money."

Reed didn't believe the girlfriend was behind the stabbing as it took a great deal of strength to inflict the wound that sliced Caulfield's neck. Plus, women typically didn't kill using such a violent method.

"And you can't think of anyone who might want to hurt your father?"

"No. But they did, didn't they?"

"Yes." Reed closed his notepad. "Is there anything else you can tell me that might help with finding the person behind this?"

She shook her head.

Reed gave her his card and stood.

She stared at the card, turning it over and back again. "I spoke to a detective, too. Who will be handling the investigation?"

"We'll be working it together. You can feel free to call either one of us if you have a question or want to share additional information." He gave her a tight smile. "For now, you're free to go."

"That's it?" She gaped at him. "My dad is murdered, and I just go home?"

"I'm afraid so."

She shook her head. "This isn't easy."

"I know," Reed said.

"Do you? Have you had it happen to you?"

"No, but sadly, I've seen others in your situation many times. Support groups for people who are victims of violence can be very helpful."

"It's a sad world we live in if such groups even exist," she muttered.

"I can walk you to the door."

She shook her head and kept shaking it. "I'm staying until they take his body."

"That's fine as long as you remain right here and don't touch anything."

"I...I..."

"I know that might be hard, but if you wander around it might confuse the forensic evidence and take us longer to find your father's killer."

"Then I won't move except to walk him out." A sob wrenched from her throat.

Reed wished he could do more for the grieving woman, but she would have to live through this and take the time to heal. He knew that from the sudden loss of his parents. "If you give me your key, I'll make sure the house is locked up when the techs finish."

She slipped a key from her ring and planted it in his hand.

"Remember to call me if you think of anything." Feeling unsettled, he left the room to look for Sierra and spotted Detective Miller staring at the patio door. Reed joined him, snapping on gloves on the way.

"I've checked all the doors," Miller said. "No signs of forced entry."

"Either Caulfield knew the killer or he had a key. His daughter had hers to get in tonight, but she might have given a copy to someone else. Or the son could've. He also had a girlfriend named Tricia. The family doesn't know her last name nor have they met her."

"Hopefully his phone or computer will reveal more about her."

"The Veritas computer expert is taking the computer into evidence as we speak, but as far as I know, Caulfield's phone hasn't been found."

Miller frowned.

"What's wrong?"

"Just don't like all these people I don't know at my crime scene."

Reed nodded his understanding, though he was glad to have Nick, Sierra, and ERT present. "You find anything of interest in your walk-through?"

Miller shook his head. "I didn't go into much depth in the office. Thought I'd leave it to you as that's your area of interest in this investigation. Just make sure I get copies of everything you find there."

"I'll forward on everything I receive. I'll also get a warrant going for his phone records and banking information. And email and social media while I'm at it."

Miller stiffened at that comment but didn't speak. His negative reaction made sense as these areas could provide many investigative leads.

Reed's best bet was to move on. "I'm going to check in with the forensic staff to see if they've located anything of interest."

Miller frowned. "You say you want this to be a joint investigation, but you've taken over." He crossed his arms over a broad chest. "With your prior affiliation with our agency, I'm giving you the benefit of the doubt here, but don't be playing me, man."

"I'm not," Reed said. "And same goes for you. I don't want to take over this investigation, but know that I will if pushed. So if you want to be involved, don't push me."

Reed left the frustrated Miller behind and went in search of Sierra. He walked through room after room, all professionally decorated with muted colors, the furnishings expensive and implying a designer's touch.

Caulfield obviously made good money as an accountant. Maybe Reed should keep more of an open mind about this guy potentially stealing the money from Eddie's clients.

In the master bedroom, Reed spotted Sierra on the small deck outside. She was frowning and staring at a hot tub on the back side of the large lot that climbed up steeply from a retaining wall. The area above was filled with scrub and wild plants. The yard—and the neighbor's yard—went on beyond what Reed could see in the dark.

A wooden walkway led from the deck to the hot tub. Maple tree branches hung over the tub and lush greenery surrounded it. Lights were strung on a pole and around the area, illuminating the large tub and casting Sierra in shadows.

Reed stepped into the cool night and briefly noted the stars sparkling overhead and the moon shining above. But his focus quickly returned to Sierra. Even in shapeless coveralls, she sent his pulse beating faster. What was it about this woman that he found so compelling?

She opened the bulging hot tub cover and gasped, then clamped a hand over her mouth and nose. Steam rose up from the tub into the cooler night air, carrying a smell that nearly brought Reed to his knees. He covered his mouth too and looked inside the tub. What should be sparkling clear water resembled sludgy red soup.

"Another victim?" Sierra looked up at him, her eyes wide, shock giving her a glazed look.

"Could be," he said, but the woman's blouse snagged on the edge of the tub told him they would indeed find another victim in the tub. It was only a matter of time.

15

The moon had darted under clouds, casting Sierra in shadows as she remained frozen in place and stared at the tub. Hand over mouth. Eyes still wide. Her body rigid. Reed's heart creased. He couldn't let her remain here staring at this horrific scene.

"Dr. Albertson is still here. Let's get her and see what she thinks." He took Sierra's hand and led her away from the hot tub.

She didn't argue or fight, telling him more about her state of mind than the wide eyes still dark with shock. Her hand trembled in his, and he had to work doubly hard not to pull her close to his side and hold her until the shaking subsided. If he did, he wouldn't mind what others thought, but once she came out of the fog of shock, he knew this fiercely independent woman would be upset with him taking over in front of her associates.

He found Dr. Albertson standing by the gurney where, with the help of her assistant, she'd loaded Caulfield's body. Caulfield's daughter clung to the gurney as if she couldn't bear to let it go.

Dr. Albertson glanced at Sierra then Reed. "What's wrong?"

Reed released Sierra's hand and stepped closer to the ME to keep the techs and Caulfield's daughter from hearing him. "Looks like we have another body. This one in the hot tub. Or at least what's left of a body."

Dr. Albertson grimaced and shook her head. "Let me get this guy into the van, and then I'll take a look."

Reed nodded and took one look at Sierra who remained pale and wide-eyed. She seemed as if she might be sick or drop to the floor. He put his hand on the small of her back and urged her to sit on the sofa.

He squatted by her and made eye contact. "Would you like some water?"

She nodded. "I have a bottle in my tote."

"Be right back." He located the bottle and returned to her. A bit of color had pinked her cheeks, but her pallor was still evident. "You okay?"

She nodded woodenly as she opened the metal water bottle. "Based on what we saw, we'll need to call Kelsey. She'll be the one to recover the remains, not the ME."

Reed liked that Sierra was coming back to life and was able to think clearly now, but he still didn't like that she had to deal with this. However, this was her job, and he had to let her do it. "Assuming we're not dealing with some animal that crawled into the tub."

"It would have to be a large animal to make such a mess. Plus I saw a woman's blouse."

"It could have been left there from before," Reed said. "The neighbor said Caulfield and his girlfriend spent a lot of time in this tub."

"The neighbor." She blinked a few times, her lashes fanning her face like a hummingbird in flight. "I forgot to ask. Is he the Ranger I talked to?"

Reed shook his head and shared his conversation with the Driscolls. "I gave the list to Nick, and he's looking for anyone with a military background."

She gave a firm nod. "Since the Driscolls said the noisy hot tubbing stopped a few weeks ago and they hadn't seen the girlfriend since then, it could very well be her body in the tub."

Reed nodded. "And the only way I can see Caulfield leaving her in the tub all this time while he continued living here is that he killed her and didn't know how to dispose of the body."

"We can speculate all we want, but we need to know for sure that we're dealing with another body and that it *is* Tricia." Sierra unzipped her coveralls and reached inside for her phone. Her hand was shaking as she made a call. "Kelsey, sorry to wake you. We've found what we think is a victim in a hot tub, but we're not sure if it's human or not. The body's been in there for some time. The ME is still here, and I'm sure she'll want you to recover the remains."

Sierra listened and stared at her feet. She gave a sharp nod. "Thanks. I'll call you back."

She shoved her phone back into her pocket and looked up at Reed. "She's getting dressed and told me to call her back if the ME asks for her."

"Doesn't she think Dr. Albertson will want her to recover the remains?"

"She said different MEs respond differently, and she didn't want to make a wasted trip if not necessary."

Reed pointed at Sierra's water bottle. "You look pale. Drink some water."

She didn't argue, indicating she hadn't come all the way back yet, and tipped the bottle to her lips with a shaky hand. "I've seen a lot of horrific things in my job, but this is the absolute worst."

143

He nodded.

She stared at him. "You seem to be taking it in stride."

"Believe me, I'm not. I'm just better at hiding it than you." He gave a tight smile and took her hand. "I can go out to the hot tub with Dr. Albertson if you want to wait here."

She opened her mouth to speak, but shook her head and jerked her hand free. "I need to look for blood near the tub and process the scene. I'm a professional. I can handle it."

He didn't want her to have to handle it. He wanted to spare her from such a thing, but she really was a tough woman, and he knew she would be okay in time.

Putting on a fresh pair of gloves, Dr. Albertson marched up to them. "Show me the way."

Sierra set down her water bottle and got up to lead them back outside. Reed noticed on the way that the horrific smell from the hot tub had drifted in through the door, and Dr. Albertson covered her mouth and nose.

If *she* thought the stench was too strong, he knew it was *really* bad.

She took one look at the steaming sludge and faced Sierra, but kept her hand over her face. "Human or not, your anthropologist will need to recover these remains."

Reed changed his focus to the ME. "Any idea on how long this body's been here?"

Dr. Albertson shook her head. "Bodies usually decompose slower in cold water, but this heat would have greatly sped up decomp. The condition of the water suggests everything but the bones have decomposed. So two weeks. But it could be as little as one. I'll consult with the anthropologist, and hopefully, together we can come up with an estimate."

"The neighbor said they hadn't seen Caulfield's girlfriend in a few weeks," Reed said. "This could be the reason."

Dr. Albertson gave a firm nod.

"I'll call Kelsey." Sierra got out her phone.

"Thank you." Dr. Albertson took another look at the hot tub, then shaking her head, she strode away.

Sierra phoned Kelsey, and when she finished her call, she looked at Reed. "She's on her way."

Reed hadn't fully appreciated what Kelsey did for a living until now. How she could deal with such a scene was beyond him.

Sierra didn't waste even a second but got out a spray bottle from her kit and looked at him. "The light switch is on the house by the bedroom door. Can you turn it off?"

"Sure thing." He strode to the house, and the moment he clicked off the switch she started spraying the edges of the hot tub, then shone her UV light over the area. Blue glowed around the lip of the tub.

"Blood." She sprayed a slatted wood wall behind the tub and the decking surrounding it, but nothing glowed.

Reed walked out to her.

"No blood on the deck, but that's definitely blood in the tub." She clicked off her light and looked up from where she remained squatting. "Lack of any spatter around the tub says the victim didn't die from a gunshot or knife wound. At least not out here. She was most likely killed in the tub."

Reed didn't point out that they didn't yet know if there was another victim, and if so, if it was a woman. "That leaves strangling, drowning, or hitting her hard enough to end her life. But there are too many variables to know at this point. Let's hope Kelsey can tell us something."

Sierra gave a resigned nod. "I need to look for additional evidence. Can you turn the lights back on?"

"Of course, but if Dr. Albertson is right that this person's been dead for a week or more, won't any evidence out here be contaminated or even have blown away?"

She lifted her shoulders. "Yes, but that won't stop me

from looking. And we need to pin down Caulfield's daughter and son on the last time they were here, and if they noticed anything about the hot tub."

"I can call them."

"I honestly can't imagine them knowing about this." Sierra glanced at the tub then frowned and sat back on her haunches.

"It's gruesome all right. I never thought I would say this, but I hope this person was murdered and didn't accidentally get trapped in the hot tub."

Sierra's gaze flashed up to his. "You think that could happen?"

"I remember reading about a suspect who ran from the police after a carjacking, hid from them in a person's hot tub, and got trapped. It was a woman, but I have no idea why she couldn't lift such a cover."

She shook her head. "I was just thinking that it was odd that the gases from decomposition didn't blow this cover off."

"Perhaps Caulfield continued to lift it to release the gases."

"So you're thinking he knew the body was in there."

"Yeah, unless he suddenly stopped using the hot tub. I'll ask his daughter about that, too."

Sierra shook her head. "I never expected finding Eddie would take such a crazy turn."

"We don't know these murders are connected to Barnes."

She got up and met Reed's gaze head on. "But what are the odds that they aren't? I mean what does your gut say?"

"My gut says you might be right. That Barnes didn't disappear on his own."

"And worse," she said and chewed on her lip. "I'm starting to wonder if he's even still alive."

Yeah, that bothered Reed, too. As did the thought that

maybe Barnes wasn't actually missing or hadn't been abducted. That he'd gone into hiding of his own accord as he was the killer they now sought.

~

Sierra wished she could give Kelsey a hug. Or that Kelsey would hug her. As she wished Reed would have done. How wonderful would it have been to rest her head against his chest while he helped her come to grips with the horrible crime. But honestly, it was bad enough that she let him take her hand—if he hugged her, she would appear weak at a crime scene.

Sierra figured Kelsey could be thinking about appearing weak too, but she'd handled tough scenes before, and she was clearly handling this one. She grimaced when first arriving on scene, but didn't show any other outward signs. She simply went back to her van to grab Klieg lights and set them up to illuminate the tub of sludge, making it even more horrific-looking, and then laid out clean tarps around the tub.

"Would you like me to take the photos for you?" Sierra asked.

Kelsey turned to look at Sierra. "I appreciate it, but no sense in both of us having to witness these details."

"You're sure?"

"Yeah, Tyler's on his way to help."

"Kind of a gruesome thing for an intern to see, isn't it?"

"He has to learn to handle scenes like this, so it will be good for him."

Sierra knew Kelsey was right, but if she'd seen something like this right out of college, she might not have continued in her profession. "Tell you what. I'll start the pics so you can get to work, and then he can take over when he arrives."

"Okay, have at it, and thanks." Kelsey took her clipboard holding a sketch pad for diagraming the scene and stepped away. Sierra had already done a scene diagram, but Kelsey would complete her own along with an inventory of the bones she collected.

Sierra lifted her camera, and first took long shots of the hot tub and surrounding area then moved steadily closer until she was over the tub that Kelsey had turned off. Steam still rose up, and Sierra had to get creative to get detailed pictures without fogging her lens, but she accomplished them. And she knew the photo quality would be better than Tyler would take, due to his lack of experience.

She finished the shots and looked up to find Reed watching her. Not idly, but intensely studying her. She held his gaze, and he crossed over to her.

He searched her eyes, digging deep. "You doing okay?"

She nodded.

He gritted his teeth, and she heard them grinding. "I'm impressed by how you're handling this."

"Thanks," she said, touched by his compliment, but she quickly changed her focus to Kelsey before she let go of her precarious hold on her emotions and threw herself into his arms. "I'm all done, Kels, so you can get started."

Kelsey nodded, put down her sketch pad, and lifted a long instrument to reach into the tub. It came out holding a bikini top. She laid it on a tarp. She plunged the tool in again and came out with a long bone.

"Definitely human." She squatted and gave the bone a thorough study before looking up. "We have adherent muscle still attached, but nothing more." She paused and tapped her knee with her index finger as she continued to stare at the bone. "I'd estimate two weeks in this heat for that to happen."

Kelsey got up and gently set the bone on the tarp with all the consideration she gave every victim. Sierra always respected her partner, but as she continued to pull additional bones from the gross sludge, Sierra held her in the utmost respect.

She removed a thick leather belt and stared at it. "This looks like a man's belt."

"A woman wouldn't be wearing that with a bikini," Sierra stated the obvious.

"We could be looking at two bodies," Kelsey said. "I've recovered nothing so far to suggest that, but I can't confirm a thing until I've removed every bone from the tub."

Reed looked at Kelsey. "If we only have a female victim, someone could've used the belt to strangle or restrain her."

Kelsey nodded and shifted her focus to her intern, Tyler. Eyes narrowed, he walked toward them from the house. He was slender—a runner's body that was tan from his time outdoors, and he had messy blond hair.

"Hey, Tyler." Sierra smiled at the twenty-something intern.

He looked at the tub. At the tarp. Got closer and turned green around the gills. He bolted away and threw up in the bushes. He dropped down to the deck, dangling his legs off the edge and hanging his head between his knees.

"Guess maybe I'll be taking pictures a while longer," Sierra said and wished she could be anywhere but here right now.

～

Reed watched Sierra as she continued to take pictures in a backyard that should be calming and peaceful with all the flowers and lush trees, but horror had wiped that all away. He hated to see her upset earlier, but he was also sad that a scene like this didn't make her sick like Tyler or like a first-time detective might react. Because that likely meant she'd seen a lot of death over her career, and it had to eat away a bit of her soul each time. At least he knew it did for him.

Still, he was impressed with her ability to do her job even in the face of horrible things. He'd pegged her as a strong woman right off the bat, and her actions continued to prove that. He might be attracted to her, but he also greatly admired her—and the rest of her team. They just didn't make his heart beat faster like she did.

His phone rang, and he was shocked to see Nathan Adair's name show up on the screen. Reed had texted his supervisor to tell him about the murder, but didn't expect a middle of the night callback from the Assistant Special Agent in Charge of the Portland field office.

Reed stepped out of earshot and answered. "Sir."

"We have a murder?" Adair asked.

"Looks like two actually." Reed quickly brought his supervisor up to speed on Caulfield and the hot tub. "The Veritas anthropologist is here recovering the remains as we speak."

Adair huffed a breath. "Any idea on the second victim's identity?"

"None. Hopefully they can still get DNA from the remains. Or maybe dental records can be used for ID, but we'd need a lead on who we think is in that tub to request the records. At this point we aren't even sure if it's male or female."

"Does this mean you're rethinking your take on Barnes's disappearance?"

"Yes and no. For all we know, Barnes could even be behind these murders so I'm keeping my options open."

"Keep me in the loop."

"Will do." Reed disconnected and glanced at Sierra to find her watching him. He instantly felt disloyal for thinking Barnes could be a murderer, but Reed had to think like an investigator, not a guy infatuated with the man's daughter.

Tyler got up and took a long drink from a water bottle hanging from his belt and joined Kelsey.

"Sorry," he said, still looking pale.

"No worries." Kelsey smiled. "It's happened to most of us at one time or other."

Sierra stepped back. "Make sure you send me all of the pictures you take."

He nodded and hung his camera strap around his neck.

"We're going to have to run every bit of this liquid through a sieve to find teeth and smaller bones," Kelsey told him.

Tyler swallowed hard and looked like he might be sick again. "Let me guess. That's grunt work and as your grunt..."

Kelsey nodded. "But once I've recovered the major bones, I'll pitch in."

He shook his head. "I've got it Dr. M."

Reed saw the guy pull back his shoulders, but Reed doubted Tyler had a clue what he just committed to. There had to be four, five hundred gallons of sludge in that tub.

Kelsey looked at Sierra. "We clear to set up in the yard to begin that process?"

"I'll clear an area for you to work." She turned to her kit.

"Any way I can help?" Reed asked.

"No," she answered quickly then tilted her head. "I mean sure. You can look through a magnifying glass as well as I can. Together we can cover an area far faster so Kelsey can finish up sooner." Sierra grabbed a magnifying glass from her kit and handed it to him. "This way."

Kit in hand, she jumped down from the deck and

walked to the area near the retaining wall lit by the bright lights Kelsey had set up.

Sierra ran her gaze over Reed and landed back on his face. "Let me get you coveralls."

He didn't argue as he didn't want to ruin his suit, but more importantly, he didn't want to contaminate the scene.

"Be right back," she said and headed for the house.

He took off his suit coat and laid it on the back of a lawn chair then rolled up his sleeves and loosened his tie. If he was going to be crawling around on the ground, he didn't want it strangling him.

She returned with an unpackaged suit and shook it out. "It's the biggest one I have. Hope it fits okay."

He slipped his legs in and pulled it up. It was a bit small but he was able to zip it up and the fabric covered most of his body.

Sierra dropped to the ground lit by Kelsey's bright Klieg lights and pointed at a spot next to her. He got down on his knees about an arm's length from her.

For a moment they knelt and just looked at each other until she jerked her gaze away. "You see anything suspicious, you give me a shout."

He nodded and started running his gloved fingers over the trimmed blades of grass in the perfectly green lawn. Caulfield had obviously taken care of his yard as the grass was thick without a weed in sight.

"He recently mowed the grass," Sierra said, sounding matter-of-fact when he knew deep down she was still shaken. She was like most everyone here at the crime scene. Putting her emotions on hold for now. Blocking them. When she was alone, she would let them all out.

"He obviously used a grass catcher," she continued. "And it would've sucked up other things, too. If his garden debris bin hasn't been emptied, I'll have to look through that."

Reed glanced at her. "That could be nasty."

"Not as bad as a dumpster or surely not as bad as draining that hot tub."

He was beginning to see she tried to look for positives in her life, and he liked that about her and liked being with someone with a positive attitude. What was he thinking? He just plain liked being with her, even if it was at a double murder investigation.

"So what made you go into forensics?" he asked as they turned to work their way back toward the fence.

She was silent for a long moment. "You're going to laugh."

He glanced over at her. "A good laugh might be perfect right now."

She sat back and looked at him for the longest time, probably trying to decide if she could trust him with her story.

"Back in the day," she finally started. "I wanted a career in law enforcement. My family pushed me to choose a safer career. Then, when I developed a crush on the guy who played Nick Stokes on CSI, my career path was cemented in my mind."

Reed smiled, so grateful that she shared something personal that he wouldn't laugh.

"Of course, that meant I watched every show and made sure I took as many chemistry and biology classes as I could take in high school." She gave a nervous laugh. "I don't suppose you chose to get into law enforcement due to a crush."

He frowned. "Actually, it's kind of related. One of my high school girlfriends was murdered."

"Oh, Reed. How awful."

"Yeah, it was tough." The memories washed over him.

"They never found her killer. I thought if I went into law enforcement I could solve it."

"And did you?"

He shook his head. "I worked on the case for years, but it went cold a few years ago, and I had nowhere else to look. Every year on the anniversary I pull it back out, though. Go through every detail and hope to find a lead."

"I'd be glad to look at the files if you want. Maybe I can see something that was missed."

"When we wrap up this investigation, I might have you do that," he said, but immediately wondered if they would even see each other after the investigation. He couldn't imagine not wanting to see where this attraction between them led, but Sierra was a different story all together. He feared she might be perfectly happy to have him disappear from her life forever.

16

"Thanks for meeting me so early, Kels." Sierra took a picture of the sketch Kelsey made of the Army Ranger and sat back in the chair by her desk. "This looks just like the guy I talked to."

Kelsey smiled, but she'd been at the crime scene all night and looked tired. She'd showered and changed, but there was no way to shower off the lingering effects of her job.

"You should go get some sleep," Sierra suggested, though she hadn't gotten any sleep and felt like a hypocrite suggesting it.

"Maybe later. I want to drop the sketch off with Blake so he can run it through facial recognition. If that doesn't pan out, we can get it running on the news right away. And then I need to begin examining the bones and ID the hot tub victim."

Sierra understood Kelsey's desire to work. Sierra would do the same thing. Not only to help with any forensics she could process, but also to keep from thinking about the horrific crime scene. "Anything you're ready to share on that yet?"

Kelsey shook her head. "You know me. I don't like to speculate."

"I totally get it." Sierra squeezed Kelsey's hand. "I owe you for this one."

"If you hadn't called me, I would still likely have been called in, so you don't owe me a thing." Kelsey got up with sketch pad in hand. "I'll let you know what I find."

Sierra watched Kelsey depart and offered a prayer for her friend. For Caulfield's family. For the family of the person recovered from the hot tub. For Eddie, her team, and Reed. For them to be able to find Eddie alive.

Feeling a little better, she sat back to prioritize her morning. She now had two investigations with plenty of evidence to process, and she figured they were connected via Eddie, so both were top priority. Sierra had promised Reed she wouldn't do any work without him, but she'd gone to Emory's lab and left the blood samples found by Caulfield's body and taken from near the hot tub, and hair located in the tub along with blond hairs Sierra recovered in Caulfield's bed. Then for the last hour, she'd listed out the leads on her whiteboard before putting them in order by the lead she felt most likely to turn up evidence and connect the two scenes. She felt okay with doing all of that without Reed, as she didn't actually process any evidence.

She studied the board. First items up this morning would be Eddie's and Caulfield's shoes. If she could place them together at a scene other than Eddie's office, she might be able to figure out why someone would kill Caulfield and abduct Eddie. Because now she was certain that Eddie had been abducted.

Eddie. Her biological father. She'd been so focused on him that she hadn't been thinking about her other dad. The man who'd raised her. The one she loved and had called father for so many years. He was in the hospital, and she hadn't talked to him since she learned of Eddie. Visions of him lying in his bed played in her brain. Pale and weak. Maybe near death's door. And she'd left him upset and hurt.

Tears quickly wetted her eyes. She tried to stop them, but couldn't. She'd been mad—furious even—at her parents, but now their secret just hurt. Deep inside. Where only emotions from someone you loved unconditionally could cause pain.

She grabbed a tissue from her desk and blotted her face, but the tears kept coming. She needed to cry, that was obvious, but she didn't want to greet Reed with red eyes and a blotchy face. She looked up at the ceiling and forced her mind to happy times. To fun outings with her parents and brothers when she was a little girl.

That made things worse.

Okay fine. Think of times when your brothers made you mad.

So many times to choose from. She conjured up the last conversation with her oldest brother, Aiden. He nagged her about her lack of a life outside work like he often did. Telling her there was more to life than a career. Just like Reed had suggested, except Reed didn't nag her about it. Just stated his point of view on the subject. Clearly and concisely. And that had made her consider his point far more than Aiden's nagging had ever accomplished.

Her desk phone rang, and she jumped. Caller ID said it was the reception desk. She looked at the clock. Eight. The time she and Reed had agreed on after they left Caulfield's house, and he must have arrived.

She picked up the handset. "Good morning, Lily."

"Agent Reed Rice is here to see you."

"Tell him I'll be down in few minutes." Sierra hung up and checked her makeup in her compact mirror. She cleaned away mascara streaks from the tears and left her lab. By the time she got down to the lobby, Reed was not only checked in but pacing in front of the door. He was dressed in a black-with-gray-pinstripes suit, and he'd paired it with a white shirt and lavender-and-black tie. Like his other suits, it fit him perfectly, tailored to his broad shoulders and narrow waist.

She felt underdressed in her jeans, T-shirt, and lab coat, but she was a tomboy at heart, and she didn't often dress up. Suddenly, she wished she had a better wardrobe. But why? She didn't want anything personal with Reed, right?

He caught sight of her, and she shifted her focus to his face, surprised to see how refreshed he looked. It seemed like he'd slept well when she hadn't even climbed into bed. She'd spent the time since they parted reviewing every single line of his case file on Eddie.

He searched her face. The concern she saw at the crime scene was still present. "You look tired."

"Gee, just what a girl wants to hear." She laughed.

"Sorry." He ran his gaze from the top of her head to her feet and back up. "I mean you look great, but tired." He grinned, a wide flash of white teeth that warmed her heart.

She felt a blush creeping up her neck. She spun, making sure the door closed behind him, and quickly boarded the elevator to hide her reaction to him. He stepped in with her. The space seemed to evaporate with his larger-than-life presence and was filled with his unique scent of leather and cinnamon mix. She was not only drawn to him because of his looks and his personality, but his scent was enticing and intriguing as well.

"What's on your agenda this morning?" he asked, thankfully breaking the tension.

"Shoes. Both Eddie's and the ones I found in the foyer at Caulfield's place. We know accounting connects them, but I was hoping we might find particles that would connect them in additional ways."

They reached her floor, and together they strode to her lab. She unlocked the door with the fingerprint scanner and Reed opened it for her. As he followed her, his now-familiar scent replaced the antiseptic smell of the lab.

He held up his briefcase. "I've got Caulfield's phone records to review while you work on that."

"Then make yourself at home at one of the tables while I grab the evidence." She crossed the room to the lockers. She felt his gaze follow her and didn't hear him moving. She couldn't work under the tension filling the room and needed to find a way to keep things light between them.

"You said evidence was handled differently depending on whether you process all of it or just some," he said. "Which do you do more of here? Specific items or the entire investigation?"

"And let the questions begin." She looked back at him and grinned, hoping to lighten the mood.

"If you don't want to answer..."

"I was just teasing you."

"Oh, right." He smiled. "Guess it's too early in the morning to pick up on that."

"Would you like some coffee?"

"Oh, man, would I."

She gestured at the pot that she recently brewed in their mini-refreshment area.

He put down his case and marched toward it like a man on a mission. As he poured, he looked up and quirked a smile. "So, my question."

She chuckled. "We used to do specific items more, but it's changing since Blake joined us. Detectives like having one point of contact for their questions, and word is getting out that we can handle full investigations. We're actually meeting this week to talk about expanding."

He turned holding her favorite mug that said *It's a foren-*

sics thing, you wouldn't understand. "Do you have the space to do that?"

She nodded. "Half of this floor and all of five and six are available."

He sipped his coffee, his face pensive. "You all have really built something special here."

"Go ahead and tell that to the Special Agent in Charge of your office and encourage him to use our services more often." She grinned.

He frowned.

She took it to mean that he didn't want a connection between his office and her lab to continue and that hurt. "I was kidding, you know?"

"I know." He went to the table where he left his briefcase and stood with his back to her, ending the conversation.

She had to admit to feeling hurt. He was really running hot and cold this morning when he'd been so consistent since she'd met him. She had no idea what changed. She thought they'd gotten to know each other the past few days and developed an understanding and respect for each other. Not to mention a personal interest, but something had put him off since she'd said goodbye in the wee hours of the morning. Or maybe she was the only one who thought this way. Thankfully, she had way too much to do today to dwell on it.

She put on gloves, grabbed Eddie's shoes, and took them to the table where she'd already placed fresh paper. She mounted one shoe, sole side up, in a clamp that she swung over the table. She adjusted a lighted magnifying glass and studied the treads.

Her cell chimed, and she spotted a text from Kelsey. She read it and bit back her disappointment. "Kelsey says the Ranger sketch didn't return a facial recognition match, and

Blake wants your permission to release it to the media along with a press release."

Reed took a seat and looked at her. "Yeah, he should go ahead with that. I'll text him a phone number for our office hotline to use." He pulled out his phone.

Sierra typed her response to Kelsey then went back to working on the shoe. She was even more determined to find a lead since the sketch didn't match. In the loosely held particles, she spotted typical sandy soil found near the beach along with little pebbles, but didn't see anything else unusual. She took a dental pick and released some of the deeply embedded soil onto the paper. Along with it came clay soil like the kind found in the Willamette Valley along with a red powdery residue that she didn't immediately recognize.

"Hmm," she said to herself.

Reed was off his stool and across the room in a flash. "Something interesting?"

"Maybe. Eddie's shoe has clay soil stuck in the treads, which means he could've recently been in the Portland area. And there's a red residue that I can't place." She scraped a sample onto a slide and went to her microscope across the room to examine it. "From the particle size, I'd say we're looking at a mixture of clay and sand."

"Which would come from where?" His voice came from right behind her.

She craned her neck to look at him. "Bricks are the first thing that comes to mind."

"Brick, huh? Not a common building material in the Pacific Northwest. Not with all of our trees." He tapped his chin. "It could mean we're looking for an older building. But for the particles to be lodged in his shoes, the brick would need to be crumbling, right?"

"Yes, or in the process of being made. I don't know of any brick factories in the area, but Nick can check that out."

"Eddie could've been on a construction site where brick was being laid. I'm assuming cutting bricks would leave some dust behind."

She nodded. "I'll check Caulfield's shoes, too."

She discarded her gloves in the biohazard bin and grabbed Caulfield's shoes from a locker then took them to a different table. She put on gloves and mounted the shoe in the vise to examine the sole under her magnifying glass. When she spotted a hint of red, excitement raced through her body, and she dislodged the soil. Similar particles rained down on the paper. "We have brick dust on Caulfield's shoe, too."

"So we find the place with the crumbling or new brick, and we might find Barnes."

"Yes." As she looked up, she caught sight of a red splotch on the back of the shoe. She bent closer, shocked that she hadn't noticed this at Caulfield's house. She looked up at Reed, her heart clutching. "There's not only brick dust here, we have blood, too."

17

Blood. The implications of Sierra's find hit her hard, and she could barely breathe.

Reed bent over the table and stared at Caulfield's shoe. "You're sure it's blood?"

"It looks like it, but I need to confirm." She used her hip to push him out of the way and slid onto the nearest stool. She set down the shoe and reached under the table for her blood test kit. A quick swab of the stain, and she added the Bloodstain Green drops. The swab turned green.

"It's blood," he said, obviously remembering the procedure from yesterday.

"Yes, but whose blood?" She grabbed a piece of sterile paper and quickly folded a section of the paper over one-third. She smoothed the crease, folded the other end over that, and repeated the process from the other two sides to create a sort of envelope. She had made these so many times on the job that she could do it with her eyes closed. She placed the middle of the paper under the shoe and grabbed a scalpel.

Reed silently watched her every move. She scraped the knife over the shoe and reddish-brown flakes dropped onto the paper below. She folded up the paper and tucked the outside two edges into each other to make a small packet.

"Couldn't you just use an envelope for the blood?" Reed asked.

"Yes." She removed her gloves. "But this druggist fold works best to store evidence because powders and fine particles can leak from the corners of an envelope."

"Interesting." He shook his head. "I've said that a lot with you, haven't I?"

"Yeah, but then what I do *is* interesting so you should say it." She grinned up at him, and this close she could see the tiniest of scars just below his right eyebrow. She gently touched it.

He sucked in a sharp breath.

"How did you get the scar?" she asked, now wondering why on earth she'd touched him in such a personal way and dropped her hand.

"I met the corner of a raised fireplace hearth when I was three."

"Stitches?"

"No," he said, his voice barely a whisper. "Just butterfly bandages."

"Must have hurt."

"I don't remember it at all, but my mom said I didn't cry."

"A tough guy even then, huh?" She smiled.

He looked at her for a long moment, his dark gaze digging deep. "If I was so tough, why would your touch scare me to death?"

"I didn't know I was so scary." She tried to laugh, but she knew what he meant—and that scared her, too.

She felt that same strong pull toward him that she'd barely been able to ignore up to this point, but managed to stay seated.

"I meant the way I feel when you touch me," he said barely above a whisper. "Shoot, when you even look at me."

"I know. I just thought I'd give you a chance to move on without having to discuss it."

He didn't respond right away, just stood looking at her. "You want me to move on?"

"I don't know. I...I can feel it, too, but I..."

"But you don't want anything permanent."

"Exactly," she said, glad he remembered her take on relationships. "I've learned from experience that if I date, it often heads that way and people get hurt."

He frowned. "You mean the *guy* you date gets hurt."

"Yes." She shifted uncomfortably. "They have expectations I'm not willing to fulfill. So I stopped dating. Now I only interact with guys as friends."

"I think it might be too late to avoid that." He took her hand and held it between his.

She looked at their hands joined together, her smaller fingers held by his strong, tan ones. A rush of longing for everything she'd avoided in life poured through her, and for the first time in her adult life, she wished she wanted the same thing as a man who was interested in her.

Her phone rang, and she jumped, pulling her gaze free. She saw her mother's name on the screen. "I need to take this. It's my mom, and it might be about my dad."

Reed nodded and went to the table holding his paperwork.

She appreciated the bit of privacy he offered and accepted the call. But before she even spoke to her mom, every reason she wanted to remain single came rushing back to her. This amazing man might be showing her how incredible he was in every way, but she would keep her distance. She had to, or she would eventually find herself smothered by a man and lose the freedom she'd worked so hard to obtain in her life.

"Good morning, sweetheart," her mother said.

At hearing her mother's voice, Sierra's pulse kicked up, and she felt shaky. How could she be feeling this jittery from a simple call from her mother? Sierra had never felt this confused before. "How's Dad doing?"

"Good news. Aiden's a match, and he's going to donate one of his kidneys."

"That's great," Sierra said, when what she wanted to say was, of course he was a match. He was their dad's flesh and blood, not like her. "When will they do the surgery?"

"Dad wants to wait until…" Her mother's voice broke.

"What, Mom?" Worry replaced Sierra's anxiety over talking to her mother. "What's wrong?"

"Nothing. Not really. Your dad just…he wants to see you before surgery. In case something goes wrong. He wants to know you've forgiven him…us."

Talk about pressure. "Nothing's going to go wrong."

"I believe that, and he does, too, but…just in case."

Sierra loved her parents, but she wasn't sure she was ready to forgive them yet. She definitely wouldn't tell her mother that when she was already so worried. "I'm really sorry, Mom, but I can't come now. I'm in the middle of an investigation that's time sensitive."

"Can't someone else do the work?"

"They could, but it's about Eddie. He's disappeared."

A long silence filled the phone. "What do you mean disappeared?"

"The FBI thinks he embezzled a large amount of money from his clients and took off with it."

"That doesn't sound like the Eddie I knew."

She was shocked, and yet, glad to hear her mother defend Eddie. "Tell me why."

"He might not have wanted to be a father, but he was a good person." She sighed. "He was as honest as the day was long. He couldn't tell a lie to save himself. And he never, never would have stolen from his father's business."

"Maybe he changed."

"Maybe, but I just don't see it. He was never motivated by money. As long as he could play golf at the country club, that's all he cared about. And me, of course. We were so in love. I used to go with him to the course all the time."

Sierra couldn't even imagine her mother in love with anyone but Sierra's legal dad. "For what's it's worth, I don't think he stole the money either, and the trace evidence I located showed signs of foul play."

"Oh, oh, my. That's terrible. Of course you need to help find him."

"No...I want to..." She didn't know what she wanted. Not with her parents or with Reed.

"You're not ready to forgive us," her mother said. "I understand. We'll be here when you are. And I'll let you know if anything changes with Dad's health."

"Tell him I love him, please."

"Of course, I will."

"And I love you too, Mom."

"I love you too, sweetheart. Talk soon."

The call went dead, and a hot tear slid down Sierra's cheek. Then another one. And another. She let them flow, wondering how to handle this. Her dad was getting sicker by the day, and she couldn't be the reason he held off on the transplant.

Her phone chimed. She spotted Aiden's name and read his text.

You made Mom cry.

How did she respond to that? She never wanted to hurt her mother or her father. Never. But she had. As deeply as they hurt her. Tears poured down her face, and her whole body ached with the pain.

Reed crossed the room and held out his arms. "Come here, honey."

His offer of comfort and heartfelt endearment snapped the last bit of her control, and she started sobbing. She couldn't ugly cry in front of him, so before he wrapped those strong arms around her, she bolted for the restroom.

She was vaguely aware of an orange smell from the cleaner they used as she splashed cold water on her face that was just as red and blotchy as she expected it would be. The cool water felt good, and it slowed her tears, but didn't stop them completely.

Emory entered, purse in hand. "Been here all night and I was on my way to check in on you when I realized I needed to...you're crying. What's wrong?"

Sierra ripped a paper towel from the dispenser and blotted her face. "I just talked to my mom."

Emory stepped closer. "Your dad. Is he...?"

"No. He's going to be okay. Aiden's a match, and Dad will get the transplant soon." Sierra explained the call.

Emory set down her bag and rested a hand on Sierra's shoulder. "I totally understand. You know that. Forgiveness in a situation like this can't be rushed." She shook her head. "I didn't want to hurt my mom either, but I did. It took me some time to get over learning I was adopted, but now we're fine."

"See that's the thing," Sierra said. "I know I'll get over this. I love my dad and wouldn't trade him for anyone else, but it still hurts."

"Maybe go see him. Tell him that. And then he can have the surgery knowing you love him, and that you know once the pain subsides that you'll find that forgiveness."

"Yeah...yeah. I can do that." She gave Emory a quick hug. "Thanks. You've helped a lot."

Emory smiled. "It's good to see what I went through help you. God doesn't waste a hurt, right?"

"Yeah, sure," Sierra said though she didn't yet know the purpose of this pain in her own life.

"I've been thinking of looking for a way to work with others who learn later in life that they're adopted. After this conversation, I definitely plan on finding a way to do it."

"That's a great idea. I'll pray that you find the right opportunity."

"By the way, I got your samples from Caulfield's place and started them running. I'll have the results by morning."

"Excellent. I also have a blood sample for you." Sierra's phone buzzed. She glanced at it. "It's Reed. Checking to see if I'm okay. Or maybe he's just getting impatient for me to get back to work."

"Law enforcement officers. You can't live with them and you can't live without them." Emory smirked.

"Ah, but it's not long before you'll be living with yours."

A wide smile crossed Emory's face. "Sixty-three days and seven hours until I walk down the aisle."

"Not that you're counting or anything." Sierra grinned.

Emory swatted at her. "You have a man waiting for you. And a very attractive man at that."

"I hadn't noticed."

Emory snorted. "I have mascara in my bag in case you want to repair yours."

Sierra held out her hand. "It's important as a partner to always look my best when I might run into clients."

Emory rolled her eyes and dug out the mascara.

Sierra used a wet paper towel to clean away black smudges of mascara and applied the wand to her lashes.

She stood back and looked at herself. "I look like I've been crying."

"No you don't. You just look a bit tired."

Sierra handed back the mascara. "Well there's no changing things, so off I go."

"I guarantee Reed won't mind what he sees. Not at all."

Reed paced Sierra's lab. He'd opened his arms to offer comfort, and she'd bolted like a terrified animal caught in headlights. Was she so repulsed by the thought of a potential relationship with him that she couldn't imagine his arms around her? The very thought made him sick to his stomach.

The door opened, and she entered. She met his gaze, but quickly looked away, tugging the lapels of her lab coat closed as if she needed armor in his presence. "Sorry about that. My mom...I..." She shrugged.

"No need to apologize," he said and truly meant it. "I take it from your conversation that things are still dicey with your parents."

She sat at the table holding the shoes. "My brother is a match for the kidney transplant, but Dad wants to hold off until he can talk to me. He wants to hear that I've forgiven my mom and him for withholding this from me."

Reed planted his hands on the table and looked at her. "And you're not ready for that."

"Exactly, but I don't want to delay his surgery." She picked up a twist tie from packaging and fidgeted with it. "I just ran into Emory. She has a unique insight on this. Not too long ago, she found out that she was adopted. Her parents hadn't told her, and she was angry and hurt for a while, but ended up reconciling with her mother. She suggested that I would eventually forgive my parents, so why not go talk to my dad now and tell him I might not be ready yet, but that I knew I would be."

"Sounds like good advice."

"Yeah. I'm just not sure I feel like I have the strength to do it."

There it was again. She didn't even think to ask for someone to go with her. To help her through this. She had such a strong need to be independent and tough. To do everything on her own. But Reed knew she didn't need to do that. Not when she had so many people who would support her.

"You don't have to be strong enough to handle this on your own," he said, hoping she'd be receptive to his comments. "God will be with you and give you the strength."

She dropped the twist tie and looked at him, her expression confused. "Sounds good, but I have to admit that's hard for me. My parents raised me to be independent. To do things on my own."

"So maybe that's why you're going through all of this now. God's taking you to a point where you can't do it on your own, and you need to reach out to Him. To rely on *Him* instead of yourself."

She seemed to ponder as she clutched her hands together. "All I know is that I've never faced anything this tough before."

Reed kept his focus on her and went around the table to take her hands. He held them tightly so she couldn't pull away. "And maybe God is also telling you that you need to let people in. To let them get closer even if it could result in them taking control away from you."

Her eyes glistened with tears and a single drop rolled over her cheek. He released a hand to brush it away. "Why don't we take time for you to go see your dad? I can come with you if you want."

She pulled her hands free and stepped back.

He had to admit her reaction stung, but this wasn't about him or how he felt. It was about helping her. "We can do whatever you want. I could drive you then hang in the lobby or the hallway."

She drew in a sharp breath and held it for a long time before letting it slowly out. "I need to see him, and I don't want to go alone. On the way, we can drop off the blood sample at Emory's lab and get Nick started on finding locations where we might find the brick dust. But I need to talk to my parents alone."

He worked hard to hide how much her agreeing to his help meant to him. "Sounds like a plan. Just know I'll be there waiting outside the room if you need me."

She gave a resolved nod and pushed to her feet to grab her backpack and the druggist fold packet. Glad to see her mood improve, Reed shoved papers into his briefcase and followed her into the hallway.

She watched until the door clicked closed behind them. "We can start with Nick on the third floor and then hit Emory's lab on the way down."

Reed trailed her into the stairwell and followed her to Nick's domain. The first impression Reed got was that the space was unusually dark to be called a lab, but Reed was used to eccentricity in tech people, so when he walked through the large room with five computers humming along one wall, he didn't question the lighting. Sierra led him into a room in the back that was filled with computer parts, and Reed was surprised that there was room for Nick inside the smaller space. Both rooms were cold, likely to keep the running equipment cool.

Nick's gaze went straight to Reed. "Tell me you brought me an image of Eddie's hard drive."

"I did."

Nick flashed Reed a surprised look. "Seriously? I thought you'd string me along and never produce it."

"That was uncalled for, Nick," Sierra scolded.

Reed agreed and didn't like Nick's insinuation. Usually Reed would let such a dig pass but he wouldn't let it go with Sierra standing here looking at him. "I'm a man of my word."

"Sorry, man," Nick said. "You've done nothing to deserve my comment, and I shouldn't generalize like that."

Reed nodded and got an external drive out of his briefcase. "A copy of all of Barnes's files."

Nick took the drive and held out his hand for a fist bump. Reed figured this was Nick's way of making sure they were good and tapped the guy's fist.

"I'll get started on this right away." Nick was true to his word as he grabbed a cord from his desk and shoved the plug into the drive.

"I have something else I need to ask you to do that takes priority," Sierra said.

Nick looked up at her. "Lay it on me."

"We're looking for any buildings in the area with red brick exteriors that are either under construction or are crumbling."

Nick's forehead furrowed. "That's not an easy task."

Sierra stepped closer to him. "I thought maybe you could write one of your famous algorithms to search for construction stories."

"Yeah, I can do that, but I doubt they'll mention brick. It'll more likely show up in any associated pictures."

"But you'll figure it out, right?" She smiled at him. "I mean you always do."

"Flattery will get you nowhere." He laughed.

Sierra chuckled, and Reed felt that same jealousy that hit him with Chad. He knew she wasn't involved with this guy or with Chad, but she liked Nick and was easygoing around him. Reed wanted her to feel at ease with him like that.

Or did he? He liked the sizzle that crackled between them when they were alone. Maybe being at ease would erase that, and he didn't want the sparks to go away.

"We need to get going," Sierra said. "Let me know if you find anything on the brick."

"Will do."

"Before we go," Reed said. "Any progress to report on the residents list I gave you last night?"

"My guy's working on it. Should have information by the update meeting this afternoon." Nick leaned back in his chair and propped his feet on the desk. "I *have* completed my background check on Eddie. Found only two points that I think are relevant to the investigation."

Reed wanted to doubt that this man found anything, but Reed had come to realize that this team pulled things off that mere mortals couldn't do. "So what do you have?"

"We all know that Eddie wasn't desperate for money, right? All of his financials were in good standing, and even your forensic review of his accounting showed that there wasn't a tie between the missing money in the business and his personal accounts."

"Right. We never connected the two, but he was the only one with authority to move the money, so he's the most likely person behind the theft."

"You'd think, but I tracked the offshore money transfer to an IP address that doesn't belong to Eddie."

Now Reed was very interested as his IT guys said they couldn't track the transmission. "Then who?"

"Not a specific who, but where." He handed Reed a piece of paper. "I tracked it through a myriad of proxies to this local address."

Reed glanced at the Portland address. "What's there?"

"As far as I can tell, a vacant building. Odds are good that whoever moved the money is no longer there, but—"

"But a visit to the facility is in order," Reed finished for him.

Nick nodded. "I've gone ahead and done virtual surveillance for you. And before you ask, I didn't notice any brick in the photos. But I found the building owner. A shell corp that I had to unravel to get to the owner. A Vasily Kuznetsov." Nick pointed at the paper. "His name's on there so you have the correct spelling."

Reed thought this lead was too good to be true. "Our guys were never able to trace the transfer transmission. You sure you got this right?"

"They couldn't track it because they're not me." Nick grinned and dropped his feet to the floor. "And I'm positive I've got it right."

Sierra was studying the paper. "Vasily Kuznetsov. Name's Russian, right?"

"Right," Nick said. "A nationality common for hackers, but also common for our city. We have many law-abiding Russian immigrants living here too."

Sierra nodded, and Reed could see she was thinking fast and furious. "Have you run background on Kuznetsov?"

"I was getting started when you showed up. All I know at this point is he's not one of those law-abiding citizens. He's been hauled in for racketeering and extortion, but the witnesses who were scheduled to testify suddenly changed their minds and none of the charges stuck."

Sierra's eyebrows drew together. "I'm heading out to

check in with my dad. I'll visit this building on the way back, so could you text me if you learn anything?"

He nodded and looked at Reed. "You going with her?"

"I am," Reed said feeling defensive and sounding it as well.

Nick held up his hands. "Hey, man. Chill. I just wanted to make sure Sierra wasn't stepping into a potentially dangerous situation on her own."

Sierra glanced between them. "I can take care of myself, you know."

"Not if you run into gun-toting criminals, you can't," Nick said. "At least not until you decide to carry, too. Then maybe I wouldn't worry about you doing something like this."

"You know I'm never going to carry."

"Then I'm glad you have super-agent with you." Nick laughed, but Reed could still see his lingering concern.

The same concern left unease roiling in the pit of Reed's stomach.

"Text me if you learn anything about Kuznetsov." Sierra spun on her heel and exited.

On the way to his vehicle through a spitting rain, Reed knew he needed more information on Kuznetsov—criminal background and activities that were available only to law enforcement. Information that even Nick with his super-human research powers couldn't find. Reed opened his phone to text the best analyst in his office.

Get me everything you can on a Vasily Kuznetsov of Portland. I need it yesterday. Lives could depend on it.

18

Reed drove them to the hospital and tried several times to start a conversation, but Sierra didn't feel like talking. And she got tired of listening to the pitter-patter of rain on the windshield as the wipers scraped the moisture away, so she clicked on the radio. A news program came on, and when the announcer mentioned Ira Caulfield's name, Sierra turned up the volume.

"Authorities are looking for a man with an Army Ranger tattoo on his right forearm. According to a witness who spoke to him on scene, he's six feet tall and muscular. He has dark hair in a military cut and a wide jaw. His eyes are blue. The witness said he claimed to be a former Army Ranger, but authorities believe he could still be an active duty soldier. A sketch of the suspect can be found on our website along with the number to call if you should recognize this man. In other news—"

Sierra turned down the radio. "It's good to hear that the media jumped on Blake's press release and even radio stations are carrying the news."

Reed nodded. "Hopefully the phone line will light up

with legitimate callers, and we won't have too many crazies to weed through to find them."

"Hopefully," she said as she knew that such a plea would bring people out of the woodwork who had no connection to this man nor legitimate information to provide.

Reed pulled into the hospital's entrance, and she started praying. She asked for God to be with her. To give her that strength that Reed said He would provide. But as she rode the elevator toward her dad's room, she didn't feel strong. She felt like punching the main floor button and waiting for the elevator to take her back down to flee this difficult situation.

Reed stepped close to her and took her hand. He didn't speak. Just held it warmly in his. That comfort she sought warmed her to her soul. Had God put Reed into her life to show her His love and support in human form? No matter the reason for Reed's presence, she was deeply grateful that he wanted to be here for her.

They exited the elevator to the smell of antiseptic and a strong cleaner that a janitor was using to mop the hallway. She carefully skirted his wet floor sign and knew Reed was behind her.

At her dad's door, she turned to him. "Are you sure you don't want to wait in the lounge or downstairs even?"

He shook his head. "I want to be here so if you need me, you can find me right away."

"If you're trying to get me to like you, you're very much succeeding." She smiled at him.

He grinned. "And here I thought I was being subtle and masking it in concern for you."

She grabbed his hand and squeezed it. "Thank you, Reed. It helps a lot to know someone is waiting for me."

He reversed their hands, holding hers between his warm

fingers. "Remember, I might be out here waiting, but God is going into that room with you."

She nodded and extracted her hand to straighten her T-shirt and pull back her shoulders. She knocked lightly on the door and entered.

Her mother sat at her father's side, but Sierra almost gasped at the change in his appearance in the two days since she'd seen him. Today he looked like a shell of himself with dark circles under his eyes and sallow skin.

Had the stress of their estrangement added to his health issues? She couldn't bear the thought.

She'd led such a blessed life until now. Her whole family had. Until her dad got sick, she hadn't had to face any real difficulty. Sure, she thought along the way that many issues were big and unsurmountable, but in hindsight, none of them were even a blip of difficulty until this.

She rushed across the room, giving her mother a tight smile on the way to the other side of the bed. She was careful to avoid all of the cords and tubes and took her father's hand. She dug deep for a smile. "Hi, Dad."

"Sweetheart," he said and his eyes brightened. "I'm so glad you came."

"Of course I came. I hear Aiden's a match. That's such good news." She tightened her grip on his hand and rested on the side of his bed. "Now tell me you have the surgery scheduled."

He frowned. "I needed to see you first."

"Well, now you have." She worked hard to control those tears that seemed to linger near the surface lately and looked at her mother. "You can find the doctor and get this scheduled, right?"

Her mother bit her lip. "I..."

Sierra knew what they were both waiting to hear, and

she closed her eyes for a moment. *God, please show me how to forgive them. Not in a month, or week, or even a day. Now.*

The thought of Jesus's sacrifice on the cross and forgiveness of the thieves hanging there brought her eyes open. She found both parents looking at her with such expectation on their faces. Memories of childhood and growing up flashed before her eyes. Falling. Getting hurt. Band-Aids and hugs. Kisses. Meals around the big table. Laughter. Joy. Love. Unconditional love. Unconditional acceptance and forgiveness. Nothing expected in return. Just two loving parents being there for her no matter what.

"I'm not mad anymore," she said and meant it. "I can't really understand why you didn't tell me, but I do know that you did it out of love. Everything you do for me is out of love, and I forgive you both for not telling me."

Her mom started crying, and her dad pulled her down for a hug. She went willingly into his arms. Even in the hospital, he smelled of the spicy aftershave he'd worn since she could remember, and she felt at home resting against him. Tears threatened again, but they were tears of joy over being able to let go of the hurt and anger.

Because of you, God. Thank you.

Her dad's arms relaxed, and his breathing quickened. Holding her took too much for his limited strength. She stood up. Her mom got up to rush around the bed and draw Sierra into her arms.

"God bless you for your generosity," she said and pulled back to kiss Sierra on the cheek. "Now I'm going to go find that doctor and get the surgery scheduled." She rushed across the room and jerked open the door to come to a stop. "Oh...oh."

Sierra saw Reed standing in the middle of the hallway facing the door. "Mrs. Byrd, I presume." He held out his hand. "I'm Reed Rice. I'm working with Sierra on an investigation."

"Looking for Eddie?"

He nodded.

"Thank you for helping her with that. I sure do hope he's okay." She looked back at Sierra. "You should invite Reed in instead of leaving him in the hallway."

And just like that, her mother was taking charge again. But with Sierra's recent flashbacks, she'd seen what Reed was trying to convince her of. Her family only wanted what was best for her. Didn't mean she had to like it or even do as they suggested, just understand their motives. She might still bristle inside, but she could try understanding.

"Do you mind, Dad?" she asked.

"Of course not."

She curled her finger at Reed, but kept her gaze on her father. "I'm not able to stay for long. I need to get back to work."

"Your mom told me about Eddie going missing." He seemed to be unfazed by talking about her birth father.

"It doesn't bother you to talk about Eddie?" she asked.

"Maybe once upon a time, but then you were born and I didn't care one bit. I had you." He smiled and shifted his focus to the door. "Now introduce me to your friend."

"We're working together, Dad." She glanced at Reed who'd barely stepped in and was leaning against the wall.

He pushed off and came closer to the bed. "Reed Rice."

He shook hands with her dad. "I'm sorry to interrupt when you likely want to be alone with Sierra."

Her dad waved a hand. "I'm always glad to meet her friends, though I have to say, she doesn't encourage that. Our little girl is all grown up and living her own life. Giving her all to her career."

That sounded terrible to Sierra. Like she was neglecting

them. And maybe in her quest not to feel overpowered she *had* been absent in their lives until her dad got sick. She had to change that. "I promise to visit more often. And once you get out of here you can drop by my work at any time."

He looked at Reed. "Do you work at the lab, too?"

"No, sir, I'm an FBI agent."

"Figured with that suit you didn't work with our Sierra. Never seen one of her coworkers in a suit."

"You've never been there when one of us has to go to court," she said, feeling like she needed to defend her partners.

Her dad didn't seem to notice her comment as he was assessing Reed. "Being an agent must be an interesting job."

"It is. Nothing I'd rather be doing."

"Not married I see."

"No."

"You another person who lives for your work?"

"Just haven't met the right woman is all." He glanced at Sierra, his gaze lingering.

She blushed.

"Oh, right. Oh." A wide grin brightened her father's face.

Sierra was so thankful her mother had left the room, or she would be planning her wedding to Reed.

"We're going to head out, Dad, so you can get some rest. Have Mom call me when she knows a date for your surgery." She bent down and kissed her dad's cheek, and when tears pricked at her eyes again, she stepped around Reed to the door.

"Nice to meet you, Mr. Byrd," Reed said, sounding sincere.

"You too," her dad said. "Keep an eye out for my little girl. We've given her quite a shock this week, and I want to be sure she's okay."

"My pleasure, sir," Reed replied.

Sierra cringed inside, but she didn't say anything, just marched down the hall to the elevator. The doors opened, and Aiden stepped out.

"Sis," he said and ran his gaze over Reed who'd come to a stop close to her and reached out to hold the elevator door open.

Her brother was tall with black hair like all of her brothers except the baby, Erik, who inherited dishwater-blond hair from their mother. As an ATF Agent, Aiden pumped iron to keep in shape, and women flocked to him. To all of her brothers, for that matter, and they took it for granted.

"Did you do the right thing so Dad can have the surgery?" He held her gaze like he could make her behave according to his plans.

She stiffened at the word *right* as she really had a huge reason to be upset with her parents, but she nodded. "Mom's looking for the doctor to get it scheduled. Now I have to go."

"And you are...?" Aiden asked Reed who introduced himself.

She was about to jerk Reed into the elevator and out of her family's realm, but that would be rude. She might not want her family all up in her business, but she wasn't rude.

"Reed's an FBI agent who's helping on my current investigation, and we stopped in on the way to another location."

Aiden's dark eyebrows rose toward equally dark hair. "You mean your investigation to find Eddie Barnes."

"Yes," she said, knowing her mom had filled everyone in on what was going on.

"I hope you find him." He frowned. "Just so you know, I think it stinks that Mom and Dad never told you he's your biological father, but it doesn't change anything for me or the others." He grabbed her in a bear hug and knuckled her head. "You're still one hundred percent our sister."

That, more than anything, made her weepy again.

"Thanks," she said, but rushed into the elevator. "Catch you later."

Reed released the door and joined her. She looked up at the bright light overhead to stop those tears.

"I like your family," he said.

For some reason that made her unreasonably happy, but she wouldn't stop to analyze it. Too much introspection these past few days, and she couldn't handle one little bit more.

Reed got eyes on the old warehouse where the Internet transfer of Barnes's money occurred. The single-level building was made of cinder block in a dirty beige color with the trim and large address numbers painted a bright turquoise. Most windows were cracked and some were covered with plywood sprayed with colorful graffiti.

His phone dinged, and he grabbed it from the holder to look at the message.

Too many past investigations on Kuznetsov to note here. He's currently under investigation for murder. Graham's case. Call him for details.

Reed swallowed hard and sent a reply. *Need a business address for Kuznetsov.*

"What's wrong?" Sierra asked.

"Vasily Kuznetsov is suspected of murder, and we have an active investigation open on him right now." He stowed his phone. "You should stay in the car."

"Doesn't look like anyone's here. And it's not like if he's here that he's going to start shooting at me for no reason."

Reed felt like demanding she remain in his vehicle, but

he knew her well enough to know she wouldn't. "But I'd feel better if you stayed here."

She crossed her arms. "You know how that makes me feel, right?"

"Yeah. Like I'm treating you like one of your brothers might do in this situation."

"You are *so* not like a brother to me, but..."

He loved hearing the first part of her response, but not the last. "But you feel like I'm trying to tell you what to do."

"Yes. And honestly, if I thought there was any danger here, I'd listen to you and stay, but I think you're overreacting."

"Yeah. I am. But I just told your dad I'd look after you."

"And if you hadn't done that?"

One side of his mouth tipped up. "I'd still be asking you to stay here. But it's your choice."

"Fine." Her arms uncrossed, and she gave him a tight smile. "Go have a look, and I'll wait here."

He returned her smile, making sure it wasn't a victorious or gloating smile. Or one that said he'd gotten his way, but a genuine smile with a hint of thanks in it. Hers widened, and he'd never been so smitten by a smile in his life.

He started to lift his hand to touch her face. Maybe to pull her close for a kiss, but he didn't want to freak her out. If he wanted to persuade her to change her mind about a potential relationship, he needed to take things slow. Her willingness to let him have his way when it came to her safety and not be mad was a huge victory and the first step.

"I'll be back in a few." He pushed out of the SUV and jogged across the street.

He really didn't like leaving her behind, but he felt she would be safer in the SUV than scoping out the building with him. He walked around the exterior and tried to look in the windows, but they were too dirty. He moved toward the back of the building, taking a quick look at his SUV to make sure all was okay with Sierra.

She sat watching him, and he gestured his intent to disappear behind the building. She nodded her under-standing, and he rounded the corner. He found the back door boarded up, but the plywood had been pulled loose, leaving an opening. As a law enforcement officer, he had no right to enter a secured building, but the opening gave him leeway, and he slipped in. His jacket snagged on a nail on the way in, and he could only hope the tear was repairable.

The building consisted of a large open room. It had large spiderwebs clinging to the corners and contained a strong musty odor that was stirred up by a cool breeze sliding through broken windows. He flipped up a light switch and dirty overhead lights came on. So there was power. Not surprising, he supposed. There would have to be power to send the wireless transmission.

Hand on his sidearm, he made his way across the space to the only inside door. He jerked it open to find a small utility closet that was warmer than the main room. On a broken chair sat a wireless router, the lights blinking. A black cable ran from it to a cable connection in the wall.

He took pictures of the device front and back in hopes that Nick could tell him something just by looking at it.

He texted the pictures to Nick.

Found this router at the address you gave me.

Not much good to me unless you can bring it back.

No can do. Will need a warrant for that. No probable cause.

Then get some, Nick replied.

If only it was that easy. Reed took pictures of everything in the space as he exited and then jogged back to the car. "Found a router hooked up to cable. Nothing else."

She swiveled to face him. "I know you can't do anything, but I could have Nick come over here to access it."

Reed shook his head. "That could jeopardize the investigation."

"So what do you want to do about it?"

"I'd love to get an agent to babysit this place, but I doubt there's anyone free for a detail."

She lifted her gaze in what he was coming to recognize as her thinking pose. "I could hire Blackwell Tactical to do it. I'm sure Gage will have someone here soon."

A good idea but... "They're probably not cheap."

"We get the friends and family discount." She chuckled, made the call, and raised the phone to her ear. "Gage, it's Sierra again. I need to hire your team."

She explained about the warehouse and money transfer, and then listened. "Yes. Twenty-four hour surveillance."

She felt silent. "Perfect. They can stay at my condo when they're not watching the building."

Stay with her?

"I'll text you the address." She ended the call and looked at Reed. "He's sending Riley and Sam."

Right. Probably two big strapping military macho men. Here. Staying with Sierra. "I take it you know these guys."

She nodded. "But Sam's a woman. I think I mentioned her. She's the team's forensic specialist and Emory's friend. She'll take day shift and spend the night at my place."

Reed let out a quiet breath and hated that he'd been jealous again, but he *was,* and it was time to face facts. He wasn't just attracted to this woman, he'd developed serious feelings for her. And there she sat, typing on her phone, oblivious to him.

He knew she was attracted to him, but for the most part she seemed quite content to do her job and ignore him. Or she was keeping her vow of not dating guys and only treating them as friends. He wasn't one to dwell on things he could do nothing about, but she was worth dwelling on.

Worth finding a way around her objection to getting involved. And worth burying these jealous feelings before they made him do something stupid.

She shoved her phone into her pocket. "Okay, so what next?"

"Next we pay a visit to Vasily Kuznetsov at his official business address. But we wait for your friends to get eyes on this place first. In case we spook him, we don't want him to send someone to grab the router."

19

The Veritas team was gathered around the conference room table by the time Reed got Sierra back to the center for the update meeting. He held the door for her, and she smiled her thanks up at him. The ease that he'd seen with Chad and Nick finally seemed to flow between them, too. He grinned back at her and couldn't for the life of him stop. She didn't move and didn't seem to want to end their connection either. When he glanced at the others, they all looked at them. Not only looked at, but assessed. Reed was used to such inquisitive looks from other law enforcement professionals, but these guys took nosy to a new level.

Blake was the only one who seemed focused on the investigation. He stood at the whiteboard, a list of leads or forensic finds written in black marker. "We're just about to begin. If you'll take a seat, I'll start with the items I'm responsible for."

Reed trailed Sierra to two empty chairs and pulled one out for her. That earned him another smile, and he couldn't resist it.

"Seriously, you two," Nick said. "Give it a rest."

Sierra cast Nick a confused look, but Reed totally understood what Nick was seeing between them. Instead of getting mad at Nick's comment, Reed was glad—it meant he wasn't imagining this connection with Sierra.

Blake tapped the word *ledger* on the board. "A copy's in the hands of a forensic accountant. He started on it right away and now we wait."

Blake put a red check mark next to the item and pointed at *Eddie's Golf Partners*. "I called the top three guys Eddie golfed with. Nothing new, I could head back to Seaview Cove to conduct a face-to-face interview, but I doubt it will help."

Reed was thankful to have a former LEO on the team as he could be sure Blake had conducted thorough interviews. "Then let's check it off."

Blake marked that item as well and then tapped the line item that said *Eddie's Business Partners*. "Okay, Nick, you're up."

"From what I could gather, and it was a lot, he was flying solo except for his accountant. Not even a business manager. The rental checks went to a lockbox in Portland, and the accountant managed that box. So he handled the intake of cash and Eddie handled the outflow."

"Separation of duties—a solid accounting principle on the surface," Reed said. "Yet Eddie still managed to take money."

"How'd he allegedly do it?" Sierra asked.

Reed ignored her allegedly comment. "He created bogus vendors that on paper looked like they provided services required for managing the rental properties, issued checks to these businesses, then deposited the checks into accounts he opened."

"And how long did it take for him to amass the $250,000?" Grady asked.

"Less than a year," Reed said. "He managed exclusive

properties up and down the coast that commanded three grand a night or more in rental income during peak season and brought in six million in rental income in a year."

Maya shook her head. "I should've sold this place and bought beach rental properties."

Reed's phone chimed, and he glanced at the screen. "Serial number of the gun found at Barnes's cottage didn't match anything in the system."

"So it wasn't recovered by police and used in a crime," Grady clarified.

"That's right."

Blake crossed the item off the board. "Back to you, Nick."

He sat forward and rested his hands on the table. "Nothing else in Eddie's background, but Reed gave me a copy of Eddie's hard drive and I'm just getting started on that."

"Since computers often give us some of the best leads these days," Blake said. "Let us know the minute you find anything."

"Will do. I also have Caulfield's Apple Watch. My guys have imaged it and are reviewing the data. I can tell you that his heartbeat stopped recording yesterday at nine p.m."

"Fits with Dr. Albertson's assessment of rigor on the scene," Reed said. "I'd hoped she could do the autopsy today, but she's swamped, so it'll occur tomorrow afternoon."

Blake moved to a separate whiteboard and wrote *Ira Caulfield* and *Apple Watch* below it. "I haven't been looped in on this murder yet. We'll finish with our follow-up on Eddie and then work this one."

He moved back to the first board and tapped social media. "What have you found, Kelsey?"

"Eddie has both a business and personal Facebook account, but he didn't post much or often on his personal account. He did list rentals on the business page on a regular basis, but it honestly looked like he had some automated software that posted those as they were all identical except for the property. I doubt a person could have done that for a long time without changing at least one thing up."

"I don't know of any program that would post rentals specifically, but he could've had custom software created," Nick said. "I'll look for that on his computer."

"Our techs didn't notice that, but I don't know if it makes any difference as the posts stopped when he took off," Reed said.

"Or was abducted," Sierra added.

Reed nodded, and then remembered he'd never mentioned to Sierra that he wondered if the brick dust connection to Caulfield could mean Barnes killed Caulfield. But Reed wasn't about to bring that up here before talking to her in private about it.

"Any other social media accounts besides Facebook?" Blake asked.

"Not that I could find."

"We didn't find any either except for LinkedIn," Reed said. "He has a business listing there, but he wasn't active on the site."

Blake checked off *Social Media* and tapped the word *Phone*. "I reviewed the call logs in Reed's case file. Other than the burner phone Reed mentioned, I didn't see anything unusual on the list. It's of interest, though, that the last person Eddie called was his accountant. Now that Caulfield's dead, the call might be more significant. And obviously, I didn't get a chance to interview Caulfield."

"We never located his phone, but I should have his LUDs by end of day." Reed didn't bother explaining LUDs, the common term used by LEOs that stood for Local Usage Details.

"Sierra dragged me out of bed at zero dark thirty to come take his computer into evidence before anyone else did, and we're imaging it now," Nick said.

"Okay, hold up." Blake moved to the other board. "Let me get this written down." He wrote fast and glanced at the other board. "Update us on forensics, Sierra."

"We have a few strong items, and to keep Blake from becoming a human ping-pong ball, I'm going to stick with Eddie for now. I recovered blood from the whale that I mentioned. Emory's running DNA on it now. I've also given her swabs from the ledger and gun."

"The whale, ledger, and Glock will finish running tonight," Emory said. "But DNA for the whiskey bottle, all glasses, and the single hair found at his office have completed. Eddie's DNA is on two of the glasses and the whiskey bottle. And the really big news is it's his blood that you found in his office."

"So Eddie was the injured party?" Sierra clarified as she looked at Reed.

Emory nodded.

"Which means he could've been abducted." Sierra gave Reed a pointed look.

He nodded at the possibility, but they had nothing to substantiate it.

"I also recovered a second DNA profile on two glasses along with the hair," Emory continued. "I didn't get a match in law enforcement or military databases for any of it."

Reed was disappointed in the results but wouldn't let it show.

"FYI, there was only one DNA source on the ledger." She smiled up at Blake. "I also don't want to see my sweetie running between boards, so I'll stick with Eddie's items."

The tough guy blushed as bright red as the marker in his hand.

"Someone help the poor guy out before he combusts from embarrassment," Nick said.

"And on fingerprints," Sierra jumped to his rescue. "Eddie has a very unique arch in his profile so I was able to quickly eliminate his prints from the ones lifted at the cottage and his office. Reed has submitted the others through AFIS."

Reed nodded. "I put a rush on them, but you all know what a rush is in the law enforcement world."

"Glacial speed," Maya muttered.

Reed took no offense at her statement. She was right.

"And last and most interesting," Sierra said. "I found brick dust in the treads in both Eddie's and Caulfield's shoes." She told them about her theory on the findings. "Nick is looking for potential places where they might have met."

"My algorithm is running, but so far no hits." Nick frowned. "And I wouldn't hold your breath. It's probably going to take a real human to search the Internet for this. With everything else my guys and I have been tasked with, we don't have time for that. I did trace the wire transfer of Eddie's money back to a local address owned by Vasily Kuznetsov."

"Sierra and I visited the place today." Reed shared what they'd found.

"And I hired Gage's people to sit on the place," Sierra added. "Riley and Sam are on the way here. Once they're in place, Reed and I will talk to Kuznetsov." She looked at Nick. "Can you get me a list of all properties in Kuznetsov's name? I want to check them out for brick dust."

"Sure thing. Is that top priority, or are the computers and watches?"

She looked at Reed.

"I'd say Caulfield's electronics will yield more than

following the brick dust lead. It even trumps Barnes's computers as our techs have scoured that already."

Nick changed his focus to Sierra. "You concur?"

"He's probably right. Do Caulfield's computers and watch first."

"Will do." Nick leaned back in his chair and put his hands behind his head. "And you should know, there's not a single military or former military member in Caulfield's neighborhood. Not even a child of any of the residents. But maybe Sierra's sketch running in the media will break this investigation open."

Sierra frowned. "I feel so dumb for letting the guy leave."

Just the thought of her near this Ranger who could be Caulfield's killer made Reed see red. He wanted to demand she be more careful. Instead, he curled his hands in fists under the table and made sure his tone remained neutral. "You didn't know he was a potential suspect, and even if you tried, you couldn't have stopped him."

Sierra nodded, but was watching him carefully. Had he failed to keep his tone level? Let in some of his angst over her being alone with a potential killer?

Blake moved to the other whiteboard, thankfully taking her attention. Blake glanced at Emory who was smiling at him. They were obviously in love and also respected each other. A very important component in a relationship.

He took a sideways look at Sierra. Did she respect him? He couldn't say. Not with how he'd cuffed her in Barnes's office and perhaps the way he couldn't just take at face value that Barnes wasn't guilty of embezzlement. Reed wanted to agree that Barnes had been abducted and someone else stole the money, but despite the things this team had uncovered, none of them cleared Barnes of the theft or of Caulfield's murder.

"I've been talking with Dr. Albertson about the woman found in the hot tub," Kelsey said.

Reed shifted his focus to her. "It's officially a woman, then?"

She nodded. "Her hyoid bone was broken. That, along with the belt we recovered from the tub, leaves us to conclude that she was strangled."

"At least that was a whole lot quicker than being trapped in the hot tub," Maya said.

"Agreed," Kelsey said and looked at Grady. "Can your team examine the belt and see if you can find anything unique about it?"

Grady nodded. "Don't hold out hope though. Belts might be great weapons for strangulation, but unless you can get DNA or prints or it has a custom buckle, belts rarely return anything unique that leads to a killer."

"And in this case, prints were obliterated by the long exposure to the heat," Sierra said.

"Now that we know it might be the murder weapon, I can swab for DNA," Emory said. "DNA can survive in water, but it will degrade over time, and in hot water like this tub? Odds aren't good that I'll find anything."

Kelsey nodded, her eyes narrowing. "Our biggest issue right now is identifying the woman. As Emory said, due to exposure to such high temperatures for so long, we aren't able to reliably get DNA. The hair might still be viable. I've taken a bone and tissue sample and given them along with hair to Emory. If anyone can find DNA in those samples she can."

"Thanks for your confidence in me, Kels," Emory said. "And the DNA finishes running early tomorrow from the blood recovered by Caulfield's body and the hot tub area, plus the woman's hair recovered in Caulfield's bed."

She looked at Blake. "Sorry to send you back to the

other board, but I can also compare Caulfield's results to the unknown DNA found at Eddie's house and cottage."

Blake smiled at his fiancée and went back to the other board to jot everything down.

"If the DNA doesn't give us the woman's ID," Kelsey said, "we can also try tracking her bikini. But honestly, it's brand-name ready-to-wear, and I doubt that will yield much."

Sierra frowned. "So how are we going to find out who she is?"

"Good detective work might give us the answer," Reed said. "If it's Caulfield's girlfriend, the woman's name could very well show up in his emails, phone, and other communications."

Maya curled her fingers in fists on the table. "If this woman *was* his girlfriend, how could he have left her in the tub for that long? That's just disgusting."

Sierra shook her head. "It really was gross."

"The belt might mean the killing wasn't premeditated," Grady said. "Like he grabbed whatever he could find. So if he killed her in a fit of anger, he might not have had a clue how to dispose of the body so he just kept putting it off."

"Maybe so," Blake said. "But that's all speculation."

Reed looked at Kelsey. "If we can get the girlfriend's name and her dental records, can we do a dental match?"

Kelsey nodded. "Yes, dental radiography matching is a good possibility here. We recovered every tooth."

"I talked to Caulfield's daughter and son this morning," Reed said. "They don't know her last name so they're not going to be of any help in IDing her."

"Let's not lose hope," Emory said. "The DNA could still pan out."

"And if none of this works?" Grady asked. "Knowing you, Kels, you must have something else you can do."

"Isotope analysis might work."

"Explain, please," Reed nearly demanded as he was getting frustrated from hitting dead end after dead end in finding Barnes.

"I'll take shavings of her tooth enamel and bones, and will analyze chemical traces in those shavings for lead, carbon, and other elements. This information can give a surprisingly detailed history of diet and environment."

Reed stared at her. "Not sure how that will help."

"Elements come in different versions, called isotopes, and they vary by mass. Geographic locations have characteristic percentages of these isotopes in rocks and soil. They're a kind of signature. Geologists have been documenting these signatures in databases for years. We can use the mass spectrometer to read the signature of elements from her bone or teeth and match it to a location. This will confirm if she's from the area or not from around here. And if not, we'll have a place to look to compare with missing persons reports."

Kelsey took a long breath. "This analysis will be a last resort thing. But you should also know, I recovered a wedding ring in the tub."

"The woman was married?" Sierra asked.

"Looks like it."

And the surprises just kept on coming. Par for investigations, but Reed thought this one was more bizarre than others he'd worked on. "If she turns out to be Caulfield's girlfriend, it could explain why he hid her from his family and neighbors. And if the husband found out and came after Caulfield, it would explain the violent death."

Blake started writing on the board again. "Now that we know it's a woman, I'll go ahead and contact local authorities for any missing person's reports that might fit here."

"Keep me in the loop on that, will you?" Reed asked.

Blake nodded. "What else do we have from Caulfield's place?"

"Tons of fingerprints," Sierra said. "I'll go through them after we break up here. And as we said, Nick has Caulfield's watch and computers."

"Have I mentioned how impressed I am with everyone's skills?" Reed asked. "Because if I haven't, I need to say you've all lived up to your reputation and more."

"Maybe hold that praise until we actually close this investigation," Kelsey said.

"Oh, I don't know." Nick grinned. "I say keep it coming. I, for one, love being adored."

Everyone laughed, and Reed finally felt like he was accepted by these amazing men and women. He was proud to know them. Even prouder to be working with them and would miss them all when the investigation concluded, but none more than Sierra.

"Any calls on the sketch?" Grady asked.

Reed nodded. "But none that have given us any leads yet." His phone rang and seeing Dr. Albertson's name he quickly stepped from the room and answered.

"My schedule changed. I can post Caulfield first thing in the morning," she said. "You available?"

Reed smiled at the good news. "Name the time and I'm there."

~

On the way out of the meeting, Sierra glanced into the lobby then turned to Reed. "Perfect timing. That's Sam and Riley at the front desk. Let's get them going on their assignment."

She hurried across the lobby to greet the pair and introduce Sam to Reed. Both Sam and Riley were blond, tall, and very fit. Sam had shoulder-length hair that was nearly straight, and Riley's hair was styled in a windblown look.

Sam shook hands with Reed. "Do you know Piper Nash?"

"Sort of," he replied, but Sierra had no idea who Piper was. "She was going on medical leave right when I was assigned to the Portland office. Is she a friend of yours?"

"Close friend to Eryn Sawyer, our team cyber expert, but we've all worked with her." Sam smiled. "Her injury's finally healed, and she's going back to work next month."

Reed nodded. "I heard it was touch and go, so good for her."

"And bad for us," Riley said. "We were hoping she might join Blackwell, but as Sam said, we're glad she's okay and can return to being an agent."

"The cyber and computer staff kind of stick to themselves in their own little world," Reed said. "But the Portland office isn't that big, so maybe I'll run into her."

Sierra looked at Riley. "Do you want to scope out the building or get checked in here?"

"I'll go with Sam and get the lay of the land," he replied. "She can drop me back here."

"Then let me tell our receptionist to call Maya if I'm not here when you get back. An escort is required at all times in the building." Sierra quickly made the arrangements then gave them the address of the warehouse, and they all walked outside together.

As they reached their SUV in the chilly damp air, Sierra pointed at Sam's ring that was glinting in the sun's rays. "Emory said your wedding was amazing."

A beaming smile crossed Sam's face. "The happiest day of my life, and honestly, I don't care where we were or what we did as long as we said *I do*."

Riley looked at Sam and grinned. He looked happy for Sam.

But Sierra saw much more than happiness in his expression. "Another happily married person, I take it."

"You know it." His grin widened. "I highly recommend it."

Reed locked gazes with Sierra for a moment, and she saw *I told you* so in his gaze.

She snapped her focus back to Riley and Sam. "With the big smiles, you two should be wedding ambassadors."

Sierra had made sure she sounded cheerful, but she felt a twinge of jealousy that shocked her to the core. She'd had friend after friend get married, and she'd never felt one pang of jealously.

Was Reed right? Were Sam and Riley right, too? Was marriage really a wonderful thing?

20

Sierra spent the next morning in her lab working on finger-prints from Caulfield's house while Reed attended Caulfield's autopsy. A postmortem exam usually took two to four hours to complete, but it was nearly one o'clock, and Reed hadn't arrived at Veritas. They'd worked in her lab late last night, and thankfully before departing, he'd said he was fine with her working this morning without him lurking over her shoulder. He was either being expedient or he'd come to trust her and accepted that she wouldn't keep evidence from him.

She thought it was more the trust factor. Their connection had long ago changed from a typical business relationship, and she sure hoped he trusted her by now. She trusted him. She just didn't trust the feelings she was developing for him this quickly. Based on her parents quick marriage, she always thought that love could come quickly. But after their bombshell explanation—that didn't include saying they were in love when they married, just that her mother was pregnant—her theory didn't hold weight.

"I finished developing prints on the photos from Eddie's

cottage," Chad announced from the fingerprint area. "They contain only Eddie's prints."

"Not surprising," she said as she couldn't imagine who else would want to look at old pictures of her.

The lab phone rang, and Chad went to answer. "Agent Rice is in the lobby."

"Thanks." She got to her feet to go check him in, but the door opened and Emory stepped inside. She was dressed in jeans, T-shirt, and her lab coat, and had a mega frown on her face. She came across the lab to Sierra.

"I have DNA results from Caulfield's place." Emory laid a folder on the table but rested her hand on top so Sierra couldn't look at the reports yet.

Sierra looked at Chad. "Will you—"

"Go get Agent Rice in the lobby?" he finished for her. "Yeah, I'm out of here."

Sierra turned to Emory. "Let's wait until Reed gets up here to review this. That way he can ask questions if he has any."

Emory nodded, but that frown remained.

"I'm not going to like the results, am I?" Sierra asked.

"Not all of them, no," Emory said. "So was Reed at Caulfield's autopsy this morning?"

Sierra nodded. "I hope it gives us something to go on, but at the very least he should have Caulfield's prints, and I can eliminate them from my stack of cards."

Emory nodded. "Are the prints the last of the evidence?"

"Yes," Sierra said. "But I didn't process all of Caulfield's house myself, so I plan to go back there to do another sweep."

Emory tipped her head and studied Sierra. "I was surprised to hear you let ERT do a lot of the work."

"Me, too, now that I look back on it. But the body in the

hot tub really threw me. I couldn't think." Sierra shook her head. "I've never seen anything like that, and I hope never to again."

"I don't know how Kelsey can handle it," Emory said. "But she doesn't falter. Ever."

The door opened, and Reed preceded Chad into the room. Sierra was vaguely aware of Chad going to his desk, but Reed smiled at her, and butterflies took flight in her stomach at the mere sight of him in his deep charcoal suit with fresh white shirt and red tie. He looked striking and confident as he crossed the room, his gaze remaining on hers and not shifting even a fraction.

She was captivated by his good looks, but it was more than that for her. He'd shown such admirable qualities. He'd demonstrated his ability to work with a team, and that he was ethical and responsible. He had great communication skills and paid attention to detail. He had a good sense of humor and was compassionate. All characteristics that made him a good agent, but also a fine human being and an exceptional man.

He came to stop in front of her and acknowledged Emory with a brief nod.

"How'd the autopsy go?" Sierra asked.

"Gave us a few things to work with." He laid fingerprint cards on the table. "First up, Caulfield's prints."

"I was hoping you would bring them."

He looked at Emory. "I should have asked if you wanted to hang around and hear about the autopsy."

"I've got DNA results to share," she said. "But you can go first if you want."

He waved a hand. "You go ahead. I know you're busy."

She smiled at him, but it quickly evaporated as she opened the folder.

"The first profile is for the blood found on Caulfield's shoe." Emory met Sierra's gaze. "I'm sorry, but the DNA matches Eddie's DNA profile."

"Eddie's blood?" Sierra's knees felt weak, and she dropped onto a stool.

Emory patted Sierra's hand. "Remember, we don't know how much blood had been cleaned up, and Eddie might not have been seriously injured. But you should also know that the hair you recovered in Eddie's office matches Caulfield's DNA. This combined with the blood on the whale and Caulfield's shoe looks like Caulfield injured and may have abducted Eddie."

"And what about your other results?" Reed asked.

Emory flipped the page. "No match in CODIS for the blood recovered by the hot tub, but the profile does match the blond hairs found in the bed."

"And the hair from the hot tub?"

She shook her head. "Sorry, not a viable sample."

"Still, the hair in the bed links the woman in the tub to someone who slept with Caulfield," Reed stated.

"Or at least slept in his bed," Emory clarified. "But yeah, it's likely his girlfriend."

Sierra grabbed her phone, tapped Nick's number, and put him on speaker.

"I have you on speaker with Emory and Reed," she said after he answered. "DNA results lead us to believe that the woman in the hot tub was Caulfield's girlfriend. Any info on his computer that gives us a lead on her identity?"

"Sadly, no," Nick said. "But you should know that Caulfield bought two burner phones about six months ago. If the wedding ring belongs to the victim, Caulfield probably used the phones to communicate with her to keep from leaving any trails for her husband to find."

"Sounds likely," Reed said.

"I'm still reviewing the drive. I'll let you know if I find anything else." Nick ended the call.

Emory tapped the folder. "I'll leave this with you."

"Is that the end of our DNA samples in this investigation?" Reed asked.

"Yes, unless Sierra finds something else when she goes back to Caulfield's house."

Reed switched his focus to Sierra, and she felt the heavy weight of his gaze on her. She assumed he wanted an explanation. "I don't like the fact that I didn't actually process the whole scene. I'd feel better giving it one more look."

"If you think it will pay off, then I'm all for taking you over there on the way to interviewing Kuznetsov."

"I can't promise that it will pay off, but I can promise it will give me more peace of mind." She smiled at him.

For some reason he didn't smile back at her, but locked gazes and held on.

Emory cleared her throat. "I should get going."

Sierra snapped her gaze free and faced Emory who was giving her a pointed look. Clearly she was picking up on Sierra's vibe with Reed.

"Thanks for everything," Sierra said, encouraging her friend to leave without saying anything or asking any questions.

Emory nodded, but her expression remained inquisitive. "Let me know if you need my help with anything else."

"Will do," Reed said. "And thank you."

Sierra looked at Reed. "So the autopsy results?"

He sat on a stool next to her. "The knife wound to Caulfield's throat severed both the carotid and jugular. He died from severe rapid blood loss. Dr. Albertson said he would've dropped immediately and couldn't have fought back. She didn't find any signs of defensive wounds or skin cells under his nails, confirming her cause of death."

"Sounds like he didn't know what hit him," Sierra said.

Reed nodded. "She also confirmed that the other stab wounds were inflicted postmortem."

"Rage maybe?" Sierra asked. "If so, this murder is very personal."

"That's my take, too," Reed said. "Otherwise, why inflict the final injuries?"

"I suppose it could just be someone with a sick personality."

"True. That's possible. Either way, Dr. Albertson didn't collect anything that could give us the killer's DNA. She did say the wounds suggest a smooth not serrated blade."

"That's something, I guess."

"And so is this." Reed pulled an evidence bag from his coat pocket and laid it on the counter. "She recovered the tip of a knife in one of the wounds by the ribs."

Sierra picked up the bag to study the thick metal point. "We can take it to Grady. He might be able to determine the murder weapon."

Reed arched a brow. "From a knife tip?"

"I've seen him do it before."

Reed just stared at the bag in disbelief.

"When are you going to stop questioning what we can do?" She grinned at him.

"Right. I need to stop that, don't I." He shook his head. "Seems like I should have learned by now that you're all superhuman."

She lifted the lapel of her lab coat. "We've got to stop hiding our capes under lab coats."

He laughed in earnest, the deep sound rumbling through her lab, and she loved how it filled such a solemn room with joy. She laughed with him and was suddenly very thankful he'd come into her life.

"I'm glad you're here," she blurted out without thinking about it or wondering if Chad was overhearing their conversation.

Reed's smile vanished, and he continued to look at her but didn't say anything. She wished she could see even a hint of whether he was glad to be there or not, but his blank expression made that impossible. It reminded her of when they first met in Eddie's office. The antagonistic atmosphere between them was long gone, but he seemed silent and withholding. Sierra sobered as well. She was responsible for his abrupt attitude change, but that was good. Neither of them needed to dwell on something that had no future.

"The AFIS report for the earlier prints came in," he said. "You compare Caulfield's prints with the other cards, and I'll review the AFIS report. Then we can drop off the knife tip with Grady on the way out."

She couldn't help but notice how he was still trying to dictate their actions. She wasn't opposed to his plan, it was sound, but she wondered if he was this controlling in his personal life. Not that it mattered. Not one bit.

She grabbed Caulfield's print card and spent a few hours comparing them to other cards and pulled matches for his prints. Then she stacked the others according to matches, leaving her with five piles. One was fairly tall, and she suspected it was for the girlfriend or maybe even Caulfield's daughter or son. She wished you could determine sex by the print size, but both men and women had varying-sized prints.

"We need to get elimination prints from Caulfield's daughter and son. I'll have Chad take care of that." She sent Chad a text. Then she put the cards back in the locker and took out the prints from Eddie's office and cottage.

Chad replied that he was willing to take the prints if she would leave him the contact information so he could arrange it.

She looked up at Reed. "Can you write down contact info for Caulfield's kids for Chad?"

"Will do."

She turned back to Caulfield's prints and compared them to the office prints.

"Bingo!" She shot Reed another look. "Caulfield's prints are on the whale."

"With Barnes's blood on Caulfield's shoes that makes sense."

"So it really *is* looking like Caulfield was the one who abducted Eddie." She paused for a moment as a more terrifying thought came to mind and her stomach tightened. "Or I have to admit, Caulfield could even have killed him."

Reed watched her carefully. "And how does the thought of Barnes potentially being dead make you feel?"

"Feel?" She flashed her gaze to him. "I don't know...I mean...I haven't really thought it was a good possibility until now." And she didn't want to believe it.

He frowned. "There's something else we need to consider here."

"What's that?"

"What if Caulfield *did* hurt Barnes at his office, and then Barnes decided to get back at Caulfield and killed him."

She gasped. "You think Eddie's a killer?"

"It's a possibility we can't rule out."

She shook her head as hard as she could, but her personal connection to Eddie motivated her response. As a forensic scientist who'd worked many cases, she could see that Reed could be right. "We can't rule it out, no."

He met her gaze. "This is a hard thing to consider, but I'm glad you're keeping an open mind."

"I guess the positive would mean Eddie was still alive when Caulfield was killed." She couldn't come up with any other positives and needed to change the subject before she started hyperventilating over the fact that her biological father could very well be a murderer.

21

Sierra couldn't keep thinking about Eddie potentially being a killer and had to move on before Reed continued their conversation. She looked at him. "Anything in the AFIS files?"

"They said none matched exactly, but we have a potential match to two of the prints. Or more correctly, we have a potential match to three different people on one print and two on the other."

"Send the results to the printer, and I'll have a look at them. I might see something your print examiner missed." She gave him a guest login to access her printer, and the pages were soon spitting out. She retrieved them and sat down to look at them.

Reed came up behind her, and he smelled fresh, like clothes brought in from an outdoor clothesline. He'd obviously showered and changed after the autopsy and maybe that's why it had taken him so long to arrive.

"What about that print?" He reached over her shoulder to tap a set of prints, the soft fabric of today's suit brushing over her wrist, sending a tingle up her arm. "Looks like it's a match."

She scooted away from him, but didn't look to see if he noticed because there was no point in checking. He noticed everything about her. All the time. And she had to admit she didn't miss a thing he did either.

She slid the print he'd questioned under the lighted magnifying glass. She scanned the details and pointed at a line on the potential match. "See this? It's called a crossover. It's where two ridges cross over each other. The potential print doesn't have that, so it isn't a match."

"Why would Quantico send it to me then?"

"To understand that, you'd have to understand how AFIS works. Do you?" She didn't look up at him—he was much too close for comfort.

"Sort of." He came to rest on the counter next to her and smiled. "But I know you're going to enlighten me."

"The FBI's fingerprint database contains around forty million records and has around seventy thousand searches a day. It's the largest AFIS in the U.S. but there are regional databases as well."

"I didn't know it was *that* big."

She nodded. "To help manage the records, collected fingerprint images are compressed and sent to an AFIS operator. They decompress the image and create a biometric template which is a numeric representation of the fingerprint. This contains information that makes the fingerprint unique. That template is stored in the database along with the actual fingerprint image."

"So two files per print."

"That's right. The template is then run against the database to filter out all non-matching records and isolate a few potential matches. These matches are given to a fingerprint expert who compares the actual images to determine a match. In this case, the expert told you none matched, but gave you the possible prints found by the database. That's unusual."

His eyes narrowed. "Why do it?"

"I'm not sure, other than the tech person did it to cover his bases. This print is close enough to warrant consideration, and if they were wrong and missed it, they could be responsible for leaving a criminal out on the street."

"Yeah, I can see that. But you say no way."

"Right. Let's look at the other ones." She reviewed them and determined that the others weren't a match to any of their submitted prints.

"So basically, we struck out with AFIS."

"Yes, but Caulfield's print looks similar to the last one you submitted to AFIS, so I can continue to compare them to the others from Eddie's office and home. Maybe that will give us the lead we need."

She looked at the print cards from Eddie's office. "Caulfield's print matches one lifted from a glass in the sink. I thought it was odd that the county techs didn't take those glasses. Maybe they were left when Eddie came back."

"So what are you thinking? They have a glass of water then go back out front and Caulfield attacks?"

"Sounds odd, right? But it could've started out friendly then escalated."

"Yeah."

She moved on to the doorknob prints from Eddie's office and home. No match. She looked at the partial from the Glock slide. "I can't be certain, but the partial on the Glock could be from Caulfield. You think he gave or sold the gun to Eddie?"

"Could be, though we have nothing to suggest that."

She flipped though the remaining cards. "That's the last of my prints, but we still have the knife tip. Let's get that to Grady."

While she returned the evidence to the lockers, Reed packed up his briefcase. She grabbed her backpack from her desk and the knife tip. On the way down to the first floor, she prayed that Grady was as talented as she claimed and could give them a solid lead.

Sierra led Reed to the back of the first floor. She knew as an LEO Reed would like this lab. She watched his face as he examined a display case holding different firearms and ammunition labeled with their particulars.

"Wow." A boyish grin spread across his face. "That's some collection."

"You don't know the half of it," she said. "He's got boxes and boxes of weapons and tools in the back room."

They entered that area with worktables holding vises and comparison microscopes used to evaluate bullets recovered at crime scenes to those Grady fired from a recovered weapon. On the far wall sat a large stainless steel bullet recovery containment system that included a water bath, and the caustic smell of gunpowder lingered in the space.

Reed turned in a circle and took it all in. "Now here's a lab where I could spend some time."

"You're like every other officer I've seen come in here for the first time." She shook her head. "I don't get it."

"You might understand if you ever took me up on my offer to learn to shoot," Grady said as he joined them.

She rolled her eyes.

Grady changed his focus to Reed. "I'd be happy to show you around."

"I'll gladly take you up on that, but not with our tight schedule today. Rain check?"

Grady nodded. "What can I do for you?"

Sierra gave him the evidence bag.

He held it up to the light. "C'mon. This is an easy one. You should make me work for my living."

Reed gaped at Grady. "Seriously, you know the knife?"

He nodded and crossed the room to a floor-to-ceiling cabinet with small drawers. He ran a finger down the labels and pulled a drawer out to set it on a table. It was filled with knives, and he lifted one out. "Here it is. A Medford TFF-1 Fat Daddy Tactical Fighting Folder."

The blade was folded into the handle, and he snapped it out then put on gloves and set the recovered tip on top of it to compare.

"You're right." Reed shook his head. "How did you do that? Just like that."

"I told you he was good," Sierra said. "He does magic."

Grady turned the knife to the side. "Nothing magic about it. I'm familiar with a lot of knives. The blade size and thickness gave this one away. This might be a folder but it's meant to take the place of a fixed blade. It's constructed specifically to be used by military and law enforcement personnel."

Reed's obvious fascination grew. "So our Ranger might carry one?"

"Yeah. Sure," Grady said with enthusiasm. "A real good possibility."

"Any way we could trace a purchase back to him?"

Grady shook his head. "Too common of a knife and too many Internet suppliers selling it. I can, however, match this tip to the murder weapon when you recover it."

"I'll check ViCAP to see if this particular knife was used in any unsolved case," Reed said.

The Violent Criminal Apprehension Program, a database that contained crime scene descriptions along with victim and offender data for homicides, missing persons, unidentified dead, and sexual assault investigations was managed by the FBI, but all law enforcement agencies had access to the data.

Grady snapped the knife blade closed. "Want me to keep the tip in a locker here so I can compare it to any recovered weapon?"

"Please." She gave him the evidence log, and he recorded his name.

"Thanks, Grady." Sierra led the way out of the lab and into the cool air. The sun was buried behind thick clouds, hinting at rain.

"We'll take the van so I have my tools if needed." She crossed the lot, got the van open, and climbed behind the wheel. Reed took the passenger seat. She was used to Chad riding with her, and he was much smaller than Reed who seemed to take up all the space.

She couldn't keep thinking about him when she needed to be focusing on her work. She snapped on the radio as a distraction from the tension.

Reed eyed her as if he knew why she'd turned it on.

"We might hear more about the investigation," she said.

They listened to the news updates for the drive, but there was no mention of the investigation. They'd gotten a bunch of calls, but none had panned out, and she hoped the lack of news reports didn't mean that the Ranger was already yesterday's news.

At Caulfield's place, she parked in the driveway and pocketed her keys. She thought she might feel unsettled coming back here, but the house looked far less threatening than it had in the dark of night.

"Need me to carry anything?" Reed asked.

She shook her head and got out to grab a portable kit from the back along with her protective suit, booties, and gloves. She slid into the suit while Reed broke the door seal and unlocked the front door. They put on the booties and gloves then stepped inside. The horrid aroma from the hot tub permeated the house. Sierra gagged and swallowed hard. She wished she could open windows, but that violated protocol. As long as the house was an official crime scene, the windows would remain tightly closed to prevent something from blowing in and contaminating the scene.

"I hate to do this, but..." Reed pulled the door closed behind them. "With this place locked up tight, it'll take some time for the aroma to dissipate."

Sierra nodded and thought about the implications. "Sadly his daughter will have to deal with this odor as well as her father's death. Not to mention learning about the woman in the tub."

"Now that Kelsey is certain a woman died there, I'll have to talk to the daughter and her brother again. They're both going to be shocked."

Sierra tried to put herself in their shoes, but thank God she'd never had to go through something like that. "I can't even imagine being in their position."

He frowned. "I can. Sort of, anyway."

She looked at him and waited for him to explain.

"The day the police came to tell us about my parents. It's a shock I'll never get over. It's lessened over time, but it's always there. Just thinking about it can instantly bring back the nausea and weakness I felt when the officer delivered the news. So I get how they will feel."

"I'm so sorry you had to go through that, Reed." She squeezed his arm.

"Thanks." He curled his hands into tight fists. "And even if I hadn't lost my parents, I still see a lot of suffering on the job that can help me empathize with Caulfield's kids."

"Yeah, I get the last part." She thought he was going to take her hand so she stepped back. "Let me get started."

He frowned, but she didn't know if it was because of her move or because he was still thinking about his parents. She felt so bad complaining about learning about Eddie when she had wonderful parents in her life and Reed had no one.

Father, please give him comfort. And give him the family he seems desperate to have.

"We should get to it," he said.

"Right." She opened her kit, got into the zone, and forgot all about Reed being in the house with her. The afternoon passed, and she didn't find any leads inside. But she did learn more about Caulfield in the sweep. He was a beer drinker and ate yogurt and salads. He smoked cigars in his office. He collected sports memorabilia, which she thought the killer would have taken if it was a home invasion. And he didn't have a picture of his family in the house. Not a single one.

That was the weirdest thing. No pictures on the walls or the tables or shelves of his son or daughter or his deceased wife. And no albums tucked into any of the cabinets or added to bookshelves that were filled with suspense novels.

Maybe the girlfriend didn't like having his family pictures around. She'd clearly staked her claim to his bathroom drawers, closet, and dresser drawers. The female items could be his former wife's things, but the fashion was more current and expiration dates on the toiletries were recent. She wondered if the girlfriend spent the night or just stayed long hours.

Reed came up to her in the bedroom. "Find anything?"

"Nothing. At least not forensically." She explained her discoveries.

"If the girlfriend was spending so much time here, maybe she separated from her husband. If so, I'm not sure why she was still wearing a wedding ring."

"Or if the Ranger is her husband, and he's still active duty, he could be deployed long enough that she felt free to basically live here." She frowned. "But since the closest army base where Rangers are stationed is Joint Base Lewis-McChord in Seattle, it's probably not likely that he's a current soldier, right?"

"You did your homework."

She nodded.

"Yeah. It's not likely, but you never know. He might be stationed in Seattle but lives in Portland."

She glanced outside and was surprised to see it was late enough that the sun had started dropping toward the horizon. "I'm going to take a look at the yard again before it gets too dark."

Reed's phone rang, and she waved at him to tell him to stay behind and answer. She went out through the main patio door and around to the bedroom deck. The hot tub was empty, except for red sludge coating the walls. She had no idea how the contents had been disposed of, but Sierra did know it had to be considered hazardous waste.

She set down her kit and got out a magnifying glass and flashlight.. Concentrating on the deck surrounding the tub, she circled it and bent down to get a better look at a splintered section.

The boom of a rifle shattered the silence.

She hurled her body to the ground behind the tub, her heart galloping.

A bullet whizzed over her head, the air pressure changing.

Gunshot. The word slammed through her brain.

A bullet grazed the tub, the plastic splintering and biting into her face. She curled into a tight ball and tried to make herself as small as possible.

Someone was shooting—at her.

Her.

22

Gunshot—rifle! Out back.

Reed bolted for the door, adrenaline coursing through his body. He jerked the door along the sliding track so hard it hit the wall and bounced back.

"Sierra!" his voice was shrill with panic. She didn't respond.

Not a word.

The crack of the rifle rushed through his head again and fear gripped him. He had to get to her. He started outside. Stopped. He couldn't go racing into a barrage of bullets. He was no good to Sierra dead. He had to control his emotions. Think rationally.

He scanned the yard.

"Where are you, Sierra? Where?"

Another rifle report rent the air. She must still be alive or the shooter would have stopped firing.

Reed needed another view of the yard. He raced to the bedroom slider. He immediately saw Sierra crouched behind the hot tub, her eyes wide with fear, but alive. Blessedly alive.

Thank you, God!

Reed jerked his gaze up to the steep hill behind the house—the only place the shooter could be firing from. Reed spotted him, dressed in camouflage and on the move heading east. Fifteen or so feet more, and it would give him a clear shot at Sierra.

Reed drew his sidearm and jetted out of the house. As he charged ahead, he fired at the gunman. He dove into the scrub.

Reed paused behind a tree to catch his breath and waited for return fire.

Nothing.

Reed bolted out and pelted the scrub with bullets as he charged down the walkway and dove for cover behind the hot tub. Splinters bit into his face, but he didn't care. He swept Sierra up in his arms, moved to the other side, and covered her with his body.

She struggled to get up. "Reed. No. He'll shoot you."

"Don't move. Shooter's on the move and doesn't have a shot right now." At least Reed prayed he didn't have a shot. He holstered his weapon and got out his phone to dial 911. "This is FBI Special Agent Reed Rice. We're taking fire." He gave the address. "Shooter on the hill behind the house with a rifle."

"Are you in a safe place?" the dispatcher asked.

"We're protected by a hot tub, but the shooter can move around to change his angle. Get help here now!"

Reed disconnected and drew his gun but remained pressing Sierra's shaking body to the deck beneath him. He hadn't counted the number of bullets he fired, but he knew he hadn't emptied his magazine. Problem was, he might only have a few bullets left, and he didn't have a backup magazine. Hopefully, if the shooter advanced on them, Reed had enough ammo left to protect Sierra.

He tucked her body closer and waited for a bullet to

come. To pierce his back. He'd made peace with this possibility the day that he swore to protect innocent life at all costs, and he'd come close twice, but God had always brought him safely through.

Father, please. Please don't let Sierra be hurt, and please spare my life too. I don't want Malone to lose someone else.

Sirens sounded in the distance.

"They're coming," Sierra's muffled voice came from beneath him. "Thank you, God. Oh, thank you."

Reed knew it was too soon to be celebrating. One pull of a trigger, and he could die. So could she, as a slug from a high-powered rifle could pass through him.

"Why is this even happening?" she cried out. "Why is someone shooting at me?"

Reed hadn't given that any thought, and he wouldn't until the deputies rolled up and cleared the area.

She started crying.

"*Shh*, honey. It's okay." He gave her a bear hug with his free arm. "I'm here, and we'll be fine."

"But you told 911 that he could get to us."

"It's possible, but I'll bet the sirens spooked him and he took off." Reed could only hope that was true.

"You really think so?" she asked between tears.

"Sure," he said, but kept a tight hold on her. Not only to protect her, but hopefully to offer comfort. He only hoped she found his arm around her comforting. He honestly didn't know.

He heard fast-moving footsteps in the house, and he glanced at the patio door where a deputy paused. "Agent Rice? Deputy Schooner here."

"We're on the other side of the hot tub. Shooter's on the hill. May have taken off when he heard your sirens."

"Stay put. I'll skirt the property to get up there and take a look."

"Copy that," Reed responded and squeezed Sierra. "See, honey. We'll be fine."

Reed heard the tall grasses rustle nearby. He assumed it was Schooner, but Reed still moved to fix his handgun on the area and make sure his body remained covering Sierra. More sirens came their way and soon deputies spilled out of the house and were swarming the hillside.

"You're clear, Agent Rice," Schooner yelled from the hill.

Reed pushed off Sierra, holstered his weapon, and helped her sit up. She had yard debris in her hair, and he scooted closer to gently extract it.

"Thank you for saving my life." She gave him a tremulous smile. "And for grooming me."

He liked that she could find humor in the situation. "Any time."

She clutched his arm. "I know I made light of it, but you shouldn't sound so nonchalant about it. You would have taken a bullet for me. I'm so..." She shook her head. "So in awe of your bravery."

He didn't want credit for doing the only thing he could do in the situation. "It's my job."

She frowned. "So that's it? You did your job to protect me?"

"No, it's so much more than that, but I figured you wouldn't want to hear about anything else."

"I don't care about anything right now except that I'm alive and you're alive." She scooted close to him, slid her hands into his hair, and pulled his head down for a kiss. An all-encompassing one that made his toes curl.

He swept his arms around her and pulled her against him. Deepened the kiss, letting every emotion about being alive fill his kiss. She matched him measure for measure, and kissing her was everything he thought it would be.

More than he thought. He never felt so alive. So enthralled. Captivated.

"Um, Agent?" Schooner's voice was far too close.

Reed gently pulled back and worked hard to get his breathing under control.

Sierra blinked a few times but then her gaze drifted over Reed's shoulder and her face turned a crimson red. "Oh...I... I'm sorry, Deputy. You didn't need to see that PDA."

He smiled, but it was tight. "Does that mean the two of you didn't sustain any injuries?"

Reed looked at Sierra and saw blood on her face. "Your face is bleeding."

She touched it. "A bullet grazed the tub and plastic splinters flew."

"I'll get medics out here," Schooner offered.

Sierra shook her head. "I'm fine, and we need to get up on that hill to collect evidence before dark."

"We?" Schooner asked.

"I'm Sierra Byrd, trace evidence expert at the Veritas Center. Your sheriff hired me to process the murder scene here Sunday night. I'm sure he'll want me to handle this, too."

"Let me give my sarge a call to confirm that." Schooner stepped away.

Reed searched Sierra's face again, still seeing hints of terror in her eyes, and a sharp bolt of anger cut through him over what had just happened to her. He wanted to cocoon her in his arms, take her far from here, and never let trouble come near her again.

But he'd have to settle for just letting her recover, then getting her away from this scene. "Maybe you should leave the forensics to someone else. Climbing a hill and scouting around after being shot at might be too much."

"Are you kidding?" She pulled back her shoulders.

"That's precisely why I'm going to do it. No one is going to shoot at me and get away with it."

~

Sierra told Reed she was fine, but her insides and knees were quivering as she carried her kit up the hill beside him —quivering from fear and also from her reckless behavior back there.

What was she thinking by kissing Reed? She wouldn't have to imagine it anymore, she'd experienced it and would never forget the way she felt. Never forget his insistent yet gentle touch. Never forget his strong arms around her or the beat of his heart in his solid chest.

"I first spotted him just ahead," Reed said, shouldering the assault rifle he borrowed.

He grabbed onto a small tree trunk and hoisted his body above the retaining wall. He said there was no way he'd take her up on the hill without a firearm in hand. He couldn't use his duty weapon after firing at the suspect. When a law enforcement officer discharged a weapon—either accidentally, intentionally, missing or hitting or killing a suspect— their agency confiscated the gun and conducted a full investigation. Firing his gun again would confuse the evidence, so he borrowed the rifle from Deputy Schooner.

Reed held out his hand and gave her a tight smile. She let out a long breath of unease over scouting out this area in the approaching dark and took his hand. He held it for longer than necessary, looking into her eyes, a question in his.

"Yes, we *have* to do this tonight," she said.

"You can read my mind now, huh?" He chuckled.

"It's what you were thinking, right?"

"Yes."

"We can't risk losing any evidence and that means processing the scene now."

"Yeah, I get that," he said. "I just don't like exposing you to danger like this."

"The shooter's gone. We both know that."

"Gone, yes, but how far?" Frowning, he turned on his flashlight and picked his way through the wild greenery in slippery dress shoes, keeping his balance. He held back branches for her and even helped her scale a few large boulders, holding her hand tightly and confidently.

He glanced back at her. "If we run across any of the bullets I fired, I'd appreciate it if we could mark them for our team to retrieve."

"Of course," she said as she knew it would make his agency's investigation go faster and he would be out of commission for a shorter time.

"There." He pointed ahead with his flashlight. "The grass is flattened. Has to be the stand the shooter took while waiting for you."

She slipped ahead of him and knelt down by the circular area in the grass to search with her magnifying glass. "Looks like he policed his brass."

"Not that a special forces guy would collect casings on a mission, but if our shooter is the Ranger you ran into yesterday, makes sense that he's smart enough to do it."

She looked over her shoulder at Reed. "Sounds like you really think it's him."

"I figure he'd be the only one shooting at you. If he's watched TV or listened to a radio, he knows you can identify him."

"But how does he know my identity? That wasn't in the news stories."

"No, but you were the only person who interacted with him."

Her heart fell. "And I told him I was on the forensic staff and our van was sitting right there. He could've connected the two and staked this place out, hoping I would show up again."

Reed frowned. "Or worse, he staked out the Veritas Center and followed us. I hate to think that happened, but I had no reason to watch for a tail."

A sudden chill enveloped her, and she shivered.

"Either way, we've got to find him."

"Seems to me the only way we're going to do that is to figure out the woman's ID. Assuming, of course, that he's her husband."

Reed surveyed the area then dropped to the ground in a prone shooting stance, placing the rifle at an angle facing the hot tub. He sighted it in. "I put the distance to the hot tub around a hundred yards. Direct and easy shot. One any sharp shooter could make in his sleep. So the Ranger shouldn't have missed."

She shuddered at the thought. "Then why did he?"

"Maybe he was just trying to scare you." Reed didn't sound like he believed his own statement.

And she didn't believe it either. Not with all the information Grady had shared over the years about sharp shooters. "If he *is* a sniper, he would follow the 'one shot, one kill' motto, right?"

Reed took in a sharp breath and nodded.

She thought back to the first shot. To that icy panic that burst through her body. Two, maybe three, more shots followed, a hot bolt of fear cutting through her. She swallowed to let the feelings pass before she hyperventilated. She had to analyze this without any emotions at all.

The gun had fired, and she bent down. "On his initial shot, I think I bent over to take a better look at the deck just before he fired. And then the hot tub protected me until you did."

"Which tells me he wasn't using a .50 caliber round."

She nodded as she knew a .50 would go through cement blocks from a mile or more away, and at this distance, the hot tub wouldn't even have slowed it down.

"Looks like a thirty-degree trajectory." She had calculated bullet trajectory at crime scenes so many times that she felt confident in her estimate even without the tools to confirm it.

And surprisingly, Reed didn't question her assessment as he came to his feet and stared down on the house in the waning light. She was suddenly aware of his wide shoulders and his powerful build. And of his mood. Tense restraint. To put it simply, he was worried about her. Her heart soared at the thought but then tightened. If he was this worried, what would he do? Treat her like a helpless female like her brothers did, or would he respect her need to do her job?

Only time would tell.

He turned to her. "We should look around to see if there's any evidence of how long he'd been here. I doubt he'd be careless enough to leave anything behind, but..."

She knew he meant something like remnants from snacks or drinks consumed while lying in wait. Flashlight aimed at the ground, he made his way around the shooter's nest, and then shook his head. "Nothing." He pointed to the west. "I tracked him this way. Let's follow his exit path."

He waited for her to start off first this time, and she thought it might be because if shooting started again, he could more easily take her down and protect her.

As they set off, she had just a moment to realize how incongruous his dress shoes and expensive suit were in this scrub. She looked at him. "Do you always wear a suit at work?"

"Except when we're on a surveillance or a takedown op." He eyed her. "Looks kind of crazy out here, doesn't it?"

She nodded, and seeing that he knew she'd been studying him, she felt a warm blush rise over her face. She shone her light ahead and focused on the ground to follow the shooter's trail. She went about fifty feet and came to a stop. "Wait, what's that?"

Reed knelt down to stare at it. "It's a Leatherman."

Sierra squatted next to him. "You think the shooter dropped it?"

Reed looked around. "Grass's been flattened in a wider path here. Looks like he took a spill. If it *is* our Ranger, he could've been wearing a duty belt and it fell out of a pouch."

She handed a marker to Reed. "Put this next to it, and I'll take a few pictures."

He set the white tented marker holding the number one next to the multi-purpose tool and moved out of the way. She snapped a few pictures then pulled an evidence bag from her kit and dropped the tool inside.

"If I can lift prints from that, and he *is* military or even former military, his prints will be in their database." Excited about the lead, she came to her feet and smiled. "I never thought I'd say this, but I'm glad the guy shot at me."

Reed frowned. "I'm not glad for that at all, but the evidence he left behind could be a godsend."

She moved on, staying low and shining her light at the ground. "There. Blood."

He stepped closer and squatted. She knelt beside him.

Reed stared at the blood. "I must've hit him. Or he hurt himself in the fall."

"Either way, we have his blood." She placed a second marker and took pictures, then got out a plastic vial and small spoon and scooped the blood into the vial.

Now that they had evidence of Reed likely hitting the

suspect, would Reed be put on leave? And if so, would he have to step away from the investigation? Worse—if that happened, he would have to step away from her.

The thought left her cold inside. She wanted to find Eddie, but she didn't want to do it without Reed at her side. Especially not after this shooting. Feeling out of sorts, she put the vial into her kit.

Reed pointed at it. "You collected plenty of blood for DNA, right?"

"Today's DNA processing requires very little blood and this is more than enough."

He stood. "Let's follow the trail."

She got up and when she bent to grab her kit, he took it from her hands.

Even though she could carry it, she appreciated his kindness, and she wouldn't argue. They followed the blood trail to where it curled down in the neighbor's yard around the side of their house to the sidewalk, and continued down the street for a good quarter mile before abruptly ending.

"He parked here," she said.

Reed nodded and looked around, his gaze stopping on one of the houses. "Looks like that house has a security camera pointed this direction."

He spun and marched up to the door. On the way he brushed off his suit, straightened his tie, and ran a hand through his hair. Sierra had to be a mess from diving away from the bullets and traipsing through scrub, but she didn't bother to try to fix her appearance. Reed would do the talking and she could stay in the background.

He pounded loudly on the door, his shoe tapping on the concrete stoop as he waited. A redheaded teenager opened the rich wood door and eyed Reed.

"Special Agent Reed Rice. FBI." He displayed his credentials.

The kid looked less than impressed. "This about the guy down the street who got whacked the other night?"

Sierra cringed at the teen's language, but Reed simply nodded. "We're in pursuit of a suspect that we think was parked out front of your house. I'd like to take a look at your security camera footage."

"Yeah, sure man. I can pull it up on my phone." He got his cell out of his jeans pocket and started tapping on the screen, then turned it to face Reed. "Hit rewind to back up to what you want to see."

Reed pressed the back arrow and the footage rewound. He suddenly punched play. Sierra stepped up closer to get a better look. The shooter came limping down the street. He wore a duty belt and carried a rifle. He was dressed in camo pants and shirt, and a green stocking cap. One of his legs had a dark stain, likely the blood they trailed.

"Dude, he's like some army dude," the teen said in awe.

Reed held the phone closer to Sierra and looked her in the eye. "But is he *our* army dude?"

She enlarged the picture, and the answer was clear. She just didn't know how she felt about it. Not at all.

23

Before stepping away from the kid's house, Reed checked his email to be sure the teen had actually sent the complete video that showed the shooter arriving early in the morning. He started playing it and fast-forwarded to the end where the shooter returned to his car.

"Thanks for the video." Reed pocketed his phone and gave the teen his card. "If you see this guy around here again, don't approach him, but give me a call."

"Sure, dude, I can do that." He shoved the card into his pocket.

Reed motioned for Sierra to precede him down the sidewalk. "Thank goodness for kids not thinking about sharing their video and knowing how to do it."

Sierra nodded, but she'd gone quiet the minute she ID'd the guy as the man she'd met out front of Caulfield's house. The fact that a special forces guy had shot at her had to be freaking her out. Shoot, it was freaking him out, too. Not in the same way. But he knew how close he'd come to losing her when he was just getting to know her and wanted to start a relationship with her.

He met her gaze. "Want to talk about it?"

She shrugged. "If I hadn't bent down when I did, I would dead right now. Dead."

He didn't care if a pair of deputies were standing out front of Caulfield's house with Detective Miller who'd arrived at some point. Reed took her hand and pulled her closer to him. "You don't have to worry. Now that I know he's gunning for you, I won't let him get to you again. You'll stay at the Veritas Center until we have him in custody."

She pulled her hand free and looked up at him. "I might be terrified, but I'm not running scared and hiding out. I'm going to find Eddie."

Reed stopped and met her gaze. "The shooter's a spec ops guy, for crying out loud. If he wants to take you out, letting you stay at Veritas isn't even safe enough. I should put you in a safe house with a couple of agents for protection."

"I knew this was going to happen."

"What was going to happen?" He was honestly baffled.

"I appreciate your concern, but you're not going to *put* me anywhere." She crossed her arms. "It's my decision on what I do."

"Then decide to follow my instructions because I'm right," he snapped and at the tightening of her eyes, he regretted it. But *come on*. A trained shooter was after her, and she wasn't being reasonable.

"You're just like my brothers." She shook her head and marched down the road.

He was decidedly not like her brothers, but he thought about calling them to ask them to talk some sense into her. He'd *do* it, too, if he didn't think it would make things worse. He trailed her to the house, still on high alert.

"Any luck on the evidence?" Miller asked Sierra.

"He's bleeding. Agent Rice might have hit him when he

returned fire. We trailed him to his car down the road. The house security camera caught him on video."

"It's the suspect we've already put an alert out on," Reed added. "And gave his sketch to the news media. Now we can distribute actual photos."

"I still need to look for slugs in the hot tub area, and then we'll be leaving." Sierra stepped inside, moving at the same brisk pace that said she didn't want to have anything to do with him.

She might be mad at him, but there was no way he would let her go into that yard alone. He caught up to her and joined her at the hot tub.

She glanced at him, her expression tight. "I can do this myself."

"I know." He faced the hill, lifted the rifle, and kept his head on a swivel. He wished he had a night vision scope for this thing, but he didn't, so he had to be extra vigilant.

"You don't think he's up there again, do you?" A worry line formed between her brows.

It hurt to see her concern and he didn't want to scare her more, but her safety came first. "It's dark now, and I won't take any chances with your life."

She sighed. "I'm sorry I snapped at you. I promise when we get back to Veritas I'll consider any suggestion you make."

His gut loosened at her change of mind. "That's all I can ask for."

"What? You're not mad that I'm not falling down and doing exactly what you want?"

"As you pointed out. It's your life. I can only make recommendations." He glanced at her then back at the hill. "But you should know that I have to report discharging my weapon to my supervisor. He could put me on leave while

234

they look into it. Means I might not be there for you in any official capacity anymore."

"Can you still help on the investigation?"

"If he puts me on leave, not officially, no."

"But you could work at the center with us, right? Just not go out and do interviews and such."

"Maybe. We'll see."

"Reed," she said softly.

Her quiet tone made him look at her.

"Don't leave me alone in this, please," she pleaded. "I've gotten used to having you around."

His heart soared, but he didn't know if he could do anything about her request. "I'll do my best."

"That's all I can ask." She sounded disappointed.

But she wasn't the only one. He would be disappointed, too, if he couldn't help her bring this investigation to a close. Especially if he couldn't be there to protect her from this dangerous spec ops shooter. He made up his mind right there with her gaze on him. He would quit his job if he had to. It was just a job and she was... What was she? The woman he'd fallen in love with? His reactions to everything that happened today said that was the truth, but he wasn't sure he could admit it.

Best to move on before he declared feelings he wasn't sure of. "Even though I'd like to get you back to Veritas straight away, we should stop to interview Kuznetsov in case I don't have any standing to interview him later."

"Then let me look for the slugs so we can get out of here." She shone her flashlight in the area round the tub. "How many shots did you hear?"

"Three," he said, remembering his heart stopping with each one.

She grimaced. "One went over my head. One hit the tub. The other one...I don't know."

"But you do know the location of his stand and his trajectory. And the shots were directed at you, so let's look at the privacy wall behind your location."

She shone her light on the wall and so did he. They quickly located two embedded slugs.

"I know you want to get going," she said. "But I won't pull these out with tweezers and risk ruining the lands and grooves."

He didn't want that either. Each gun barrel was individually machined, making it unique and the bullets fired just as unique. In the machining process, spiral grooves were cut inside the barrel to give bullets a spinning motion. Bullet diameters were slightly larger than the bore diameter of the barrel it was fired from. As a result, this barrel made a negative impression of itself on the sides of the bullet, leaving grooves that could be tracked to a specific gun. If Sierra didn't alter the bullet in removing it, they might be able to match it to the shooter's gun once they located him and his weapon.

She placed a ruler next to the slugs and took pictures, then dug a couple of wooden sticks from her kit and gently started maneuvering a slug from the wall. When a quarter of it was out, she used her gloved fingers to gently remove it. She held it up in the light. "Not too deformed for evaluation."

She put it in a bag and moved on to the next one. He took the time to search for the third slug by estimating how far the shooter had headed west before Reed got outside. He stepped off the deck at that spot and only walked a few feet where he found the slug lodged in a wooden planter.

Excellent. Finding the third slug meant he could get Sierra out of this backyard where the highly-trained Ranger had nearly taken her life. Then after a quick visit to Kuznetsov, he'd make sure she was locked up tight under the watchful protection of Sam and Blake and any of her other partners who could prove their expertise with a gun.

~

Sierra rarely got to interview suspects or persons of interest, and looking at Vasily Kuznetsov's sinister stare, she wished she hadn't accompanied Reed to the interview. He stood behind his expensive desk in the most lavish office she'd ever seen. He had intense blue eyes below bushy black eyebrows, and his face was weathered and so wrinkled he reminded her of a Shar Pei. Strands of gray mixed with inkiest of black hair. He wore a black turtleneck and black slacks. But it was the deadly intensity in his eyes that sent a shiver creeping down her spine.

She had no idea what this man had seen or done in his lifetime, but the two armed men as big as refrigerators standing behind him told her it had certainly involved danger.

"Agent Reed Rice." Reed displayed his shield clipped to his belt.

"I know who you are agent." Kuznetsov shifted his focus to Sierra.

She felt his power and the danger and instinctually took a step back.

"And you, Ms. Byrd. How are you?" Kuznetsov sounded like they'd come for a social visit, but she had no idea how he knew her name. He likely knew Reed from an investigation, but Kuznetsov knowing her wasn't at all likely.

"How do you know my name?" she fairly demanded of him.

"I am well acquainted with your father. Eddie Barnes, not the man you call *father*."

She gaped at him. "You know Eddie's my biological father. But how?"

"He spoke of you many times."

"How do you know Barnes?" Reed asked, stepping closer to her.

Kuznetsov scared her, and she was thankful Reed was only a fingertip away.

"He manages a few of my beach rentals." He waved a hand over chairs by his desk. "Please. Sit. Sit. And I'll have drinks brought in."

Sierra dropped into a chair, thankful to sit before her knees gave out. She took a deep breath of the air laced with a lingering smell of garlic as if he'd just finished a meal. Reed moved a chair right next to her and sat. She wanted to reach out to him. To let him know this man was terrifying her, but she didn't want to appear weak.

"Nothing to drink for me," Reed said.

"Me neither," she said.

"Suit yourselves." Kuznetsov lowered his body into a high-backed leather chair.

"When was the last time you saw Eddie Barnes?" Reed asked.

"Hmm. It's been some time." He turned to look at one of the refrigerator men. "When did we last go to Seaview Cove?"

"Fourth of July," Refrigerator One said, his voice as deep as the ocean and his stature as threatening as a storm.

"And you saw Eddie at the fireworks," Refrigerator Two added.

Kuznetsov didn't look happy with the added bit of information from the second man, and she knew he was going to pay for speaking without being asked. She could easily see Kuznetsov pummeling this man with his fists or even killing him for a simple step out of line.

A sneering smile slid across his face. "We did indeed see him there."

"Did you visit his office?"

"No."

"When was the last time you *did* go to his office?"

"Years ago, when he took over his father's business. Otherwise he came to me."

Could Eddie have visited this creep when he came to take those pictures of her? "And have you spoken to him since then?"

"No, my dear, I have not. Is Eddie in some kind of trouble?"

"He's missing," Reed said matter-of-factly, but she saw his fingers curl where his hand rested on his leg. "Has been for a month."

"I am sorry to hear this."

"Are you?" Reed asked.

"But of course. He is my friend."

"Then why did you move his money to an offshore account?" Reed's tone and voice turned deadly cold.

Kuznetsov's friendly façade evaporated, icy blue eyes impaling them as he leaned forward. "I have no idea what you are talking about."

Reed didn't flinch. Didn't move. "We have it on good authority that you were involved in an Internet transaction that involved moving Barnes's funds."

"That's ludicrous." Kuznetsov sat back and held out his hands. "Look at this place. Does it look like I need other people's money?"

"Some people aren't content no matter the amount of money they've amassed," Sierra said.

He speared her with a look. "I am not one of those people."

She forced herself not to squirm under his burning

239

intensity. "Do you have any idea where Eddie might have gone?" she asked, changing tactics.

"I'm afraid not. We are friends, but just business ones. You know, superficial."

"And do you have the same relationship to Ira Caulfield?" Reed asked.

A muscle in Kuznetsov's face tightened, but he released it so fast that Sierra wondered if she'd actually seen it.

"He is my accountant."

"Was?"

"I beg your pardon?"

"Oh come, Kuznetsov. Don't pretend you don't know he was murdered Sunday night."

"I did not know this." His tone seemed sincere, but Sierra figured he was a practiced liar.

"We also located a body in Caulfield's hot tub," Reed said. "Know anything about that?"

If he was surprised, he didn't show it. He didn't even blink. "Of course not. I'm not in the business of murder, Agent Rice, no matter what you think."

"Thank you for your time." Reed abruptly stood and gestured for Sierra to exit before him.

In the hallway she looked at him. "Why the sudden departure?"

"He's had years of practice lying. We're not going to get him to tell the truth without some leverage." He met her gaze. "Time to get you safely behind Veritas's secure walls and hope since I mentioned the money transfer that this guy retrieves the router at his warehouse."

They went to the door, and as she was about to step outside, Reed stopped her. "Let me take a quick look, okay?"

She nodded, thankful that he asked but still raising her worry again. He disappeared into the dark and soon came back. "We're clear. Mind if I drive?"

She handed him the keys, and he pulled her tight against his body while rushing toward the van. She didn't argue as he'd done the same thing when they arrived. He was certain they weren't tailed, but he said he would rather be safe than sorry.

He got the vehicle on the road and kept checking his mirrors. He made a few left turns that weren't necessary, and she knew he was checking for a tail.

When they neared Veritas, he looked at her. "I assume you have a secured parking deck."

"Around back. Access is by fingerprints."

He pulled behind the building, and at the gate, he stopped. She leaned over him. He put his hands around her waist and held her there as she pressed her fingers on the reader. She couldn't even count how many times she'd touched him this afternoon, but each time they made physical contact, she wanted more of it.

Including now. It would be so easy to kiss him again as she settled back into her seat, but she had more control now, and she wouldn't. Kissing him once was bad enough. She didn't want to lead him on and make him think she'd changed her mind about a relationship. She'd simply been vulnerable after the shooting. That was all.

24

Reed didn't want to call his supervisor. Once he did, he would have to leave Sierra. But he should have reported the shooting while still at Caulfield's house, and he needed to report in before Adair heard about it from someone else.

Reed dialed and moved as far away from Sierra as possible so he didn't distract her while she worked on printing the Leatherman. He looked down at the Veritas Center badge swinging from his dirty lapel. Even after all that Sierra had been through, she followed protocol and insisted he check in at the front desk when they arrived. Her strict adherence to procedure, doing the right thing no matter what, made him even more sure that he had to call Adair.

"Adair," his supervisor answered.

"It's Rice. I discharged my firearm today and need to report it." Reed gave him the details.

Adair muttered something under his breath. "And you're just now calling?"

"I had to be sure that Ms. Byrd made it to a safe location."

"No," he snapped. "Her safety was up to the locals."

Reed figured he'd say that. "You're probably right, but it's already done."

"That it is." Adair hissed out a wheezy breath.

Reed ignored his supervisor's displeasure and continued, "Ms. Byrd retrieved evidence from the suspect, but we left my slugs alone. I know you'll want ERT to recover them."

Adair didn't respond for the longest time, and Reed wished he was looking at the guy to get a read on his thoughts.

"I'm still in the office," he finally said. "You better be on your way here in less than five."

"Actually," Reed said. "Could you give me a little more time? We recovered the shooter's Leatherman, and Ms. Byrd is looking for fingerprints right now. If she finds any, I'd like to bring the card in for someone to search military databases for a match."

"I'll give you thirty minutes. But that's it. Don't take advantage of my generosity."

"I won't, sir." Reed ended the call and crossed the lab to Sierra, but as he neared her, the door burst open and her partners flooded into the space.

Maya eyed Sierra. "You weren't going to tell us you were back and that you had a near brush with death?"

Sierra looked like she wanted to sigh, but didn't. "How did you know?"

Blake crossed his arms. "Trent heard it through the grapevine and called me."

"You *were* planning to tell us, right?" Grady asked.

"Yeah, sure," she said. "After I developed prints on the Leatherman we think the shooter dropped."

"And if she didn't tell you, I would have," Reed said, trying to get them to back off a little. "I fired at and may have hit the shooter. Means I need to turn in my weapon while my agency investigates."

Blake nodded as if he was glad Reed was following protocol, but now Reed was having second thoughts about leaving her behind. He glanced at her and wished she would look at him, but she'd been avoiding his gaze. Likely because of the kiss. Or because of his hot-headed statement about locking her up in a safe house.

Blake firmed his stance. "We'll keep an eye on her. Make sure nothing happens to her."

Leave it to a former law enforcement officer like Blake to figure out what was bothering Reed.

Emory looked at Reed. "Does this mean you can't come back and work with us any longer?"

Reed didn't even want to think about that, but he had to. "It'll be up to my supervisor. But even if he takes me off the investigation, I can work with you all in an unofficial capacity."

Blake frowned. "If you value your career, you won't come back here before you're cleared."

Sierra finally looked at him. "Please don't risk your job for me."

"A job is a job," he said and hoped she understood he was trying to tell her she was more important than that. "God will provide another one if needed."

She shook her head. "I won't let you throw away your career. I'm fine. Everyone here has my back."

"Yeah, but how many own a gun and are experienced shooters?" he asked and was surprised that all of them but Sierra raised their hands.

"I'm the odd one out," she said.

"And Grady takes us all to the range and makes sure we understand gun safety," Maya added.

"Well, tonight, I'm glad you all have weapons training and experience."

"Since we're all together," Blake said, focusing on Reed, "I should mention that I heard back from the forensic accountant. The account numbers in Eddie's ledger and dollar amounts all match companies who provided services for the rental properties. Could be for the bogus companies you mentioned."

"Forward the information to me so I can have my analysts compare them to the accounts they flagged."

Sierra frowned. "So that means Eddie knew about these accounts."

"Seems like it," Blake said. "Also, there hasn't been any women reported missing in the area in the last month."

Sierra ran a hand over her face. "Are we ever going to figure this out?"

Reed didn't want her to dwell on these discoveries, so he pointed at the Leatherman. "Did you find any prints on the Leatherman?"

"I didn't finish yet. Gonna take a bit longer."

Reed nodded. "Wish I could hang around to see what you find, but I have to go."

Nick stepped forward. "Before you go, I should mention I was able to go deeper into Caulfield's computer and found a few heated emails between him and Kuznetsov."

"What about?" Reed asked.

"Caulfield said he was leaving the country. Kuznetsov told him he didn't want to find another accountant, and he didn't want Caulfield to leave. Caulfield said he could keep doing the books from long distance. Kuznetsov didn't like that idea. He said, and I quote, 'I prefer to have my employees where I can keep an eye on them.'"

"What did Caulfield say to that?" Sierra asked.

"He refused to change his mind, and said as soon as his

girlfriend sorted out a few things with her husband—yeah, she was married like we suspected—Caulfield would be leaving with her."

"Do you think Kuznetsov killed the girlfriend to keep Caulfield here?" Sierra asked.

Reed recalled their meeting with the thug and his goons. "After talking to him, I wouldn't put it past him. And if he didn't personally do it, he could've had one of his bodyguards take care of her."

Sierra shuddered. "They certainly seemed capable of it."

Reed looked at Nick. "Did you find anything else that gives us a lead on her ID?"

Nick shook his head. "Caulfield was super careful about that, which in itself should tell us something."

"Like what?" Sierra asked.

"Like the husband must have been a seriously jealous guy if Caulfield resorted to burner phones and wouldn't have any written communication with her."

"It's looking more and more like this husband killed Caulfield," Maya said. "Especially with the military style execution and stab wounds."

"Not to mention him shooting at Sierra," Grady said.

Reed nodded his agreement and wished he could stay to talk about this, but Adair was waiting.

"I need to go." He made eye contact with Blake, compelling the guy with his gaze to keep his promise and watch out for Sierra.

Blake gave a crisp nod.

"I'll see you out." Sierra went to the door.

Reed followed her. At the elevator, he took her hand, stopping her from pressing her fingers against the print reader. "Promise me you won't leave this building without me."

Her gorgeous honey-brown eyes narrowed. "I'm not sure

I can promise that. An urgent lead could come in that I need to follow up on."

He didn't like her answer. Not one bit. "Nothing is urgent enough to potentially risk your life over."

"You do it every day. Risk your life, I mean."

"But I'm trained on how to minimize that risk. You aren't."

She tipped her head, seeming to buy into his explanation, but he still didn't get that promise he needed.

"Look," he said. "I shouldn't be at the office for long. I just have to fill out a form or two and turn in my gun. Then I can come right back here to make sure you're safe."

"I appreciate that, but..."

"But nothing." He cupped the side of her face. "You know I care about you, and I protect those I care about. So please—*please* say you'll stay here for the few hours it takes for me to do this."

"Okay, fine. But only if you stay available by phone so if something breaks, I can get ahold of you."

"I can do that." He smiled and received a warm smile in response. He wanted to kiss her, but he wouldn't in the hallway where one of her partners might see. So he dropped his hand and gestured at the fingerprint reader.

They boarded the elevator and with the future uncertain, he knew he had to kiss her before he left. He crossed the car in three steps, looked deeply into her eyes then pulled her close. He plunged his hands into her hair and tilted her head back. She gave a small gasp before he lowered his head and kissed her. Hungry, needy, he let his kiss transmit every emotion he couldn't put into words. She returned it. Matching him again.

When the door dinged and opened, he gently stroked a thumb over her jaw while he got his breathing under control before he had to face their security guard.

247

She blinked up at him, her breathing uneven. "What was that for?"

"I want you to remember that while I'm gone. Remember what we could have together if only you'd be willing to risk it." He caressed the side of her face with a gentle touch. "I know it's all I'll be thinking about."

～

Sierra stood outside, the night cool, the sky overcast as Reed walked to his car. Each step he took felt like a literal punch to her gut. She didn't know when she would see him again, and the thought troubled her more than she would have thought.

At his vehicle, he turned to look at her. "Go back inside, honey."

She was suddenly catapulted back in time to the shooting. He'd called her "honey" then, too, and she hadn't really thought about it. But now, here, while she was thinking straight again, she could hardly breathe for thinking of the implications. Honey implied something. Definitely something more than coworkers and more than just two people who were attracted to each other. It implied a future. A relationship.

"Sierra," he said firmly. "Go inside or I'm not leaving."

"Sorry." She gave an innocent wave of her hand when her brain was still wrapped up in his intentional use of the endearment.

She backed to the door and pressed her fingers on the print reader to hurry inside.

Pete stood by the door watching her. "Heard about the shooting. You okay?"

She nodded.

"You don't look okay. You look shell-shocked."

Yeah, but not from the shooting. From the implications of this amazing man falling for her. Or more likely, from the fact that she found herself wanting the man to fall for her. Something she'd never felt before. Never. And oddly, it didn't panic her in the way she thought it might. Just scared her a tiny bit.

"It will get better with time," Pete said.

She forgot about Reed for a moment to smile at Pete. "Thanks."

"And if you want to talk about it, I've been through the same thing—and more—and would be glad to help."

She squeezed his arm. "You're the best, Pete, and maybe I'll take you up on it."

He gave a firm nod and walked her to the inner door that he unlocked and held open for her. He considered the partners his children and wanted to protect them. She didn't want him to worry so she pulled her shoulders back.

She stepped into the elevator, and the memory of Reed's intense kiss came rushing back. She touched her lips and remembered how his touch felt. Thought about him just like he told her he would be doing with her. Yeah, she wanted to see where this thing with them might go, but was she ready?

Can you help me with that, God?

She gave it more thought as she exited the elevator and headed toward her lab. She knew God could help, but it would still take action on her part to trust in God and let go of her fear of commitment and step out in faith.

She pushed open her lab door, not at all surprised to find her partners waiting for her. They wouldn't have left until they were sure she was okay, and they had all worked together to form a game plan to investigate the shooting.

"We need to call hospitals," Maya was saying. "If this guy

was injured enough to leave a blood trail, he likely needs medical attention."

Grady shook his head. "If he's a former Ranger and the wound hasn't damaged muscle or bone, he'll most likely handle it himself."

"Either way, I figure he won't go to a hospital for fear of being arrested," Blake said. "But we should still make those calls."

Sierra tipped her head at the fingerprint station. "I need to finish processing the Leatherman and the slugs before I do any calling."

"You do your thing," Blake said. "I'll distribute a list of hospitals, and we can each take a facility or two. That way if he *has* gone in for care, we'll get a jump on finding him. And if he hasn't, we can alert the ER staff to be on the lookout for him."

Sierra was coming to appreciate Blake's investigative thinking more and more with each passing day.

Grady clamped a hand on the back of his neck. "This guy leave any brass behind?"

Sierra shook her head. "Just blood, the Leatherman, and slugs."

He nodded his understanding. "Get those slugs to me the minute you're finished. I know we don't have a gun for comparison, but there might be something about them that gives us a lead."

"Will do."

"And I want to look at the video," Nick said. "Maybe I can enhance it and see something that could help ID this guy."

If she'd been thinking clearly, she would have asked Reed for a copy, but first the shooting and then the kissing left her brain foggy. "I'll text Reed and ask him to send it to you."

Nick gave a firm and very serious nod for the usually easygoing guy. "If I don't have it within the hour, I'll be nagging you for it."

"Understood," she said and got her phone out so the minute they left she would remember to text Reed.

Emory held out her hand. "I'll take the blood sample with me."

Sierra went to her kit sitting on the first table where she'd dropped it when she and Reed had arrived. She pulled out the vial, the sight of the blood raising her anxiety and she had to swallow hard to be able to hand the vial to Emory without tears in her eyes.

"Okay, people." Blake clapped his hands. "Let's move. I'll email the list within the next five minutes."

"Thank you," Sierra smiled at the men and women who'd become a second family to her.

Kelsey ran her gaze over Sierra, looking for what Sierra didn't know.

"You want someone to stay with you for moral support?" Kelsey asked.

Tears threatened again, but Sierra shook her head. "I have work to do, and that'll keep me occupied." At least she hoped the work was enough to keep her mind off both the shooting and her unexpected feelings for Reed.

The team trooped out the door, and Sierra suddenly felt very alone and instead of liking being on her own as she usually did, the solitude disturbed her. She fired off a quick text to Reed, but didn't expect to hear back from him as he would still be driving.

She crossed the room, noticing the space that was usually comforting felt big and even more empty without Reed. She already missed him, and he'd only been gone for a few minutes.

How would she feel when the investigation ended if they didn't pursue a relationship and she never saw him again?

~

Reed's CarPlay app announced a text from Sierra, and his heart nearly stopped beating before he played the message asking him to send the video to Nick.

Reed took a long breath and let it out, thankful for the rest of the drive to calm down. If he showed up a wreck in front of Adair, the guy would think Reed's stress was from the shooting when the only stress that Reed felt was from not stopping the Ranger in his tracks.

He pulled up to the secured parking structure, and while he waited for the security barrier to lower, he sent the video to Nick and replied to Sierra telling her he did.

Thank you, came her reply.

He imagined her saying it to him person. Maybe while she was still remembering that kiss. The one that told him in no uncertain terms that he'd fallen in love with her, and that she had feelings for him if only she would admit it and be willing to pursue them. He could only hope that she took his comment to heart and was thinking about a potential future together.

The barrier lowered to ground level. He parked in the structure and rushed into the building as he was already late for Adair's deadline. The Portland office was the second FBI location he'd been assigned to, and in addition to Portland being his hometown, he appreciated the newness of the building. The office used to be located in downtown Portland, but after 9/11, the building was deemed no longer secure enough, so this building had been constructed. Now about six years old, it felt nearly new and had state-of-the-art security.

He went straight to Adair's office. His boss turned from looking out of his window that had a clear view of Mount Hood. He wore a white shirt, sleeves rolled up, and gray-and-blue striped tie. His hair was short, inky black and laced with silver, and his body was toned from hours at the gym. He looked up, his green eyes piercing Reed who froze on the spot.

"About time," he said. "I was about to track you down."

Reed didn't explain his delay. He simply stepped forward and laid his handgun on Adair's desk.

"Sit," Adair commanded.

Reed perched on a chair and waited.

Adair opened his laptop and looked over it at Reed. "Let's get the paperwork started."

Reed nearly groaned. This report could take hours, and he mistakenly hoped Adair would just order Reed to complete it, not sit here and fill it out together.

Reed shoved his hand into his pocket and rested it on his phone. He'd set it to vibrate and didn't want to risk missing a text or call from Sierra. She was his top priority, and if she needed him, he would gladly bolt from this office.

25

Sierra swirled a brush over the back side of the Leatherman. A beautiful latent print developed before her eyes. She grabbed her camera to take a close-up picture and lifted the print to a card. She wanted to share her excitement with Reed and would text him, but he couldn't do anything about it right now, and she didn't want to distract him from his meeting.

She dialed Blake instead. "I found a print on the Leatherman. Do you have anyone who could run an army print this late at night?"

"I do," he said eagerly. "Be right up to get it."

"I'll have a digital file ready for you." She disconnected and at her desk, she transferred the pictures from her camera to her computer and put them on a flash drive.

The door lock clicked, and Blake barreled into the room with his phone to his ear.

She held out the flash drive. "How long do you think this will take?"

He repeated the question into the phone and listened. "He says five minutes or less once he receives the file."

She didn't want to waste even a second. "I can send it from here to save time."

Blake nodded and grabbed a pen from her desk to jot down his buddy's email address. She entered it into her email program, doublechecking to be sure she had it correct. She'd hate for it to get lost in cyberspace and lose valuable time.

Blake told his friend to expect the file from her.

She attached the photo files to her email and clicked send. "Done."

"Call me back when you have something," Blake said into the phone. He pocketed the device, but remained standing by her desk, watching her like he might do when interviewing a suspect. She felt the heavy weight of his study.

"It finally feels like we might be getting somewhere," she said to break the tension. "Too bad Reed's not here to see it."

Blake continued to watch her, looking like he was waffling over what to say. She got up and took the slugs to the fuming chamber.

He followed her. "You seem to have gotten close to Reed."

She didn't know Blake all that well. Definitely not well enough for him to bring up a personal topic that she hadn't even processed yet. She settled the slugs in the chamber and kept quiet.

"Same thing happened with me and Emory," he added.

Wow. Now he was sharing about his private life. Totally unexpected and she didn't know how to respond. She put the water into the chamber door and closed the machine. She should probably face him, but she still didn't know what to say.

"I'll take your silence to mean you don't want to talk about it," he said. "So what are you going to work on now?"

Yeah, what *was* she going to work on? They might have the print for Caulfield's killer—maybe a way to ID the woman in the tub—but that might not lead to finding Eddie. So what would?

On solid footing now, she turned to look at Blake. "Do you need me to call hospitals?"

He shook his head.

"Then I'm going to ask Nick for any articles his algorithm located on the brick and start looking at those pictures."

He nodded. "Sounds like a plan. I'll head back down to make more calls. I'll let you know the minute I hear anything about the print."

He strode to the door, but paused hand on handle to look back at her. "You're probably thinking all of this with Reed is too fast. Maybe it is. Only you know. But he's proved time and again that he's a good guy so trust your gut."

He pulled open the door and stepped out, leaving her stunned for a moment. She started to ponder his comments, but what good would that do. Finding Eddie was what she needed to concentrate on.

She texted Nick and was soon sitting at her desk behind her computer with the list he'd emailed. She read through several stories including one that held a picture of an old brick church with profanity spray-painted on the exterior. The story talked about a recent epidemic of graffiti that hit northeast Portland and about how the congregation had donated extra money to have the brick sandblasted.

"Of course," she said, sitting back. "The brick dust mixed with sand. Why didn't I think of sandblasting?"

But it wasn't like Eddie had been held at this church for a month. She moved on to additional articles until she came upon one about an older warehouse covered in similar graffiti. The building was undergoing sandblasting before the owner put it up for sale. He was quoted, and at seeing his name, she fell back into her chair.

This was Ira Caulfield's building. Ira's!

She didn't know what to do next, but before she could act, her phone rang with a call from Blake. She quickly answered.

"We have a match for a former Ranger," he said. "Name's Brody Everson and wife's name is Tricia. They live in Portland, and I've already called in a favor at PPB and have units on the way over to the address."

Her heart soared at the news. "That's wonderful. Will you let me know what they find?"

"You got it." He disconnected.

Could this Brody guy shed light on where Eddie was being held and this bizarre investigation would finally be over? Or was Caulfield's death only about Tricia?

One thing was sure. No matter how excited Sierra was about this lead, she couldn't quit working on the investigation until she located Eddie. She returned to the article, but the story really held no additional information except that the city hoped the new owner would restore the building and help revitalize the neighborhood.

That didn't matter to her. What *did* matter was that Eddie and Caulfield likely picked up the brick dust at this location. And maybe Eddie was being held in this warehouse. If Caulfield had abducted Eddie, and with Caulfield dead, there wouldn't be any danger in going over there to look for Eddie. And especially not if PPB arrested Everson before she left.

Still, Sierra wouldn't go busting into that building alone. She could do a drive-by, though. Just take a quick peek to try to determine if Eddie was or had been held there and come straight back to the lab.

The fuming chamber dinged, and she raced across the

room. She searched each slug for prints, but the cyanoacrylate didn't produce any. She bagged the slugs, grabbed her backpack and phone, and charged down the stairs to Grady's lab. She nearly threw the bag at him.

He held the bag up to the light and turned the slugs around. "Interesting—.264 Winchester Magnums."

"Interesting, why?" she asked, already starting for the door.

"Not commonly used ammo. It's often—"

"Okay, thanks," she interrupted as she didn't need more of an explanation.

"In a hurry much?" He laughed.

"Following up on a lead," she said as she stepped into the hallway.

She took the elevator to the parking garage and raced into the chilly night, even more eager to find Eddie. At her car, her phone rang, and seeing the call was from Blake, she quickly answered.

"PPD has Everson," he said. "He sustained a bullet wound to his leg, and they found a Medford Fat Daddy tactical knife with a broken tip."

It was official. He'd killed Caulfield, but had he shot at her? "They didn't by any chance find .264 Winchester Magnums, did they? Grady just said that was the caliber of the slugs we recovered from the shooting today."

"Yes! We have a trifecta." Blake's enthusiasm was contagious and her heart soared. "Everson is definitely the guy who tried to kill you and likely killed Caulfield."

She could never be happy about learning a man was a killer, but she was ecstatic that they'd taken him into custody. "Did he say anything about his wife or Eddie?"

"He clammed up, but I'm headed in to brief the detective on our investigation and sit in on the interview. I'll let you know what I learn."

"Thanks, Blake." She ended the call and slid into her car.

One thing in this drawn out and bizarre investigation was resolved. Now to look for Eddie at Caulfield's warehouse.

~

Adair closed the laptop and peered at Reed. "Now tell me where we stand on the Barnes embezzlement investigation."

Reed brought him up to speed on every lead. "I have to admit I thought Barnes took off, but after everything we've uncovered and the murders, I'm starting to believe he was abducted."

Adair steepled his hands on the desk. "You thinking he's still alive?"

Reed had been too focused on how the murders effected Sierra, and then of course the shooting, and he hadn't really given it any additional thought.

"Rice?" Adair asked.

"I honestly don't know, but if Kuznetsov is involved in this somehow, we could be looking at Barnes's death." Reed felt like he was betraying Sierra just by saying it, but Kuznetsov could totally change the case dynamics.

Adair nodded, those green eyes fixing on Reed again, mining deep. For what, Reed didn't know, but he was probably trying to assess Reed's mindset after the shooting. Trying to determine if he was fit enough to remain on the job.

Adair suddenly gave a single nod and reached into his drawer to pull out a Glock and magazine that he placed in front of Reed but didn't let go of either item. "If you're not one hundred percent after the shooting, tell me right now."

"I'm good, sir." Reed didn't add that he wished he'd

nailed the shooter, as that could lead to a lengthy discussion, and Reed was eager to go.

Adair released the gun and magazine, and Reed resisted showing any hint of his relief. Law enforcement officers were used to carrying on duty, and it had unsettled Reed when he had to place his weapon on the desk. But now he wouldn't have to walk out of this office unarmed.

Reed inserted the magazine and chambered a round before holstering it. "We done here, sir?"

"I am, but you're far from done. I want a written report on the shooting and a written update on the Barnes investigation on my desk or in my email by seven a.m."

"Understood." Reed got up, his mind going to Sierra. No way he would leave her alone all night while he typed reports. "Does it matter where I write my reports?"

"Where?" Adair arched a black eyebrow. "I could care less as long as I have the report by seven. Don't be late."

Reed nodded and rushed from the room to his workstation. He grabbed his laptop and put it in a file box with all of his investigative files then rushed out of the building. He wanted to go straight back to the Veritas Center, but he needed to clean up in case he didn't have a chance to before coming back to the office in the morning.

He got in his vehicle and connected CarPlay so he didn't miss a call or text while on the road to his apartment. He made the ten-minute drive in five and was soon in his shower, scalding hot water pouring over him. He'd turned up the ringer on his phone and left it on the counter. He wanted to stay under the water to wake up a bit, but he wanted to be with Sierra more. He cut off the water and toweled dry, his focus pinned on the phone.

He expected to be up all night working on the report and keeping an eye on Sierra's safety and couldn't face putting on another suit, so he dressed in casual attire. He did put one in a garment bag in case Adair called him into the office in the morning. He packed some toiletries and took everything to his car. He wanted to run with lights and siren, but that could endanger motorists, and he wouldn't do that just so he could get to the woman he loved faster.

~

Nearing seven, the sun dipped below the horizon as Sierra cruised slowly past the warehouse that was dark and appeared to be empty. Vacant lots sat on either side of the building with an alley in the back. The perfect place to hide Eddie as no one would go near the building. She wanted to stop but kept on going. Still, about a block away, she turned around, and drove down the alley behind the building. No lights. No cars. Nothing.

She parked across the street to watch for a while. She wasn't in the best neighborhood, so she made sure the doors were locked and the engine running. She tapped her foot on the floor, watching and waiting. For what she didn't know. But now that she was here, she couldn't make herself leave.

What would it hurt to take a quick look into a window? The ones on the side were too high, but the one in the back was at eye level.

She shoved her phone into her pocket, grabbed pepper spray from her backpack, and before she gave it another thought, she turned off her engine and got out. She left it unlocked in case she had to race back inside. She crossed the road and eased up to the building, checking her surroundings as she moved. She hurried around back, but the streetlight's beam faded. She shone her phone's light ahead and made her way to the window.

She flashed the light iron bars covering the window. She spotted movement inside. Startled, she jumped back and

261

turned off her light, her heart pounding like a drum in her chest.

"Help!" A man called out from inside. "I'm being held prisoner here."

Eddie? Was it Eddie? Should she try to find out or call someone? If she called and waited for backup and Eddie hadn't been taken by Caulfield, then Eddie's captors might return, and she would miss the chance to free him.

She moved back to the window. "Who's in there?"

"Eddie. Eddie Barnes. Please help me."

Her heart leapt at the confirmation of her biological father being alive. "Hold on. I'm coming."

She turned her light back on and flashed the beam over the lot littered with rubbish. She spotted a steel post from a sign that had collapsed. She grabbed the post, rammed it into the door, and worked the metal open wide enough until she could scoot inside. She rushed to the corner of the large empty room and found a dead-bolted steel door where Eddie had called out from.

This door was more secure than the exterior one and the lock looked new and sturdy. She ran back outside to grab the post and slammed it into the door. She dented the metal, but the door didn't budge. She hit it again. And again. And again. Over and over until the lock gave way and the door popped open.

She groped around for the light switch and flicked it up. The single bulb above shone rays into the dark recesses of the room, and she made a quick assessment. A portable toilet and dorm-sized refrigerator sat near the back wall. Food wrappers and empty water bottles littered the floor. A man rested on a sleeping bag. He had a full grayish-blond beard, and greasy blond hair. She searched his face, but in his scruffy state, she wasn't positive it was Eddie.

"Water." He blinked against the light. "Please. Water."

She wanted to help him—after all, he could've been without water or food since Caulfield died, and that had been days. But in case this really wasn't Eddie, she was going to get a few answers before he felt stronger and was better able to deceive her. "How did you end up here?"

He continued to blink. "I was abducted by my CPA, Ira Caulfield."

At last. An explanation. "Why would he do that?"

"He ganged up with an evil man to steal money from my clients." The words poured from his mouth in a disgusted tone. "Guy's name is Vasily Kuznetsov."

Kuznetsov. So he *was* involved.

Eddie cleared his throat. "Some of my clients complained, and I found out what they were doing. I confronted Ira. He hit me over the head and brought me here. He said he was just keeping me here until he could get away from Kuznetsov. Then Ira promised to let the authorities know where he left me. Did he call you?"

She shook her head.

He squinted up at her, confusion replacing his angry expression. "Sierra? Is that you?"

"Yes."

His mouth fell open, and he ran his gaze over her. "It really *is* you. How did you find me?"

She quickly explained about her dad's transplant. "I freaked out and rushed to Seaview Cove to see you, only to discover you were missing. So my team and I partnered with the FBI to search for you."

"And here you are. Rescuing me." He shook his head, but abruptly stopped. "If you hadn't searched for me, I don't know who would have. I have no one else." He frowned. "Thank you for caring enough to come after me."

Emotions she couldn't put a name to welled up inside, nearly closing off her throat. She had to get them moving before she started blubbering. She grabbed an empty water bottle from the floor. "Let's go see if the water's turned on here."

"It is. Ira came by every day to make sure I had enough food and water, but he hasn't been here for a couple of days. I thought he left me to die."

Sierra clasped his hand and got him up. He wobbled then righted himself. He smelled terrible, but she did her best not to gag.

"Restroom is on the far wall," he said.

She settled him in a rickety chair and filled the water bottle in the dirty sink. She handed it to him, and he started guzzling it.

"Slow down." She rested her hand on the end of the bottle. "Your stomach won't be used to it."

Eddie nodded. "I wish you didn't have to see me like this. I haven't showered or changed clothes in so very long." He ran a hand down his shirt and pressed on the wrinkles.

"Don't worry about that. I'm just glad I found you."

He took another long pull on the water bottle.

"The FBI thinks you embezzled the money from your clients," she said not willing to mention Reed's name just yet. "That Caulfield didn't have withdrawal privileges for your accounts so he couldn't have stolen the money."

His chin came up in the same way hers would if accused of something she didn't do. "He did it. He set me up the minute he started managing my business. I had zero interest in running it. The less I had to do with it the better. I was a fool."

"How's that?"

"Ira handled all of the contracts and companies we did business with. He entered the bills into accounting software for me. All I did was print the checks and mail them. I didn't have a clue what they were for." He shook his head. "And I sure didn't know that he set up bogus service accounts and lockboxes. When the checks came into the boxes, he deposited them into an account he set up in my name. He had all of the passwords to access the accounts online."

She wanted to believe him, but his story had holes. "He couldn't have set up that account without your knowledge, could he?"

"True that. I signed it all right. He routinely had me sign things that I never really looked at. Yeah, I know. I'm the worst business manager in history. But the clients were happy with his work until a few of them started questioning the charges. So I looked into it. That's when I found out he'd partnered with Kuznetsov."

She believed him now, but would Reed? "Is there any way you can prove that to the FBI?"

"Actually, when I confronted him, I recorded the conversation. Camera's in my office, mounted in the return air vent. But Ira found out about it. So I took off for a while to figure out how to handle it. Decided to confront him. We met here. He promised to pay it back." Eddie shook his head. "I believed him. But turns out he followed me back to my office and whacked me with the whale from my desk."

She heard a sound by the door and jerked around.

Kuznetsov charged into the room waving a gun. "Thank you for leading me to your father, Sierra."

She gasped, her heart thundering to life. Had she really led this creep here?

"And Eddie," Kuznetsov continued. "Thanks for telling me where that camera is."

Eddie's chin lifted higher, and he glared at Kuznetsov.

"You've been such a naughty boy, haven't you, Eddie?" Kuznetsov asked, grinning.

"If you mean that I let you and Ira meet in my office so you could keep your association a secret. Plus recorded the dates and times you met and the account numbers and money you talked about. Then yeah, you got me. You knew that already. But you don't have my log." Eddie snickered.

Sierra was overjoyed at Eddie's explanation of his innocence, but she didn't say anything. She raised her hand to warn him not to irritate Kuznetsov any more than he already had.

"We'll see who laughs last." Kuznetsov charged forward and planted his gun on Eddie's forehead.

Eddie's face paled, and he seemed to melt in the chair.

Sierra's insides churned, and she could hardly think. She needed to buy time. To find a way out of this. "Eddie was just telling me you helped Caulfield steal money from Eddie's customers."

"Helped, no." Kuznetsov sounded offended as he glanced back at her. "More like looked the other way while Caulfield took the money and framed this loser. Until Caulfield said he was taking off with Tricia."

"Is that the name of Caulfield's girlfriend?" Sierra asked, hoping if she played dumb, he would give her more information.

"You haven't IDed her yet, huh?" Kuznetsov chuckled.

"Her name is Tricia Everson." Eddie scowled at Kuznetsov. "What did you do to her?"

"She went for a dip in the hot tub." Kuznetsov's thin lips narrowed in a sick smile. "And never got out."

"You killed her?" Sierra's anger took hold, and she rushed him.

He spun, pointing the gun at her, and she stopped in her tracks, catching that same garlic smell that she noticed at his office.

"I couldn't let Caulfield leave town," Kuznetsov snapped.

"And now he can't, can he? Tricia's husband saw to that."

"You think *he* killed Caulfield?" Kuznetsov scoffed. "That's priceless."

"Wait. *You* slit Caulfield's throat?"

"He was gonna leave even without his precious Tricia." Kuznetsov's eyes narrowed into venomous slits. "No one leaves without my permission. No one."

"And that meant you had to stab him ten times, too?" she asked, though she knew Everson's knife was used to stab Caulfield.

"Didn't stab him. What would be the point when he was already dead?"

So he killed Caulfield and then Everson must have arrived on scene and stabbed him in rage over stealing his wife.

"Okay, Eddie," Kuznetsov said. "Tell me where you hid the ledger, and the two of you can walk out of here."

"Don't say anything," Sierra warned. "No matter what he says, he just confessed to murder, and he's not going to let us live."

26

Eager to see Sierra, Reed parked in the Veritas Center lot. He reached for his phone to send a text and tell her he'd arrived, but decided to surprise her instead. He grabbed his jacket and rushed through the dark night to knock on the door.

Pete opened it and stood back. "Surprised to see you here after business hours."

"I was hoping to surprise Sierra. Mind signing me in and taking me up to her lab?"

"I shouldn't," Pete said. "At least not until you tell me what this surprise is about."

"It's personal."

"So you're not here on business?"

"That too, but the surprise is personal."

"See, now you had to go and ruin it. The minute you said you were here on business was the minute you made me have to call ahead." He went to the desk and picked up the handset. "Might as well sign in while you wait."

He set the iPad on the desk, and Reed filled in the form. He'd been here so many times that he should have a completed form that he could pull up and just sign. He would suggest that to Maya the next time he talked to her.

"That's odd," Pete said. "She's not answering. You sure she's at the lab?"

"She was when I left, but that was hours ago. Maybe she went to her condo." He thought she would still be working on finding Barnes and a niggle of worry took hold.

"I'll try her cell." Pete made the call.

Reed heard the phone ringing. Once. Twice. Three times. And more, but no answer.

Pete's expression tightened. "Not answering her cell either. Let me page her."

He made the announcement over the speakers, and Reed tapped his foot as he waited for her to call Pete back... but she didn't.

"Let's go check her lab." Pete led the way to the elevator, and they rode up to the fourth floor.

Reed's gut tightened with every level. When the doors opened, he bolted for her lab and had to wait for Pete to unlock the door.

Reed pushed it open and made a quick sweep of the room. "Not here."

"Restroom, maybe." Pete crossed the hall and knocked on the door. "Sierra?"

They waited. No answer. Reed pushed the door open. "Sierra, you in here?"

No answer. He went in and checked the stalls. All empty. "No one here."

"Condo next," Pete said and took them up to the skybridge and down to her condo.

Reed's worry was growing with each step, and apparently so was Pete's, as the older guy moved at a pace that surprised Reed. Pete knocked on Sierra's door.

Reed heard footsteps from inside and let out a long breath. Finally. They'd found her.

The door opened and a sleepy Sam stood in the doorway.

Reed's tension returned. "Is Sierra here?"

Sam yawned. "Not that I know of, but I crashed on the couch a few hours ago, so I'm not sure."

Reed brushed past her. "Sierra? Sierra? You here?"

He raced through the rooms. One by one. Family room. Guest bedroom. Bedroom. Bathrooms. No Sierra.

He hurried back to the door. "She's not here."

"She's probably in her lab," Sam said.

Reed shook his head. "We checked there, and she's not answering her cell, either."

Worry tightened Sam's face. "Maybe she had an errand to run or something."

"She promised me she wouldn't leave the building." Reed didn't know if he was more upset that she broke her promise to him or that she had vanished.

"Oh, well, then," Sam said. "She could be in another lab."

"We paged her." Pete looked at Reed. "Let's check the parking garage for her car."

Pete spun and jogged toward the exit door. They quickly covered every floor of the garage, and Sierra's cherry red Honda wasn't anywhere in sight.

Reed slammed his fist into the column, the sting taking away some of his anger and fear. "How could she go somewhere with a killer gunning for her?"

"So you haven't heard," Pete said. "They arrested the guy who fired on her. A Brody Everson."

Reed spun to look at Pete. "When? How?"

"She found his print on the Leatherman, and Blake got a friend to run it through the army database. It returned Everson's name and Blake sent PPB to Everson's house. He suffered a bullet wound to his leg and was in possession of a broken knife that matched the one used on Caulfield. Plus he had ammo matching the slugs you two recovered from Caulfield's place."

Reed let out a long breath. At least a killer wasn't after her, but why didn't she text him to tell him about Everson? Or tell him where she was going?

"So you see," Pete said. "At least a killer isn't gunning for her."

"Yeah, but where is she?" Worry rose up and grabbed Reed around the throat.

"Maybe she told one of the partners where she went. Nick always seems to know what's going on. I swear he has every room bugged." Pete called Nick and put the call on speaker. "Hey, you know where Sierra is?"

"Nah. Last I heard was when I sent her a list of buildings my algorithm turned up."

"You don't think she found something and went looking for it, do you?" Reed asked.

"Wouldn't surprise me."

"We have to find her," Reed said, shocked at the panic wedged in his tone.

"We have GPS trackers on our phones," Nick said. "Let me see if I can track her." He stopped talking, but Reed heard him typing, and then he provided a Portland address.

Reed didn't recognize it. "What's there?"

"Let me look," Nick said and then another pause. "An old building. Brick front. She might have found this address in the list of articles I sent her."

Reed looked at Pete. "Take me back to her lab. Now!"

If Pete minded being yelled at, he didn't show it, but marched toward the door.

"I'll meet you both there," Nick said.

Reed and Pete reached her lab as Nick came barreling out of the stairwell.

Reed went straight to her computer, woke it up, and spotted an article about an old warehouse being sand-blasted.

Nick came up behind him. "Sand and brick dust."

Reed scanned the story. "It's the address you gave me. Get this. The building's owned by Caulfield."

"For real?" Nick asked.

"For real." Reed tapped the screen by Caulfield's name. "And if Caulfield abducted Barnes, it would be a perfect place to stash him."

"Sierra would've figured that out, too," Nick said.

"But why didn't she tell someone she was going?" Reed asked, panic totally consuming his voice.

Nick met Reed's gaze. "Because she knew we would stop her if she did."

"And for good reason," Reed snapped. "She could've walked into a hotbed of danger."

Sierra wanted to bolt. To take her chances, but Eddie wouldn't be able to move fast enough to get out of this building. Shoot, she couldn't move faster than a bullet either.

"Okay, fine. You want to play it this way?" Kuznetsov jerked his gun toward the door. "Get moving. Both of you."

Sierra's heart started pounding. "Where are you taking us?"

"Somewhere no one will overhear your screams when I get the information I need from you." He shoved Sierra forward, and she could barely breathe for fear of what this evil man had planned.

Eddie slowly got up and teetered on his feet. Sierra took his arm to steady him and help him outside. She felt him trembling next to her, but wasn't sure if it was from fear or weakness.

"It'll be okay," she whispered. "My team will come for us."

"But how will they know where we are?"

Kuznetsov hadn't taken her phone. Maybe Nick could track it. *If* he was even looking. *If* anyone was looking. She'd felt her phone vibrate against her leg moments ago, so maybe they'd discovered she was gone and one of them had called to find her.

Or it could be Reed, but he might not even come after her. Not when she'd broken her promise to remain at the lab. She made that promise when Everson was out there looking for her, but Reed wouldn't understand why she felt safe in going out because she hadn't told him about Everson. And she didn't deserve his understanding. Not when she put herself in this position. Worse than that, she led Kuznetsov to Eddie and put him in more danger.

Kuznetsov's two goons stood by the door, and when Kuznetsov stepped outside, they both rushed to his black SUV and opened the doors.

Kuznetsov shoved her and Eddie in the back seat, and one of the guys slid in next to them. Kuznetsov and the other man got in the front.

"Where are we going?" Sierra asked again.

No one answered.

The lack of response sent her heart pounding harder.

Father, please. Please let Reed or someone on the team have noticed I'm gone and come to our rescue. Please!

~

Reed turned to leave Sierra's lab, but Nick grabbed his arm. "We can't just go rushing out there like Sierra did. We need a plan."

Reed didn't want to plan. Not with Sierra's life riding on the line. He wanted to act. To get to her. Help her. But Nick was right. None of them would be any good to Sierra if they raced onto the scene only to be killed.

"I'll page everyone to the conference room for you." Pete crossed to the phone on Sierra's desk.

"C'mon," Nick said. "The sooner we formulate an action plan, the sooner we can go after her."

Reed didn't have to be told twice. He bolted out the door and stood tapping his foot as Nick got the elevator open.

"Who on the team can we count on for tactical support?" Reed asked.

"Grady, Blake, and me, but Blake's interviewing Everson with PPB. Sam and Riley can help, too. I'll drop you at the conference room then get Sam, and she can call Riley."

Reed jetted into the elevator. He would rather be charging down the stairs, but the elevator was faster, so he tapped his foot to let out some of the pressure building inside. He couldn't fathom that Sierra left the building when she promised not to go. He wanted to be mad at her, but his fear for her life trumped everything.

The elevator jarred to a stop, and the door split open. Grady stood waiting.

"Take over," Nick said to his partner and remained in the elevator. "Be right back with Sam."

The doors whisked closed, and Reed brought Grady up to speed on the situation while they hurried down the hall.

Grady ground his teeth as he opened the conference room door. "Sierra came to see me just before she left. She bolted out of my lab so fast I should've known something was up and followed her."

"You couldn't have known," Reed said, though he knew if he'd been in the same situation, he'd be blaming himself.

As Reed waited for the team to assemble, he paced the room. Praying. Pleading. Begging God to keep Sierra safe. To show them the way to safely rescue her.

Emory and Maya stepped into the room, their expressions tight as they sat. Nick, Sam, and Kelsey soon joined them.

Reed stopped at the head of the table. "We believe Sierra went to a building owned by Caulfield where he could be holding Barnes."

Kelsey gasped. "Alone?"

Reed nodded.

"Riley's not too far from there," Sam said. "Nick told me where she went, so I texted Riley on the way down here and asked him to do recon."

Reed was thankful for their help, but he needed to control this op if he wanted to make sure it went well. "He knows not to approach, right?"

She nodded. "At this point he's only looking for her car."

"I'll bring up the building on the screen." Nick opened a laptop and tapped on the keys. The image soon displayed on the wall-mounted TV.

"Let me also bring up satellite footage." Nick typed again, and the satellite view of the warehouse loaded in a split screen. He rotated the shot, giving them a full three-hundred-sixty-degree view of the place.

"One way in and one way out," Reed said. "Windows are too high for a quick exit but someone could make it through them."

"Which means we need to cover all four sides of the building," Grady said.

"Can we get a map view to see nearby buildings?" Sam asked.

Reed looked at her. "Your reasoning?"

"Riley's a former PPB sniper. If we have the right building nearby he could provide overwatch."

"He have an appropriate rifle with him?" Grady asked. "If not, I've got something he can use."

Sam snorted. "Are you kidding? The guy doesn't leave home without his favorite weapons."

Reed had expected Grady to argue and say as a former Marine Scout Sniper, he should provide the overwatch, but he was clearly a team player.

"Okay, here you go." Nick moved the mouse around until he lighted on a tall building with a good view of the warehouse. He zoomed in on the building. "It's an old fire station turned museum. Should work."

"We should also consider Grady for overwatch," Maya said.

"I could take a stand near the rear of the building," Grady said calmly. "Between Riley and me, we should have the whole place covered."

"Let me find another location." Nick moved the mouse over the nearby businesses.

"That warehouse would be perfect," Grady pointed out.

"Okay, I'll locate contact information for both locations so we can get permission to use their rooftops." Nick started typing again.

"Once you do, I'll make the calls," Reed said. "They're more likely to say yes to the FBI than a private agency."

Nick nodded and began typing.

"Okay, so Riley and Grady are on overwatch," Reed said. "I'm going in through the front door. Alone. Nick take the back. Sam one of the sides. But we need another person for the other side."

"I can do it," Maya said. "I've been shooting since I was a kid."

276

"Yeah, but shooting at what? Paper targets at the range." Reed asked, trying his best not to sound skeptical when he was. Very.

Maya firmed her shoulders. "I grew up hunting with my dad and can handle moving targets."

Reed thought about it and then decided her limited skills were better than leaving a side unprotected. He nodded. "Okay, we know the assignments. What about weapons and protection? I've got my go bag, but what about everyone else?"

"Riley and I have appropriate weapons and our vests in his car," Sam said.

"My collection of assault weapons has us covered," Grady said. "And I have vests for Nick and Maya."

Sam's phone chimed. She glanced at it and looked up with a frown. "It's Riley. Sierra's car is across the street from the warehouse. She's not in her car, and she's nowhere in sight."

A vise tightened Reed's stomach, and he felt like he might hurl. "We need to get moving. Now!"

"I've got contact information for the building owners." Nick jotted it down and slid the paper over to Reed.

"I'll make the calls on the way to the warehouse, and we'll fine-tune the plan as well." Reed planted his hand on his sidearm. "Let's move people."

27

Reed stepped out of the SUV and ran his binoculars over the building that looked forlorn and abandoned in the thriving Portland landscape. Sierra's car sat right where Riley had reported finding it, but she still wasn't inside.

"Overwatch report," Reed demanded over the communication device that connected the assault team together.

"All's quiet in the front," Riley said.

"Ditto in the back," Grady said.

"Let's move, people." Reed gestured for Sam, Nick, and Maya to follow him. Reed still wasn't one hundred percent confident in Maya's skills, but she seemed to be sure of herself and that was half the battle.

He reached Sierra's Civic. "Hold here while I check her car out."

He grabbed a handle and found the door unlocked. He leaned in and scanned the interior. No sign of a disturbance. No blood. Nothing to indicate she was injured. But Reed didn't relax. Not one bit.

He joined the team again and they set out, four strong. They split at the sidewalk, and he reached the front door and paused. Making entry into an unknown space, facing an unknown subject, kicked up his pulse. Maybe he shouldn't have created this plan. Should've brought in SWAT. It wasn't too late. He could still abort.

And what would he do if SWAT rushed in and botched the job? Reed couldn't live without Sierra. That he knew for sure. And that meant he had to handle this himself.

God, please watch over all of us and let us bring Sierra home safe.

Mentally ready now, he leaned toward his mic. "Overwatch report."

"Clear," Grady said.

"Clear here, too," Riley said.

"Ground team?" Reed asked.

Maya and Sam reported all was clear.

"Back door's been jimmied," Nick reported. "But no action."

"Breaching." Reed swung a battering ram that Grady provided from his collection of tools.

The door swung in. Reed dropped the ram and raised his rifle. He stepped inside and ran his gaze over the large, empty space. The back wall held three doors. A restroom sign was above the one on the right. Exit above the middle one. And office over the third door located on the corner.

He wanted to race over to the office, but he needed to be sure there wouldn't be a flank attack. He strode across the room to the restroom where a half-filled water bottle sat on the floor by a rusty chair. He kicked open the door and confirmed it was empty. Kicked open the exit door that led to a small mudroom, confirming the outside door and that area was also empty. He went to the office and caught a whiff of a similar odor that often clung to his clothes after running. He clicked on the light and spotted a sleeping bag, empty water bottles, and food trash. But no Barnes and no Sierra.

His heart fell, and he pressed his mic. "Looks like Barnes was held here, but he's gone, and so is Sierra."

∾

Panic clutched Sierra by the throat as Kuznetsov turned into a driveway leading to a dilapidated cabin in the woods. She needed to do something, but what? She couldn't stop a big man like Kuznetsov from shooting her, not to mention stopping his huge bodyguards. And she didn't want to do something stupid and put Eddie's life in danger.

But time was running out.

She couldn't wait for rescue any longer. She had to act. She leaned close to Eddie and whispered, "When he stops, I'm going to bail. Go for help. I'm sorry to leave you behind."

"Go. Don't worry about me."

"Shut up," Kuznetsov said.

She placed her hand on the door handle and prayed he hadn't clicked on the child lock so she couldn't get out.

He took the circular drive by the cabin and pointed the vehicle to face the road, leaving her direct access to the wooded area surrounding the cabin. He planted a foot hard on the brakes.

The car rocked. She squeezed Eddie's leg then jerked the handle.

The door latch released.

She bolted out, got her footing, and barreled straight into the woods. She heard Kuznetsov yelling at his men. "After her."

Loud footfalls sounded behind her. Panic exploded in her chest, but she kept going.

Branches snapped at her face. Grabbed at her clothes, reaching out to take her down. The dark nearly blinded her.

She crouched behind a tree to listen. The men were tromping closer.

Fear nearly paralyzed her.

God, please.

She bolted to her feet and took off in a different direction. She wanted to race, to plow ahead, but she couldn't make a sound or they would find her.

She swallowed to calm her fear, but her mouth was dry. Bone dry.

She glanced up at the endless sky and prayed. Prayed hard that they didn't find her, because if they did, they would kill her.

"Got her GPS," Nick said from the passenger seat in Reed's SUV. "She's on the move. South on I-205. Ten miles from here."

"Plug the address into my navigation system." Reed turned on lights and siren, then shifted into gear and floored the gas in his SUV to get them onto the interstate heading south. He cruised past the traffic, thankful that cars actually got out of his way and pulled over.

"She still moving?" he asked.

"Not since I last looked."

Fear pounded through Reed, and his hands were sweating on the wheel. He had to gain control of his emotions if he was going to be any good to Sierra when they reached her. But God help him, his brain was spinning, and he couldn't seem to control the terrible thoughts peppering him.

"Moving?" he asked again.

"No," Nick said. "I promise I'll tell you when she does."

"We'll get to her," Grady said from the backseat where he sat with Maya.

They left Sam and Riley behind in case Sierra returned, but right now Reed was wishing for more firepower in the group. At least more skilled firepower.

The GPS voice told him to take the next exit which would lead them into a rural area. He careened down the ramp and hung a right.

"Hey, slow down," Maya chastised. "We're no good to her if we don't make it there alive."

Reed knew his driving capabilities, and there was no way he was going to slow down. Not until they reached Sierra's location.

He swerved around cars that refused to get out of his way and pressed the gas harder on straightaways. They were making good time, but was it good enough?

Sierra kept heading west, knowing she would eventually reach the main road. She hadn't heard the goons in a while and had picked up her speed. Running full out now, ignoring the branches clawing at her skin. Scratching. Ripping. Her mind was a mass of worry and thoughts.

She thought about Kuznetsov and the careless way he killed Tricia and then Caulfield just so he wouldn't leave town. He was a cold-blooded killer who was used to getting his way.

Had she made a mistake in running? Would it make him so mad that he would take it out on Eddie?

Fear for Eddie tightened her chest already straining under the exertion.

She had to stop. Take a quick breather. Give Reed a call. Or call one of her partners. She dropped to the ground and called Reed first because it was his voice she wanted to hear. It was him she wanted to come for her. Him she wanted for more than a day. Or a week. For a lifetime. She knew that now. Knew he was the man who could change her mind about marriage.

"Sierra," he rasped out her name. "Where are you?"

"Reed! Thank God you answered."

A gun came out of the dark and pressed against her head. She jolted, nearly dropping the phone. She clutched it tighter but otherwise didn't move.

"End the call before I end it for you," one of the thugs said from behind.

He was smarter than she expected. He must have been silently tailing her. Of course. Kuznetsov wouldn't hire idiots. He was too smart for that.

"I mean it." He pressed the gun harder, the cold metal biting into her skin. "End the call."

"Sierra," she heard Reed's terrified voice calling out to her, and she couldn't sever the connection. She'd wait. Make the man grab her phone and disconnect the call.

He clocked her over the head with the butt of the gun. Pain ripped through her skull. Her hand relaxed. Her fingers opened. She saw the phone fall in slow motion. It tumbled. End over end and thumped onto the thick layer of fir needles.

She felt the darkness come for her.

Take her.

She dropped to the ground. As the strong woodsy scent of the forest floor engulfed her, a question ran through her mind. Would she ever see Reed again?

28

The phone went dead.

Reed slammed his fist against the wheel. "How far? For the love of God, tell me how far."

"In the woods, a mile on the right, but she's moving deeper into the woods."

"Do you think she got away from the creep who was yelling at her?" he asked.

"No." Nick's tone had such a finality to it that Reed felt like hurling on the spot.

Instead, he floored the gas.

"Up ahead," Nick said. "Two hundred feet."

Reed slowed and whipped the SUV off the road. He bolted out before it stopped rocking and ran to the back. He ripped the liftgate open. Shoved a box of ammo into his pocket and grabbed his rifle. The others had piled out but he didn't care. He had to move. Now!

He raced off the road and scrambled down the ditch. He ran hard. Fast. Hurdled fallen logs. Ducked low branches. Forced his feet through knee-high grass and weeds. Inhaled the fresh evergreen scent as he gulped in deep breaths.

A gunshot sounded ahead. Maybe fifty yards.

No-o-o! Sierra?

Was he too late?

His heart nearly stopped. He halted. Listened. Heard nothing but the team coming up behind him. He signaled for them to cover him, and he cautiously advanced. He skirted several large trees, and then he saw her. In a small clearing with the moon shining down on her.

She stood over a man. Handgun in hand. The huge man lay unmoving.

"Sierra," Reed said her name softly.

She looked up, her eyes wide and tortured. She lifted the gun, looked at it, and dropped it at her feet.

Reed raced forward, picked up the gun, then checked the man. He was alive but had a gunshot to his gut.

"What happened?" Reed asked.

She dropped to the ground and started crying. Reed went to her, knelt, and circled his arms around her. He saw crusted blood in her hair, and he wanted to pummel something. But he swallowed it down to tend to her.

"*Shh,* honey. Don't cry."

"He-e-e hit me over the he-ead. Knocked me out." She gulped in a breath. "I came to. He didn't know. I grabbed his gun. It went off. The gun was in my hand. I ki...ki..." Her crying ramped up.

"*Shh. Shh.*" He tightened his arms around her trembling body. "He's still alive."

He was vaguely aware of the others coming up to them.

Maya dropped down by the man and wiggled out of her jacket to press it on his wound.

"I'll call an ambulance," Nick said. "And Blake to get some backup out here."

Sierra looked up, and her eyes cleared. "Eddie! Kuznetsov and the other bodyguard have Eddie! A cabin.

Deeper in the woods. We have to go." She tried to stand, but fell back down.

"I'll stay with her," Maya said. "You all go for Eddie."

Reed couldn't fathom leaving Sierra behind, but he knew she would want him to rescue her father.

"Nick, you stay here, too," Reed said not willing to risk Sierra's life with Maya alone. "Grady and I'll go after Barnes."

"Hurry!" Sierra said.

Reed kissed her on the forehead and got up. He hurried ahead, Grady at his side. They silently made their way through the forest of trees and thick undergrowth until they could see the silhouette of a cabin in the murky light ahead. They both took a knee.

Grady lifted his rifle and looked through his scope. "Guy at the door. I can take him from here if you want."

Yes—Reed wanted him to, but he wouldn't just kill a man when they might not have to. "Can you skirt around the building and create a distraction to lead him away? I'll come up behind him and get the drop on him."

"On it," Grady said and slipped away, moving quietly as only a sniper could.

Reed made his way around the building, and when Grady made a noise to catch the guard's attention, Reed moved in and came up from behind. He pressed his rifle barrel into the man's back. "Drop your weapon."

The guy stilled and didn't try anything but let his gun fall. Reed whistled for Grady, and when he arrived to cover Reed, he cuffed the man and shoved him to his knees.

"Keep an eye on him," Reed said. "I'm going for Barnes."

Reed turned back to the cabin. A dull light spilled from the back window. Reed crept onto the small porch and twisted the knob. It turned under his hand, and he slowly pushed it open.

He saw a bearded and unkempt man sitting in a chair in the room ahead. Had to be Barnes. Kuznetsov was standing over him, weapon in hand.

He shook his gun, his face turning red. "Where's the stupid log?"

Could he be talking about the ledger Sierra found?

Barnes clamped his mouth closed and lifted his shoulders.

"Then I guess the secret is going to die with you." Kuznetsov dropped his finger to the trigger. "Last chance."

"Is it going to die with me?" Barnes asked. "Or did I tell Sierra where it was before she took off?"

"You think you can buy time while my guy finds her? And find her he will. Then if she can't tell me where the log is, I will kill her too."

"No, I..." Barnes's voice fell off.

Reed had to get Kuznetsov away from Eddie.

He reached into his pocket. Grabbed a coin and hurled it at the corner. Kuznetsov spun. Barnes lurched into Kuznetsov, knocking him down, and his gun skittered across the floor. Kuznetsov tried to scramble forward.

Reed raced into the room. He planted a boot on Kuznetsov's arm and the barrel of his rifle on the man's temple.

"Don't move! Don't even breathe!" Reed's fury came out.

Kuznetsov didn't move. Probably expected his bodyguard to rescue him. Or waited for a chance to escape.

Reed calmed himself down. "Hello, Mr. Barnes," he said to Sierra's father who smelled like he hadn't bathed the entire time he'd been missing. "FBI Agent Reed Rice. Sierra is fine. Her partners are with her."

Barnes sat up, but his shoulders sagged.

"Hold tight, and I'll get an ambulance out here to look after you," Reed said.

"No need. Some water and food will put me right."

Reed made the call, but he didn't have a second set of handcuffs so he remained in place until he heard sirens and saw lights through the window. Footfalls approached the front door and it soon swung open.

"FBI Agent Reed Rice here," he called out. "Suspect detained."

A deputy poked his head into the room for a quick look then shot back.

"We're clear," Reed called out.

The guy took a longer look and then entered. Reed got it. The deputy was being careful.

Reed made sure the deputy saw the FBI logo on his shirt. "I used my cuffs on the guy outside. Mind taking care of this one for me?"

The deputy nodded and holstered his weapon to cuff Kuznetsov. Reed lowered his rifle and got out his phone to call Nick.

"Put Sierra on," Reed demanded.

"Hello," she answered, her voice still trembling.

"Your father is fine. Kuznetsov is in cuffs and so is his other bodyguard. I'll head over there as soon as—"

"No. I'm coming there. I have to see Eddie."

He didn't like the thought of her traipsing through the woods with the head injury, but he knew that tone. She wouldn't be talked out of it.

"Put Nick on the phone again please."

"Yeah," Nick said.

"You clear to bring Sierra to the cabin?"

"All clear."

"She's in no shape to make the trip, so carry her if you have to."

"Understood," Nick said. "But man, you know how independent she is, and you're gonna owe me if it comes to that."

Sierra's head pounded, and her legs felt weak, but nothing was going to stop her from getting back to Eddie. And back to Reed. She had to tell him about Caulfield stealing the money. And as important, she had to apologize to Reed for breaking her promise and hope he would forgive her.

She stumbled, and Nick caught her by the elbow.

"Hey, slow down," he said. "You could already have a concussion, and you don't want to add to that."

"I'm fine." She looked up at the guy she often took for granted. "But thanks for coming for me. And for being there for me and the rest of the team. We can always count on you."

He waved it off, and she knew if she could see his face clearly, she would see him blushing. "It's Reed you need to thank. He's the one who discovered you were missing. Might've taken the rest of us days before we noticed you were gone." He laughed.

She swatted a hand at him as they made their way into the clearing. Two patrol cars sat behind Kuznetsov's car, and Grady was settling the other bodyguard into the back of one of them under a deputy's watchful eye.

The guy she shot came to mind, and guilt hit her like a tsunami. The medic said the wounded man would be fine, but still, she *shot* someone. Accidentally, sure, but she shot him. Maybe it was time she learned to at least handle a firearm safely. And she knew the perfect man to teach her. If he could forgive her.

They climbed the cabin stairs just as a deputy hauled out a scowling Kuznetsov.

She stepped aside. "Glad to see you're in good hands, Kuznetsov. May you spend the rest of your life in prison."

Reed exited behind them. "Barnes told me all about Kuznetsov's confession and about Caulfield's theft."

She was so happy to see Reed that she could hardly stop from throwing her arms around his neck and kissing him, but she didn't know how he would take that. "Does that mean you believe Eddie's innocent?"

Reed nodded. "But we'll need evidence to back that up. Like the log he claims to have."

"It's in my closet." Eddie stepped up to the door. "False wall."

"A ledger book?" Sierra asked. "I found that already."

"Good," Eddie said as he dropped into an old wooden rocking chair.

"And I found a gun."

"Yeah, I swiped it from Caulfield after I found out about Kuznetsov."

"So you don't know where the rest of the bullets in the magazine were fired."

He shook his head. "Honestly, I didn't even pop out the magazine. I'm not a gun guy and figured Caulfield had it loaded."

"You called a burner phone several times," Reed said. "Why was that necessary?"

He shrugged. "Must've been the PI I hired to look into Kuznetsov. He was a pretty paranoid guy."

Reed's phone rang, and he answered. She watched him standing strong in the doorway. She finally noticed he wasn't wearing a suit but was dressed in khaki tactical pants, a navy shirt with a gold FBI logo embroidered on this chest, and black tactical boots.

If she thought a suit made her heart pump, this attire made it beat triple time. He looked so darkly dangerous that she felt short of breath.

She searched for something to say or do to keep her

emotions under control. She noticed his sidearm. If he hadn't been required to turn it in, she was extremely happy for him. Though, with his earlier comment about getting a new job, she didn't know how bothered he was at the thought of losing this one. She'd never met a guy who seemed to love his job, was very good at it, and yet, didn't care if he lost it. This man truly had his priorities right.

He ended his call and shoved his phone into one of the big cargo pockets.

She pointed at the gun. "You're still carrying. Does that mean you're still working?"

He nodded. "Adair replaced my Glock with a fresh one."

"So you're in the clear?"

"Not fully, but I doubt there'll be any blowback from the shooting."

Surprised at his casual response, she looked at him hoping to find an explanation, but found nothing in his expression to help. "Why don't you sound happy about it?"

"I am. It's just that I have to write up a report on the shooting and one to update Adair on the Barnes investigation. Which, after this, will likely take until morning when I want to—" His phone rang again, cutting him off.

She watched him dig it out and answer. He listened and quickly ended the call. "The detective wants to talk to us, and the ambulance is here for your father."

Eddie raised his chin. "Said I didn't need one. Just some food and water."

"Come on, Eddie." Sierra took his arm. "You need to be checked out. I'll walk you out there."

"You gonna be that bossy all the time?" He poked his chin out further.

She nodded.

"Reminds me of your mother." He smiled and started down the steps.

"When this is all over," she said to him, "we'll need to sit down and have a chat."

He looked at her. "I'd like to get to know you."

"And I'd like that, too."

He beamed a wide smile at her and went willingly to the ambulance. After they loaded him on a gurney, she stepped back and noticed that Maya had brought Reed's SUV to the cabin and her partners congregated around the vehicle. Two suited detectives standing near an unmarked car caught her eye and headed her way.

"You should have an ambulance of your own," Reed said coming up behind her.

She turned, and before the detectives reached her, she needed to apologize. "I'm sorry, Reed. I should never have left the center. With Everson in custody, I thought it would be safe to drive by the warehouse. That's all I was planning to do. Honest."

"But your curiosity got the best of you."

"Yeah, it did." She clutched his hand. "I am so sorry to have put you through this."

"Don't think twice about it. I understand." He squeezed her fingers.

"You forgive me for breaking my promise?"

"Of course." He tipped his head at the detectives. "We can talk about this later."

She nodded, but his serious tone left her feeling unsettled. She had so much to say to him and she didn't want to wait, but what choice did she have?

29

The detectives couldn't finish their interviews fast enough for Sierra and clear her to leave. Reed insisted the team take his SUV and drive her to the hospital to get checked out while he cleared things up and reported in to his supervisor. She almost argued with his heavy-handed demand, but as it turned out, she had a concussion, and he'd been right. She did need to be seen by a doctor.

As soon as the doctor gave her instructions and she was allowed to leave, the team drove her back to Veritas. She ignored the doctor's orders to rest and did what she always did when she was stressed—went to her lab to work. The place felt comforting again, the usual caustic aroma of chemicals making her feel right at home. She finally felt safe after the crazy night she'd been through.

Her cell rang, and she glanced at it, her heartbeat rising the second she saw Reed's name.

"Hi," she said, the word coming out breathless, reflecting the many emotions racing through her body.

"I'm in the parking lot." His tone was as serious as it had been at the cabin. "Can we talk?"

"Sure...yeah...great. I'll be right down." She ended the

call and got up to leave but then stopped to take a few long breaths and gather her thoughts.

She'd come to care for him and wanted to pursue a future with him, but she felt very self-conscious about going to meet him right now. She'd already taken the time to shower and put on clean clothes, but she didn't expect to see him tonight and was taken off guard. And her lack of long-term relationship experience left her wondering what to say to him. She'd have to figure it out as she went.

She ripped off her lab coat, grabbed her lip gloss and comb from her backpack, and stopped in the bathroom to freshen up. She looked at her reflection in the mirror and was sure her feelings were written all over her face. Reed was an astute FBI agent—he would see them—and she wasn't ready for that yet. The realization of her feelings for him was too new for her, and she wasn't used to trusting other people, especially a man she didn't truly know.

By the time she got down to the lobby, Reed was waiting at the desk talking to Pete. Reed had obviously cleaned up, too. He was dressed casually again and held a thick file under his arm. She briefly wondered about it, but let it go when he pushed off the desk and strode her way, his gaze fixed on her face. He smiled and seemed to let out a relieved breath, and his focused attention on her kicked up her pulse.

He ran his gaze over her, lingering on her face. "Can we talk?"

She nodded and headed to the stairs. No way she would get in the elevator with him, as she wanted to kiss him more than anything, and that was *not* a good idea while she was trying to work out her feelings for him.

She opened the stairwell door, stood there only long enough to hold it for him, and then charged up the stairs to her lab, glad he followed without asking. Inside her lab, she didn't know what to say, so she waited for him to speak.

He looked her over again. "You were cleared by the doctor?"

"Mild concussion. I'll be fine." She couldn't think under his intense study, so she pointed at the file. "Something you need help with?"

"Oh, right." He set it on the table. "I forgot I had it. You mentioned that once Barnes was safe, you'd be willing to look at my investigation into my high school girlfriend's murder."

"Sure," she said, glad he provided something for her to think about other than wanting to kiss him. She lifted the folder and noted a few floppy disks. "I don't have a disk drive, but Nick does. He can move the files to a flash drive for me."

He nodded, but he didn't really seem to hear her. She figured his thoughts were on their potential relationship going forward, and she couldn't talk about that yet. "I'll text Nick to see if he can do it right now so I can read this right away."

"You should get some rest."

She waved a hand as she knew despite how tired she was that her mind was still racing with all the events that had just unfolded, and she wouldn't likely sleep anyway. She grabbed her phone to send the text. Nick responded immediately. *Come on down. The price is right.*

"He's available." She gathered up the disks and headed to the door.

Reed rushed ahead and held it open for her. "You look nice. Like you're headed to the beach instead of working in a lab."

She blushed and looked down at the outfit Sam had picked out while Sierra was in the shower—gauzy white beach pants and a powder blue knit shirt. Comfy white sandals. At the time, she figured Sam was trying to make her completely forget about shooting a man in the woods, which the cute outfit Kelsey had convinced Sierra to buy had done. Now she was glad she was wearing something pretty and not old sweats like she would have grabbed.

She looked up to find Reed still running his gaze over her. "You look great, too. I like the non-suit look a lot."

He surprised her by coloring at her compliment.

"Listen to us. A mutual admiration society of two." She chuckled and set off down the hall, feeling his focus pinned on her every step. She rushed down the stairs and into the hallway. She pressed her fingers on the print reader outside Nick's office but before she could push the door open, Reed grabbed her hand.

He turned her to face him. "Just so you know, I'm very glad to be here. To be with you."

She met his gaze and was stunned to see the depth of caring in his eyes. He really had fallen for her. Just like she'd fallen for him. She couldn't very well kiss him with Nick waiting for them, but she touched his clean-shaven jaw. Gently and quickly. "I'm glad you're here, too."

He tugged her closer but the door opened, and he released her hand.

"Why are you hanging out here?" Nick asked, shooting a look between them. "Oh, I get it. Want me to go back inside and give you some privacy?"

Reed looked like he was going to tell Nick to get lost, but she shook her head before he did, and Nick disappeared into his office.

As she stepped after him, Reed took her hand and held her back. He met her gaze. "To be continued."

"Is that a promise or threat?" she asked, loving that she suddenly felt free to flirt with him.

"Either way you look at it, that conversation and more will be happening." He gave her a flirtatious grin that sent her pulse racing faster. She was mesmerized and couldn't move. Not an inch, much less into Nick's office.

"Sierra?" Nick called out. "I thought you wanted me to help you."

She got moving, but not before Reed planted a sweet kiss on her cheek. "More later."

She blushed tomato red at him realizing the impact he was having on her, but her heart lifted at his honesty, and she only hoped she could soon be as honest with him.

Reed had very little time before he had to leave and write his reports for Adair. So as Nick copied the files, Reed took Sierra by the hand and led her into Nick's outer room. Surprisingly, she didn't shake off his hand but came with him.

He faced her. "I'm sorry, but I have to go write those reports."

She narrowed those amazing eyes. "You probably shouldn't even have come over here tonight."

"Like I had a choice." He cupped the side of her face, his gaze focused on her. "Don't you know by now what you do to me? Just one look at you, and I forget everything else."

"I didn't know I was such a distraction," she said, that breathless quality to her voice again.

"Are you kidding?" He grinned. "Look how long it took us just to get in here."

"Yeah, I guess." She took his hand and held it tightly. "We can talk in the morning."

He was so glad she didn't say they wouldn't see each

other again since Barnes's investigation had ended. He hoped she finally might be open to a relationship.

"Seriously, you two," Nick said as he joined them with a flash drive and the disks in his hand. "If you have to keep this up, at least do it in your own lab."

Sierra freed her hand and swatted it at him. He shook his head and handed her the drive and disks.

She turned to Reed. "I'll walk you to the lobby."

At the elevator, Reed looked at her. "I guess you don't let anyone roam the building without an escort."

"Only spouses," she replied.

"So if I want to wander around here, it looks like I'll have to marry you."

Her mouth fell open, and she gaped at him, her expression horrified. He stepped over to her and used his index finger to lift her chin and close her mouth. But she sputtered like she didn't know what to say. He'd been feeling confident in her response to him since he'd arrived, but he'd obviously been a bit *too* optimistic, and his comment was likely going to send her running from him.

"Hey," he said. "Don't look so worried. I was just joking."

She nodded, but when the door opened on the first floor, he got the feeling she was glad he was leaving.

She walked him all the way to his vehicle and looked up at him. "I'll see you in the morning. Call me if something comes up and you can't come by."

The urge to pull her to him and kiss her senseless was almost too much to ignore, but he just bent down and gave her a soft kiss on her cheek. "Sweet dreams, honey."

Sierra did try to catch some sleep, but the sight of the man she'd shot kept flashing back, giving her nightmares. So she'd gotten up and spent the wee hours of the morning reading Reed's file. She found the information as thorough as his file on Eddie's investigation. But she found nothing to help him. Nothing at all. So she returned to her lab to take another look before he arrived in a few minutes.

She flipped through the pictures on her computer. Pictures that included a few of Reed as a teenager. Seeing him as a boy warmed her heart toward him even more as she saw his vulnerability. He'd lost his parents, and here he was gazing with love at the girl who he was soon to lose too.

She sat back to think. He'd been through so much, and yet, he trusted in a bright future. He opened his heart for more pain and heartache with others, and she wasn't even willing to open hers once. That had to change. Starting right now. She would be brave enough to let go of her need to be in control. She had to if she wanted to be with this man and she did.

God help me with that. Please, please help me.

She looked back at the pictures and it hit her. The suspect. The one and only suspect had been ruled out because he was right-handed. Due to the trajectory of the bullets and blood spatter found at the crime scene, investigators were certain Reed's girlfriend was murdered by a left-handed male.

But in this picture, the suspect stood on the tennis court holding his racket in his left hand. He could've held the gun with his left hand, too. It was called cross-dominance. Had no one noticed that and checked it out? If so, it wasn't in the file.

The door opened, and she looked up.

Maya poked her head in. "Look who I found in the lobby."

Dressed in another black suit with pale gray shirt and

red tie, Reed pushed past Maya. He looked tired, yet jazzed about something.

"Thanks for the escort, Maya," he said and came straight across the room, the door closing as Maya backed out.

Sierra remembered his comment last night about marrying her so he wouldn't need an escort, and surprisingly, today it didn't bother her nearly as much. In fact, it didn't bother her at all. She wasn't ready for marriage—far from it, but she could at least tell him she was open to pursuing a relationship with him. First, his investigation.

"I found something." She pointed at her computer screen and explained.

He came behind her to look at the picture. "How could I have missed that? We all did."

"The obvious doesn't always stand out."

He shook his head and swiveled her stool so she was facing him. "Thank you. I can look into this guy now."

"Glad to do it." She smiled up at him.

He brushed a strand of hair from her cheek. "How's your head this morning?"

"Hurts, but it'll be fine." She smiled again, but it felt nervous and forced. "I wanted to tell you again how sorry I am that I broke my promise to you last night. I still feel so bad about it."

"*Shh.*" He took her hands and pulled her to her feet and against his chest. "All is forgiven, and I can't kiss you when you're talking."

His arms circled tightly around her and his lips settled on hers. He kissed her with a new urgency. She raised her arms around his neck and slid her fingers into his hair as she kissed him back and didn't care that her head hurt. She loved this man, totally and completely, and she wanted him in her life.

She leaned back, and couldn't stop smiling as she wondered what to say to him. How to explain.

He tilted his head. "What's the smile for?"

"For being the kind of man who I can't say no to."

"Does that mean—"

"I've fallen for you and want to find out where this thing between us goes? Yeah it does." The words rushed out, one tumbling over the other, and she was glad it was finally out there. "But I'm scared, Reed. I've never let a man get this close, and it feels kind of like I'm losing myself. I can't let that happen. I have to be who I think God called me to be and falling for you has consumed me the last few days."

He rested his forehead on hers. "Don't worry. I won't let that happen."

"How are you going to stop it?"

"By promising right here and now that I will *never* push you to do anything you're not ready for. That I'll never try to convince you of something you know isn't right for you." He leaned back. "I fell in love with the independent, super-strong Sierra. I don't want her to go away either. I love it when you're feisty. When you push back."

Her heart soared, but it was almost too good to be true. "And you'd do that for me? Not push, I mean. Not even if you want something badly enough?"

"Oh, honey, trust me." He grinned happily. "If that's what it takes to have you in my life, then I promise I will never pressure you into anything. Never."

She returned his smile, but oddly enough, she was wishing he might push just a little harder at the moment to confirm a future together. That was a first for her. No matter. She had all the time in the world to work on their future plans.

EPILOGUE

One month later

Reed shoved the gearshift into park and looked out the front window to stare at Sierra's childhood home. It was completely different from Eddie's place. They'd visited him several times this month as she got to know her bio dad. Reed was interested in seeing her interactions with her family after the stilted talks with Eddie.

Reed thought this formal two-story house fit her better than the laidback vibe of the cottage. This place had five windows on the second story and four on the main floor. And it looked like an addition had been added onto the left side. The house was beige with black trim, nestled in tall fir and maple trees.

"Nice house." He pulled out the key and looked at Sierra. "Reminds me of where Malone and I lived before our parents died."

Reed remembered everything about that place. Even the day the realtor came to list it for sale, calling it a "five, four, and a door." Real estate slang didn't do his family home justice and had added pain to his wounds that day.

Sierra clutched Reed's hand and stared up at the house. "I never realized until now how much it means to me."

"The change makes sense with the way you've started enjoying your family more."

She nodded. "About that."

"Yeah," he said, worried about meeting everyone for the first time.

"You should know that my dad is a retired Multnomah County Deputy and all of my brothers are in law enforcement."

"All?" He swallowed hard. "Man, oh, man. I'm toast."

She tilted her head. "I've seen you in action. You can hold your own."

"But I wasn't trying to impress anyone then. Now—"

"Now it will be fine. But I thought I should tell you so you know the family culture."

He eyed her. "Why didn't you ever mention this before?"

"Once I got over not wanting to be with you, I didn't want to scare you away."

He cupped the side of her face and smiled. "You could never scare me away. Honest. I'm in this for good."

She took his hand and kissed his palm. "We should probably go in."

"Or we could stay out here and make out instead." He winked.

"They'd come looking for us, and that wouldn't make a good impression on my brothers."

"I suppose not."

"Besides." She pointed out the window at a silver sedan parking out front. "Malone is here, and she's so pretty my brothers won't even notice you."

"I'm not sacrificing my sister to save myself." He laughed and got out of the car. Sierra joined him in the driveway.

"Sis." He kissed his sister's cheek then hugged her. She

looked so much like their mother that it shocked him at times. She had dark hair like his and the same dark eyes, but her chin and nose were fragile and delicate. She was nearly six feet tall in her boots and slender. She'd also inherited their mother's fashion sense.

He released her, and she hugged Sierra. They'd gotten to know each other this past month, and though they didn't have a lot in common, he was ecstatic that they liked each other.

"Sierra says you need to protect me from the big, bad Byrd men." He smiled at Malone.

"What?" She laughed.

"They're all law enforcement officers and my dad is a retired deputy," Sierra clarified. "So they might give Reed a hard time."

"And you think I can help with that?" She looked honestly confused.

Sierra nodded. "Just smile at them, and they'll fall into line. Maybe fall all over themselves trying to be the one you're most impressed with."

"You're kidding, right?"

"I've seen it happen in high school, but I'm sure they're more mature now." Sierra rolled her eyes and laughed.

"It sounds like it's going to be a wonderful evening." Malone's eyes twinkled.

"Don't you dare make it worse," Reed said. "You're here to help me."

She started up the steps and gave him that wickedly cute smile she used on him as a child, and Reed knew he was in for trouble. Big trouble.

Reed took Sierra's hand, and she wasn't sure if it was from

panic or if he was claiming his territory right up front. Whatever the reason, she was all for hand-holding and followed Malone up the walkway. His sister had nearly black hair cut just below her chin and big brown eyes with long lashes. She always dressed fashionably, tonight in white skinny jeans, brown suede ankle boots, and a soft beige knit top that tied at the waist.

Sierra glanced down at in her worn jeans and sneakers. She hadn't even thought to dress up to come to her parents' place. What was she saying? She never really thought to dress up. It was amazing Reed fell in love with her when she looked like one of the guys all the time.

He tugged her to a stop at the small stoop and kissed her soundly.

"For courage," he said and laughed.

"In that case, how about more?" She raised up on her tiptoes and locked lips with him.

"Are you two coming in or what?" Malone asked. "Oh, I see...it's *or what*."

She laughed, and Reed pulled back.

"I'm glad to see my big brother so happy, but maybe cool it a bit for Sierra's family." She marched into the house.

Sierra really liked Malone. She was so real and outspoken. A what-you-see-is-what-you-get kind of woman. Sierra almost snorted every time Reed kissed Malone's cheek and treated her like a delicate flower, which Sierra was discovering happened whenever he saw her. Her brothers would as soon sock her in the arm as anything. Maybe if she and her brothers had lost their parents, they wouldn't take each other for granted as much. She wondered what they might say if they learned she'd been taken hostage by Kuznetsov, and she actually shot a man.

Because the incident happened outside of all of their jurisdictions, hopefully they would never find out. At least she didn't plan to tell them, and she'd sworn Reed to silence, too. She convinced him not even to tell them about her bonk on the head or the resulting concussion either. She didn't want any negative news given to her parents when her dad was recovering from surgery.

They stepped inside, and her father met them in the foyer. He looked great. Standing tall. Strong again. And he had the same commanding presence he'd had before his illness.

He held out his hand to Reed who looked surprised.

"Dad looks a little different from when he was in the hospital," she said.

Reed shook hands. "You're looking good, sir."

"Please, it's Russ."

Her mother joined them. "And I'm Peggy."

Reed nodded, but Sierra could see he seemed uncomfortable with the thought of calling her parents by their first names.

Sierra introduced Malone, and Sierra's parents welcomed her.

"Everyone's in the kitchen, but a word of warning," her mother said. "The boys are watching the Seahawks and Steelers game. Seattle is down by seven and the boys are in a feisty mood."

Sierra resisted groaning as she knew that meant they would be tougher on Reed. Something he didn't miss, and his gaze turned more uncertain. He glanced at her. Here was this big strapping lawman who faced down a killer for her, and he honestly feared meeting her brothers, but he pulled his shoulders back and took her hand. He loved her enough to brave the boys, and she never loved him more.

She squeezed his hand, and they entered the kitchen behind Malone. She didn't back away from the loud shouts, but left Reed and Malone to sit on a stool by Sierra's brothers. Their backs were to an island loaded with game day snacks like hummus, nachos, and a cheese tray. Her brothers didn't even notice Malone until the Steelers scored a field goal, and she shouted at the screen. Normally, they would erupt in loud boos, but they swiveled almost in unison to stare at her.

She stood. "Malone Rice. Reed's sister."

Malone went down the row of brothers and shook hands. None of them said a word, just continued to stare.

"You guys are acting like you've never seen a woman enjoy football before. Glad to talk the sport with any of you, any time." She laughed.

"A woman after my own heart." Sierra's youngest brother Erik, the real charmer in the group, got up and mocked a faint.

Malone laughed and dipped a carrot in hummus, totally ignoring Erik and the others. They came to their senses and turned to grab snacks, and their gazes landed on Reed. The intense force of their study had to be stressing Reed out. Nothing like five lawmen scoping you out. Reed assertively returned the same force-filled stare.

Aiden got up, stepped over to Reed, and jutted a hand at him. He'd recovered well from the kidney donation, but he was still off work. It was risky for him to return due to having only one kidney. She hated that his sacrifice might have cost him the job that he loved.

He eyed Reed. "Might've mentioned you two were a thing when we met."

Reed accepted Aiden's hand, and her brother's grip looked like it was meant to punish, but Reed took it in stride. "We weren't at the time."

Sierra clapped her hands as loud as she could to gain everyone's attention. "I want to make this easy on Reed, so line up in order."

Reed let go of Aiden's hand to look at Sierra. "Order?"

"Mom and Dad graciously named these brutes in alphabetical order as they were born. Makes it easier to remember their names."

"Hey, we're not forgettable," Brendan complained, but Sierra was glad to see he went to stand next to Clay, and the others fell in line.

"The loudmouth is Brendan who you might remember from Caulfield's murder scene," she added, but made sure her tone was light. "He's the family sniper and likes to shoot down ideas, so be wary of him."

Brendon shot out a hand. "Good to meet you, even *if* you're a fed."

Reed took Brendon's hand. "Multnomah County Sheriff's Department, right?"

"Is there any other?"

"Hear! Hear!" her dad said.

Sierra looked at her bother. "He's also SWAT and a literal sniper."

"Next up is Clay." Sierra tapped her middle brother on the arm. "ICE agent and the idea man. You get stuck on anything, just ask him. He's full of—"

"Ideas," Clay jumped in. "Hey man, don't let these guys get to you. They aren't nearly as tough as they make out."

Reed smiled, seeming to like Clay.

"Before you sign onto Clay's fan club." Sierra eyed her tallest brother coming in around six foot three. "You should know he's just protecting you because right now you're the underdog. Once you're part of the family, he'll give as good as he gets."

"Yeah, what she said." Clay grinned, turning on the charm as he glanced at Malone.

"She's off limits," Reed snapped out. "Malone, I mean.

The last guy I'd want her to end up with is someone in law enforcement."

"Is that so?" Drake bristled, lifting his shoulders and looking Reed directly in the eye. Sierra might be the black sheep of the family, but Drake was the bad boy, living life on the edge, which likely made him better at his job in fugitive apprehensions as a U.S. Marshal. "Odd comment coming from a G-Man."

Malone waved a hand with nails tipped in light pink polish. "He thinks he has to protect me, but don't take it personally. No man, no matter his occupation, meets Reed's criteria."

"Sounds like he's a good brother." Aiden clapped Reed on the back and everyone except Drake nodded.

Sierra resisted groaning. Reed could very well have made enemies of her brothers with the law enforcement comment, but Malone just redeemed him.

"We think the same thing," Drake said. "We know the dangers of our jobs and don't want to see Sierra wind up being a widow."

"Hey," Clay said. "Remember Fibbies are paper pushers for the most part. Never heard of an LEO dying from a paper cut."

Sierra looked at Reed and expected him to grimace or snap, but he laughed and held out his fist to Clay. They bumped hands and both gave a nod of acceptance.

"Guess I gotta like a guy who can laugh at himself." Drake reluctantly shoved out his hand to Reed.

"Besides, now that Sierra's going to the range with me to learn to shoot, she can protect *me*," Reed said.

"She went to the range with you?" Aiden gaped at Reed. "And shot a gun?"

Reed nodded.

Drake shook his head. "Don't know how you managed

that, but you're a more convincing man than all of us. Including Dad."

"Now that we got all that man posturing out of the way," Malone said. "Commercial's over. Can we watch the game again?"

"Sure can," Erik said. "Want to sit with me?"

Sierra rolled her eyes. "And last but not least, the charmer is my youngest brother, Erik. He's a PPB officer and thinks he's God's gift to women."

"Can't argue with that." He laughed and shook Reed's hand.

"The game," Malone pointed out. "Let's watch already."

She got a ready acknowledgement from her brothers. Clay mocked holding out her stool for her, but instead of falling for his obvious attempt to flatter her, she rolled her eyes.

Sierra faced Reed. "I don't think Malone needs you to protect her. If she can hold her own in this room, she can hold her own anywhere."

Worry narrowed Reed's eyes. "Maybe."

"Remember, I don't much appreciate the brother protection act, and she might not either."

"She's never complained."

"Have you ever asked her about it?"

He shook his head.

"Might want to do that."

He frowned and drew her into the hallway. "Are you going to get upset when I get protective, because I gotta tell you, it's going to happen? I protect the people I care about, and I care about you more than I can put into words."

She opened her mouth to say she wouldn't like it, but then realized she *did* like it coming from him. She twined her arms around his neck. "I very much like your willingness to protect me no matter what."

His mouth fell open.

She chuckled.

He circled his arms around her back and pulled her against him. "Glad to sign up for the detail. I can even protect you from your brothers."

She smiled at him. "Since you turned me into a gun-toting person, I'll protect you right back."

He threw his head back and laughed. "From the looks of things, I might need it because I plan on becoming a permanent part of this family."

"You sure you want to do that?"

His expression sobered. "I'm sure I love you and want you with me for the rest of my life. If those guys come along as part of the package, I can tolerate them."

His declaration of a lifetime commitment should have her running scared, but she honestly wanted to spend her life with him, too. She'd learned this past month that loving someone as intensely as she loved Reed didn't mean giving herself up. It meant finding a way to weave love into the tapestry of her life. And they'd both managed to do that. To love, and yet, be who God intended them to be.

But she still needed to take things slow, and it was way too early for her to make an official commitment.

She leaned into him and softly murmured in his ear. "I love you, too, Reed Rice. I never thought I would find a man as incredible and amazing as you are. I think we'll be spending a *lot* more time together."

He groaned and settled his mouth on hers. He kissed her with intensity, and she kissed him back and didn't care if her entire family walked in on them. This man changed her mind about relationships, and that included her thoughts on her family, so if they did pop into the room they should be thanking him. At least that's what she would tell them. If she ever decided to come up for air.

~

Enjoy this book?

Reviews are the most powerful tool to draw attention to my books for new readers. I wish I had the budget of a New York publisher to take out ads and commercials but that's not a reality. I do have something much more powerful and effective than that.

A committed and loyal bunch of readers like you.

If you've enjoyed *Dead End*, I would be very grateful if you could leave an honest review on the bookseller's site. It can be as short as you like. Just a few words is all it takes. Thank you very much.

~

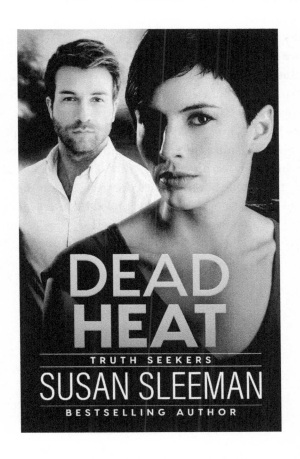

PRE-ORDER DEAD HEAT - BOOK 4
Nick Thorn, computer cybercrimes expert with FBI Agent
Piper Nash

Tracing cyber criminals is what he lives for...

When hackers breach hospital security to steal patient records and begin blackmailing them, Veritas Center's cybercrime expert, Nick Thorn is hired to locate security holes and patch the system. But he doesn't stop there. He wants to bring down the hacker and make her pay. Problem is, he inadvertently inserts himself in FBI Agent Piper

Nash's sting to catch the same hacker, and Piper has no choice but to arrest him and force him to stand down.

But the job is suddenly hitting too close to home.

Nick finds himself attracted to Piper and wants to comply, but when his grandmother falls prey to a cyber-attack by the same hacker, he takes the assault very personally and will stop at nothing to find the hacker. Not even stop for Piper's warnings to take care. They're in a dead heat to the finish line, but what Nick doesn't realize is the hacker has no intention of going to jail, and she's reserved a bullet with Piper's name on it. With time ticking down can Nick partner with Piper to find the killer before a point-blank shot takes her out?

Dear Reader,

Thank you so much for reading DEAD END, Book Three in my Truth Seekers series.

Book 1 - DEAD RINGER - April/2019
Book 2 - DEAD SILENCE - July/2019
Book 3 - DEAD END - September/2019
Book 4 - DEAD HEAT - March/2020
Book 5 - DEAD CENTER - April/2020
Book 6 - DEAD EVEN - May/2020

I'd like to invite you to learn more about the books in the series and my other books by signing up for my newsletter and connecting with me on social media or even send me a messsage. I also hold monthly giveaways that I'd like to share with you, and I'd love to hear from you. So stop by this page and join in.

www.susansleeman.com/sign-up/

Susan Sleeman

THE TRUTH SEEKERS
People are rarely who they seem

A twin who never knew her sister existed, a mother whose child is not her own, a woman whose father is anything but her father. All searching. All seeking. All needing help and hope.

Meet the unsung heroes of the Veritas Center. The Truth Seekers – a team, that includes experts in forensic anthropology, DNA, trace evidence, ballistics, cybercrimes, and toxicology. Committed to restoring hope and families by solving one mystery at a time, none of them are prepared for when the mystery comes calling close to home and threatens to destroy the only life they've known.

For More Details Visit -
www.susansleeman.com/books/truth-seekers/

BOOKS IN THE COLD HARBOR SERIES

Blackwell Tactical – this law enforcement training facility and protection services agency is made up of former military and law enforcement heroes whose injuries keep them from the line of duty. When trouble strikes, there's no better team to have on your side, and they would give everything, even their lives, to protect innocents.

For More Details Visit -

www.susansleeman.com/books/cold-harbor/

HOMELAND HEROES SERIES

When the clock is ticking on criminal activity conducted on or facilitated by the Internet there is no better team to call other than the RED team, a division of the HSI—Homeland Security's Investigation Unit. RED team includes FBI and DHS Agents, and US Marshal's Service Deputies.

For More Details Visit -

www.susansleeman.com/books/homeland-heroes/

ABOUT SUSAN

SUSAN SLEEMAN is a bestselling and award-winning author of more than 35 inspirational/Christian and clean read romantic suspense books. In addition to writing, Susan also hosts the website, TheSuspenseZone.com.

Susan currently lives in Oregon, but has had the pleasure of living in nine states. Her husband is a retired church music director and they have two beautiful daughters, a very special son-in-law, and an adorable grandson.

For more information visit:
www.susansleeman.com

Made in the USA
Monee, IL
09 October 2020